My

Helga Jensen is an award-winning British/Danish best selling author and journalist. Her debut novel was a winning entry in the 2017 Montegrappa First Fiction competition at Dubai's Emirates Literary Festival. Her debut was also a contender for the coveted 2021 Joan Hessayon Award for new writers. Helga holds a BA Hons in English Literature and Creative Writing, along with a Creative Writing MA from Bath Spa University. She is currently working on a PhD.

Also by Helga Jensen

Twice in a Lifetime
A Scandinavian Summer
Fly Me to Paris
My Heart is in Venice

HELGA JENSEN

My Heart *is in* Venice

hera

First published in the United Kingdom in 2024 by

Hera Books
Unit 9 (Canelo), 5th Floor
Cargo Works, 1-2 Hatfields
London SE1 9PG
United Kingdom

A CIP catalogue record for this book is available from the British Library.

Print ISBN 978 1 80436 227 3
Ebook ISBN 978 1 80436 226 6

Look for more great books at www.herabooks.com

Printed and bound in Great Britain by Clays Ltd, Elcograf S.p.A.

1

To my two favourite Jens.

My writing bestie Jenny, and my fantastic editor, Jennie. What would I do without you both?

Prologue

The gondola wobbles from side to side like a seesaw as I attempt to step on-board. I can already picture myself plopping head-first into the canal beneath me with my bum in the air. I am conscious that the pink leopard-print G-string I bought especially for my honeymoon will not be a good look for the poor witnesses if I end up bobbing about. In hindsight, I don't even know why I bought this uncomfortable contraption. I am certainly regretting it now.

Around us, all the other couples appear to glide smoothly onto the neighbouring gondolas, and I curse myself for being that awkward one. I never was good at stepping onto anything on the water. Perhaps that is because I never learned to swim. I have always been the clumsy one and was the last to be picked for any team sport during PE as a child.

I watch as a glamorous lady effortlessly boards her gondola and kisses her partner as she sits down. Her white panama hat doesn't even move an inch from her head as she kisses him. No doubt, if I had worn a hat, it would be over my eyes by now. I realise that I should probably stop people-watching and concentrate on getting on my own blooming gondola, but there are so many interesting people here that I can't resist.

A bit of concentration, that's what I need. I look down at the gondola and start to move one foot in front of the other, focusing fully on the task at hand. Surely it can't be that difficult.

'Argh, Will, I'm going to drown,' I half laugh, half cry.

'Don't be silly. I've got you. You should know by now I'll always have your back. I'll always keep you safe.'

My heart melts as Will takes my arm and leads me safely onto the gondola. Looking at Will's kind face, I can't believe how lucky I am to be on honeymoon with such a wonderful man. Me, non-sporty Libby, ended up married to the popular rugby player. Sometimes I think we couldn't be more opposite. I mean, I don't have half the friends that he has, and I wouldn't know what to do with a ball if it hit me in the face, which it probably would if I was anywhere near a sports field. But, whilst Will might be a popular superstar on the rugby pitch, here in Venice, he is my devoted husband and giving me every bit of his undivided attention. He may appear to be a tough, well-liked rugby player on the outside, but when we are together, he is a big softie. Nobody knows that he secretly loves snuggling on the sofa with me watching rom-coms, although he has made me promise never to tell his friends. To marry a man who loves rom-coms, makes me tea in bed and pampers me with massages almost seems too good to be true. My *husband* also adores animals as much as I do, which is always a good sign.

Gosh, *husband*! I say it once again in my head.

'I'm so glad we're married. It's only been three days and it feels different between us already, don't you think?' I say.

'It does indeed, Mrs Jones. I'm only sorry we couldn't afford to do more.'

Will lowers his voice.

'I mean, the price to ride on a gondola for thirty minutes. I'm afraid this is the last treat we can afford, Libby.'

'It doesn't matter. We have each other, that's all that matters. As long as we are together, I don't care what we do,' I say.

I look around at all the beautiful crooked little alleyways that lead from the side of the canal as we sail along.

'We don't need money to walk around here. Holding hands and walking doesn't cost a button.'

Will strokes my arm and smiles.

'You can't deny that this isn't worth it though,' I add.

Will's eyes tell me that he would probably prefer to be back at the hotel right now. But I whisper and remind him that there is plenty of time for all the honeymoon shenanigans.

I want to spend a little more time discovering this wonderful place before the sun goes down. After all, we could have just booked a hotel room in Tenby otherwise.

When I take my eyes off Will, I turn to the gondolier. He is identical to the man in the Cornetto ice cream advert, and I am half tempted to ask if he is on the TV. I am sure I wouldn't be the first to enquire. But I realise that the person on TV is probably an actor and not him, as this guy is obviously a highly skilled gondola driver. You can see his professionalism by the way he steers around corners and avoids the crowded waterways, which are packed with other boats. He is not only an expert gondola driver, but he is a highly knowledgeable historian too. He leads the gondola down the narrow canals, telling us all about the history of Venice. I am captivated by the tales of the patron saint of love, Saint Valentine, that he recalls between pointing out historic landmarks. Dressed in a blue and white striped top, black trousers and one of those famous straw boater hats, he then points out a building and says, 'That is where Casanova lived,' in his delightful Italian accent.

I look up at the old building, scared to blink in case I miss something. I wonder what sort of wild things this historic old building has witnessed.

'I can't believe Casanova lived there,' I say, grinning at Will.

'I'll give you Casanova when we get back to that room,' he says with a laugh.

I tap him on his leg and tell him to behave. But secretly, I feel all gooey inside like one of the chocolate cakes we had as dessert at the wedding reception.

Despite Will's desperation to get back to the hotel, I enjoy the gondola driver's history lessons. They certainly didn't teach this stuff at secretarial college.

I am disappointed when our gondola ride is over, although Will is no doubt happy that we have done our touristy bit.

Next, we head across the Rialto Bridge towards our hotel. I swear Will is almost skipping as we get closer to our destination.

But there are still so many things to see en route, and a man with a huge bouquet of roses springs up in front of me and stops us in our tracks as he hands me one of his blooms.

'Please take this,' he smiles.

'Umm, is there a charge?' I ask.

'You take. It's okay,' he says.

'Oh, wow, are you sure?'

'Yes, you take,' he says.

4

I hold the rose in my hand as I watch the gondolas float underneath Rialto Bridge, unable to believe how romantic Venice is. I am beginning to wonder whether the tourist board gives out free roses to spread the amore. Perhaps it is some kind of government initiative. Hand in hand, lovers smile as they cross the bridge with their roses; what a wonderful place this is. We couldn't have picked anywhere better, and I am grateful to Will for choosing this. I would have thought his dream holiday would probably be attending a Rugby World Cup final somewhere like New Zealand, but he knows how much I love culture and history, so he surprised me with my dream honeymoon. It couldn't get any better than this for me. He is such a romantic.

'Wow, what a week. Getting married on Valentine's Day and coming here for our honeymoon. It's like a dream come true,' I say with a grin.

Will holds me tight and kisses me and I am a gooey mess once again. Oh, how I love this man.

When he lets me go, I start to walk ahead. Perhaps it is time to get back to the hotel after all. However, I notice that Will isn't beside me any longer. The man with the roses is pleading with him for something. I strain to listen to what he is saying.

'Give me money. Sir, please. I need money,' he is saying.

'I don't have anything on me. I spent it all on the gondola,' Will explains.

I rush forward to help.

'I'm sorry, there's been some confusion. I thought the rose was free. Here, take it back,' I say.

The man grabs the rose back and rushes over to another unsuspecting couple to start his tactics again.

'Oh my gosh, I never expected that,' I say.

'I'm so sorry. I wanted you to have that rose,' says Will.

'Hey, don't even think about it. That was actually incredibly naughty of him.'

I grab Will's hand and we walk back to the hotel, which Will's father kindly paid for as a wedding present. We pass the souvenir shops as we hurry along. They are full of Venetian craftsmanship, and I sneak a peek in the window at the merchandise we probably can't afford.

The sun is starting to set by the time we reach the hotel and I catch a glimpse of the beautiful Venetian sunset.

When we get back to the hotel, as soon as the door swings open, I immediately spot the woman on the gondola with the panama hat in reception. She is clutching one of the roses that they must have agreed to pay for.

I am not surprised that she is staying here as our fifteenth-century palazzo overlooking the Grand Canal is spectacular with its carved marble walls and Gothic architecture. I can't help but glance enviously at her designer bag. Oh well, she may have the best of everything, but I bet her partner isn't as kind as my lovely Will.

I eavesdrop as she talks to the receptionist. I have always been rather nosy. Will teases me about it sometimes.

I pretend to look at a vase in reception as I strain to listen.

'Can you book us one of the private water taxis tomorrow for the airport? And can you pop a chilled bottle of champagne in there too?' I hear her say. I have seen those water taxis out on the canal. They are like luxury motorboats and look like something a spy in a movie would chase a villain on.

'I can't believe they're getting one of those boats... And asking for champagne!' I whisper to Will.

'One day we'll do that. When it's our twenty-fifth wedding anniversary, we'll come back to Venice and go to the airport in a private water taxi, just like them. I promise,' says Will.

'Oh, I don't need all of that,' I say with a smile.

'Yes you do. I saw the way you looked at that woman's bag. It makes me sad that I can't give you everything you dream of right now, but I will. You deserve to be spoiled. I promise I'm going to give you the best life ever. Just you wait and see.'

Chapter One

The dust flies up my nostrils and makes me sneeze as I open the glass cabinet door to pop the latest of the new stock inside. I don't know why Will bought these miniature china figurines at a car boot sale when we already have very little room left in the shop. Perhaps he thought they were a bargain and that he would make a handsome profit, as he does with everything else that he hoards. Sorry, I shouldn't say *hoard*. I mean lovingly chooses. Goodness knows why he chose to go stock-hunting for even more figurines though. He must have seen some sort of potential in them since he knows antiques better than I do, having been brought up with the family business.

To my untrained eye, I have no idea what they are worth. So I leave the pricing to Will and help where I can by manning the till in the shop. Only, the till isn't getting much manning at the moment. I only seem to open it when I need petty cash for milk and tea bags. The stock doesn't appear to be moving. Everywhere I look there are antiques and curiosities squashed together. At this stage, if we do get any customers, there will be hardly any room left for them to walk. Thank goodness for my steady supply of reading and sudoku puzzles or I would go stir-crazy waiting for business. But as Will keeps reminding me, the tourists simply aren't around during a wet and windy January in Tenby. So, since the tourists are away, Will feels that he should make the most of this time to look around for unusual goodies for the shop. Then, when it is summertime again, he will be well-equipped with all the stock he needs. Although, as he leaves me and our apricot Cavapoo, Monty, here all day, he seems to forget quite how many treasured goodies he has hoarded. Sorry, carefully selected.

Of course, some of the items Will finds are special. That is when he gets super-excited. Like when Will found the Victorian doll's house that he picked up at an auction a few months ago. That is perhaps our one jewel in the crown. I am surprised this hasn't shifted yet. Will told me it is dated from the 1800s and thus it does have a hefty price tag. He was positively beaming when he found this. Will loves the history of the items he stocks, all the memories that they carry through generations. I wonder what the story behind this doll's house is. It is particularly beautiful with its miniature four-poster bed, teeny dolls sitting on chairs and a Victorian-style kitchen with all the dishes, pots and pans that belong to the era. The craftsmanship is magnificent. I would love to take it home if only we had a daughter. However, we have two grown-up boys. Sensitive Dylan and rugby-mad Ewan, who takes after his dad. Ewan is in his last year of university studying economics, and Dylan will leave home for the first time later this year. In September, he will leave the nest that I have worked so hard to make happy and cosy for everyone. I can't believe the years have flown by so fast and now he is off to study at a university in Cardiff. I know it is selfish, but I am already dreading it. No more dinners around the table with my lovely, kind boy; instead, he'll be in his student accommodation far away from his mam. I hope he'll remember to eat his veggies. I may have to send him food parcels otherwise.

Most of my married life has been preoccupied with bringing up the boys, having got pregnant a few years after our honeymoon. I won't know what to do with myself once my second born has left home too. Since the death of Will's dad five years ago and then Will having to take over the family business, I have had to concentrate on all the domestic stuff that comes with running the house and juggling everyone's needs before my own. I always spent my mornings in the shop, before rushing back home to get tea ready and organising the pick-ups for after-school activities for Dylan. I have enjoyed being a taxi driver, chef and general dogsbody if I am truthful. It gave me a sense of purpose. My life has mostly revolved around the boys and that is exactly how I wished it to be. Other women might not find that satisfying or remotely acceptable, but for me, I never asked for much. All I ever wanted was a family to look after. When I was a child, I would play with dolls and lay out afternoon tea for them and that was what I enjoyed. I have always cooed after babies and love children. My sister, Emily, on the other hand, was climbing up trees and looking for her next adventure. She never did have children. Chalk and cheese, our mam would call us.

What will I do now though, when Dylan leaves? I guess Will and I need to get used to being a couple again, just like in those early days. I am only too aware that we have got to the stage of our marriage where we need to make a bit more of an effort with each other, so I decide tonight I will make a special family meal.

Just like the boys, the way to Will's heart is always through his stomach, so I lock up the shop early and head to the local butchers to get some nice food in for tea.

Welsh lamb chops and fresh veg around the dinner table will be just the ticket. I secretly hope that Dylan doesn't have any Friday night plans so that we can all be a family tonight. Maybe I could even bring out the Scrabble after dinner, although Will has warned me enough times that Dylan is too old to be stuck at home playing Scrabble with the oldies. I keep telling him that he may think of himself as an oldie, but I certainly don't. Fifty is the new forty, I remind him. I even bought an updated version of Scrabble to show him that I am up with the times.

'Hello, love, how much did we make today?' asks Will before I can even put down the shopping. He is home earlier than I expected, so I am guessing his latest networking meeting with a local businessman's group didn't go as well as he'd hoped.

'Oh, I don't know really. The usual sort of amount,' I say.

I could do with a cuppa and to remove my shoes before breaking the news that it is the princely sum of zero for yet another day.

'Did we take *anything*?' asks Will.

'Oh, let me go to the loo first. Pop the kettle on, will you?' I say.

I look at my tired reflection in the bathroom mirror. Perhaps looking after everyone else is taking its toll. But I remind myself that my family are my world. Still, I know that I can turn my forthcoming empty nest into a positive. I just have to get used to having time for myself. I probably need to consider a hobby. I smile at myself in the mirror as I think how I always fancied skydiving. How wonderful it must feel to be free as a bird flying through the sky. Will doesn't like that sort of adventure though so the thought of a tandem skydive is out of the question. I did hint a long time ago that it might be the ideal Christmas present, but Will got me a new tea set instead. To be fair, it was one I wanted, but still.

Will is pacing up and down by the time I get out of the bathroom.

'So, how much did we make today?' he asks again.

'Nothing. It was very quiet,' I explain.

I see the worry etched on his face. It hasn't been easy for him since he took over. I have never said this to him, but there were already rumours around town before his dad died that Tenby's Timeless Treasures wasn't doing too well. Will, however, believes he is solely responsible for saving it. He is convinced that he can turn the business around and that he won't be the one who has to close it down. Like me, family is everything to him and this is his family's baby. He has been given this family responsibility, although some may call it more of a burden than a responsibility, and it is his job to ensure that the business is passed down to the next generation. That means it goes to Dylan and Ewan who, I must add, have no interest in it whatsoever. The problem is that five years of running an ailing business can't continue, but Will won't have any of it. It worries me that he is so adamant about keeping it, although one of the things that first attracted me to Will was his tenacity. All those rugby caps he won and how determined he always is to give his family everything, have always made me love him all the more. But I fear that this tenacity is now what is bringing him down. I love this man dearly and would do anything for him. It is so hard when you see the husband you know so well become a shell of his former self because he insists on doing the right thing for the family business.

'Tenby's Timeless Treasures will be around for generations, I promise,' Will always repeats.

He is a man of his word, but I know in this case, it might not be within his power to make this promise come good. Quite honestly, I don't know how the business can survive much longer. I remember his promise that we would return to Venice for Valentine's Day to celebrate our twenty-fifth wedding anniversary. I am beginning to think he may have forgotten all about that one since the date is fast approaching, and I doubt our financial situation can manage it.

On the bright side, at least I won't have to leave Monty, who is sidling up to my legs as the smell of the lamb chops wafts through the kitchen. Monty will be good company after Dylan goes. He is always such a loyal companion in the shop as he sits there on his pillow, hoping that the local butcher will take pity on him and offer him some sausages. He doesn't ask how much the takings are before I can sit down either.

'Dinner's ready,' I shout.

Since my comment about the lack of takings today, Will has mostly been in the living room with his calculator. Meanwhile, Dylan offered to peel the spuds earlier, so he has had to sit down and watch some YouTube videos since he has exhausted himself.

'Looks fab, Mam,' says Dylan.

'She's a good cook, your mam is,' says Will.

This is exactly what makes me happy. Seeing the faces of my most precious loved ones as they tuck into a home-cooked meal warms my heart. My mam was a good cook, and I hope that I have followed in her footsteps. I think I get the domestic goddess side from her. I don't know what happened to my sister, Emily, though. She eats raw food when she is at home to save her from cooking and washing up. I suppose she can do what she wants as a divorced woman of fifty-five who flits back and forth to the Costa Del Sol to top up her tan when she feels like it. She has no commitments. Ultimately, we both live the lives we want to lead, even if they are polar opposites.

'So, how do you think I can increase sales? Dylan, any ideas?' asks Will over dinner.

'Burn the shop down and claim insurance?' He laughs.

'Dylan, what a thing to say. It's a beautiful shop filled with things that people once loved, and it's our responsibility to find the items a good home,' says Will.

This is also part of the problem. Will believes that he is responsible for finding good homes for loved ones' heirlooms. However, people don't necessarily want someone's old silver teapot, candlestick or indeed those figurines that are taking over the shop and giving me nightmares.

I don't join in with the conversation. I am really not convinced that the haunted-looking doll that Will brought in the other day will ever find a new home, let alone a good one.

'Do you have any more gravy, Mam?' says Dylan.

'You've got legs, Dylan. In the kitchen.'

As Will and I sit there alone, I look over at him. He looks completely down tonight since I mentioned the lack of takings yet again. I don't think I have ever seen him so drawn-looking since we have been married. Of course, he was devastated when his dad died, and it took a while before he could even function properly. However, with the business left to him, the only son, he couldn't dwell on the grief for too long. Shortly afterwards, he had to open the shop back up with a smile on his face and brave the customers. In those days, there used to be a handful of regular customers coming in that kept the shop just about ticking over. The older generation quite enjoyed perusing the antiques. Now the town is full of millennials and generation this and that, and nobody wants a cabinet full of antique ornaments that meant so much to their former owners. The hard truth is that many of his dad's regular customers have passed on, and nobody has replaced them. Also, a lot of collectors trade online nowadays. They are not going to park up, come into our shop and hunt past all the bric-a-brac to find a work of art.

I attempt to cheer Will up with the idea of Scrabble, but he isn't keen.

'No thanks. I think I'll get a little glass of brandy,' he says.

As he sits down with his drink, I try to get him to open up about his troubles. I know it isn't easy running the ailing shop.

'So, what did you find on your travels today anyway?' I ask.

'A box of miscellaneous stuff really. A bit of this and that. It came from a house clearance. I'll drop it in the shop tomorrow.'

'Sounds great,' I say, rubbing his shoulder.

We don't mention the shop again until morning when we head there together. Thankfully, Will seems a little more upbeat than last night as he carries his box of new stock to the shop. As always, whenever he has more items, he seems happier. Sometimes it feels like, for all his stead-fastness, he has the soul of a gambler, always attracted to the next bright thing, convinced every new item is the one that is going to save our fortunes.

As we walk along with Monty, we chat about the boys, the weather and everything other than the lack of sales, and when a seagull tries to steal the cereal bar I am munching on, we have a giggle and laugh like we haven't done in ages.

'Oi, cheeky thing,' I shout as I shoo the seagull away.

It is only when we get to the shop door that Will mentions the dreaded topic of takings.

'I hope we get some sales today,' says Will as he unlocks the door.

I shuffle my feet nervously.

I am almost relieved when, as I stand beside Will, waiting for the door to open, the naughty seagull gets his revenge on me for not sharing my cereal bar. At least it will distract Will from the subject of sales.

'A bird doing his business is supposed to be lucky. I bet we make a killing today,' I say, smiling.

Of course, I don't truly believe my words. But when you love someone, sometimes you have to exaggerate a teeny little bit to protect them. In our hearts, we both know full well that there won't be any takings today, just like every other day.

Chapter Two

When I have finished turning the alarms off and putting the kettle on, I come out onto the shop floor to find that Will is still standing with the box in his hands, looking around. I think he has had a bit of a shock. He hasn't been here for a few weeks as he has been so wrapped up in buying stock and doing paperwork stuff.

'Are you going to empty that box?' I ask.

'Nah, it's okay. I didn't realise how crowded everything was. Think I'd better stop getting anything else in now,' he says.

'I think that's probably wise. Why don't you put the box out the back and we can do a bit of re-merchandising in here?' I say.

'A busy Saturday isn't ideal to do a bit of merchandising,' says Will. *Busy* and this shop definitely don't go hand in hand, but I refrain from saying that.

'Okay, not merchandising as such, just a tidy up. Why don't we put the doll's house in the window and do a bit of a reshuffle around here,' I say.

'Sure, perhaps that's where we're going wrong. We need to change things about a bit,' says Will.

'Absolutely, we need to think like the modern person. What do they want? What are their shopping habits? Let's try to bring them in through the doors,' I say.

Had I not had the boys and helped with the business, I always thought I wouldn't have minded a career in marketing. Perhaps I can plan a marketing campaign for Tenby's Timeless Treasures.

'But that's the problem. Everyone's shopping online now. It's preposterous. How can they even see the items properly?' says Will.

He picks up a white china dog and strokes it.

'You need to touch the antiques. Feel their energy. You don't get the same experience online,' he says.

'I know, love. I know you don't agree with online shopping, but do you think perhaps it is time you took the shop into *this* century?'

We have talked a few times about having an internet shop, and my suggestion is usually met with repugnance. However, I think even Will can finally see, as much as he doesn't agree with it, that it is the only way forward. For once he doesn't shout me down.

'Oh, I… I just really don't want to do that,' he says.

'I know you don't, but it's the only chance to save the business. Why are you so against this?'

'Quite honestly, Dad would turn in his grave to see precious antiques bought in the same way you'd buy a potato peeler on some big consumerist website. Shocking.'

'He may have had his funny beliefs, but I know your dad wouldn't want to see you struggling like this. That's for sure.'

I put my arm around him and we have a good Welsh *cwch*. A good *cwch* is the answer to everything and may even make the idea of taking the business online a little easier to accept. He hasn't stopped looking around at all the stock, and I can see he is anxious about it. I just need to work on him a little harder, and I think today is the day. If only I can make this work, I might get the old fun and carefree Will back. I would do anything for that.

By lunchtime we finally have a customer who purchases a few old postcards of Tenby.

'You see? Business is booming,' says Will.

I remove the £1.50 that we have just taken from the till and hold it in the palm of my hand.

'Yup, this is definitely going to pay the rent for the shop this month.'

Will looks down, and I feel terrible for blurting that out. But he can't put his head in the sand any longer. It is time for some straight talking.

When he looks up, I notice he has tears in his eyes.

'Oh, no. Look, I shouldn't have been so sharp. I'm just trying to help you. We can't go on like this. Do you see that? Perhaps if we put the business online, it is our one chance of saving the shop. I know it goes against everything you have ever believed, but please… Let's try. If it doesn't work, then at least we know we did our best.'

'Put the kettle on and I'll think about it.'

I make Will a nice strong brew and hand it to him as he sits there with his head in his hands.

'Come on. Is it seriously that bad that you have to get yourself in this state to put a business online?'

'I like living in the past. It's what the shop's all about. It goes against the ethos of my business.'

I gently stroke his hair, like I used to with the boys when one of them had a bad day at school.

'I know how strongly you feel, but it'll be okay. Let's just give it a shot.'

Will sips at his tea and finally smiles.

'What choice do I have?'

'Not much.'

I pick Monty up in my arms and walk around in circles as I come up with how we can go about this.

'Now, how about I take a photo of the doll's house first? It is one of the most valuable items we have here. I'm sure there'll be a collector online out there somewhere. It is rather beautiful. Just think, instead of a local audience, you can reach the world,' I say.

'To be fair, you are good at taking photos,' says Will.

'Right, that's what we'll do then. You do some research for platforms that we can sell stuff on and I'll be the professional photographer. We'll have this lot gone in no time.'

Reluctantly, Will finds a site where he can list some items. Technically, it isn't an online shop as such, as it is more of an auction site. So, this is a bit of a compromise.

Will begins to list a few chosen pieces whilst I upload the photos for him. Thankfully, he isn't too bad with the internet, it's just his old-fashioned beliefs that make him so reticent.

When he has finished listing the items, I am surprised that Will actually seems quite pleased with himself.

'We make a good team, don't you think? Maybe I should listen to you a bit more often,' says Will.

'Stick with me and you won't go far wrong,' I say, winking.

Will kisses my forehead and it reminds me quite how much I still love him after all these years. We definitely make a good team. He is the ambitious worrier, and I hope I am the calm influence on him. What would we do without each other? I have always thought that if something happened to one of us, we would be like one of those couples who die within hours of each other. It doesn't bear thinking about.

Before we close for the day, I check with Will to see if we have had any interest in the online shop.

'There's a lot of people watching things. The doll's house has ten people watching it,' says Will.

'That's amazing. You see, it will get snapped up for sure.'

'What if it's other dealers watching what price it's going for though? It might not necessarily mean a sale,' says Will.

'Oh, don't be so negative. I'm going to call you Worrier Will in a minute. That's all you do is worry, even when we have a potential solution to our problems. You have to stay positive,' I say.

'Yeah, you're right. Tell you what, let's treat ourselves to a fish supper from the chippy tonight. There's no point cooking for ourselves with Dylan out tonight.'

'That sounds lovely. You're such an old romantic,' I say with a smile.

After we lock up, we head with Monty to our favourite chippy in Tenby. I am glad to see that our usual bench overlooking the bay where we can see right across to Caldey Island is unoccupied.

When we were first married, we often used to get the boat across to the island, which is inhabited by monks. The monks make the most beautiful handmade chocolate to sell on the island. Will would always surprise me with a bar on the boat on the way back. We don't seem to do surprises for each other any longer. Maybe Will thinks we are a bit past surprises at this stage in our relationship.

'Remember when we used to go to Caldey?' I say.

'Oh, that chocolate! You hated sharing it with me.'

'Well, it is very good chocolate,' I say teasingly.

'You know I'd always share everything with you,' says Will.

'I know, I'm sorry, but you know what I'm like. Chocolate, cream cakes and wine are simply things I don't share. You can have anything else though,' I say, laughing.

'If you won the lottery or were given any inheritance, would you share it with me?' he asks.

'Of course I would, silly.'

'Me too. I'd give you more than half of it if it made you happy,' says Will.

'I've told you before, I don't need money to make me happy. I need my family.'

'I know, but we also need to eat,' says Will.

'We are eating. And, I must say, the batter on this fish is very delicious,' I say. Monty seems to agree as he sniffs at my wrapper.

I crunch into a big piece of batter and feel so happy. It might be cold on this bench, but the sun is shining, I have food in my belly, and I am sat beside my lovely husband. Who needs to win the lottery? I already did.

'Are you going to check the online shop again? I mean, I don't want you to get obsessed, but it would be interesting to see if there are any bids yet,' I say.

'Good idea,' says Will.

We pop our rubbish in the bin and head towards the car as Will checks the online shop, which he has handily installed onto an app on his phone.

I can already imagine Will checking sales from bed in the night. He never really switches off as it is and is often searching online for auctions or whatever. I do worry that he may end up packaging stock to send at all hours with his new shop. I can just imagine the state of the living room as he boxes stock up at all hours.

I can tell by Will's face that the online shop is already taking off, as he punches the air. He always does that whenever there is good news.

'Yes! We've had a bid of two thousand five hundred pounds for the doll's house!' says Will.

'Didn't I tell you this was a good idea?' I say.

'I should have known you were always right. Why didn't I agree to this earlier?'

Will gives me a high five and insists we stop on the way home to pick up a 'good' bottle of wine. As we settle down for the evening and enjoy the Pinot Noir, Will looks much more like his old self. It is only now I can truly see how worried he has been. I thought he had everything under control, but the business was obviously stressing him out more than I realised. That is probably the reason he has been waking up in the night and going downstairs for a cup of tea. I should have probably said something earlier, but Will has always been one of those men who doesn't talk about his feelings. If I asked him if he was okay, he would usually make some joke. He has always used humour to avoid any intimate conversations. He doesn't like to talk about things, so I haven't pushed him. So it is such a relief to see him acting more relaxed as I snuggle on the sofa with him. He is so switched off tonight that he doesn't even have his trusty calculator close by. Instead, he has a very relaxed hand on my leg!

'You know. I think things are on the up. I have a really good feeling about everything. We're going to be okay, and it's all thanks to you,' says Will.

I give him a kiss and he puts his arm around me.

'I always said I'd spoil you, and I know I haven't been very good at that since I took over the shop. But I promise you, this is a new chapter in our lives. I want to thank you for everything you've put up with. Just wait, I'm going to give you the best surprise ever.'

Chapter Three

The auction for the doll's house is due to end at two p.m. on Monday. Will and I watch in amazement as more bids come in. There are now twenty-five people watching it.

'We really should have done this ages ago,' I say.

'Can you believe it? Three thousand five hundred pounds, and one more hour to go,' says Will.

I don't know how he is going to control his enthusiasm over the next hour. He has been pacing up and down the shop all morning.

We watch the last few minutes and can't take our eyes off the screen as the timer starts to count down. It is only seconds to go and its current bid stands at £3,750.

Then, right at the last second, there is another bid for £4,000.

'Oh my gosh! That's amazing.'

I am grinning like a Cheshire cat. Our very first item has sold for a small fortune. I try hard to stop myself from saying 'I told you so'.

Will takes me in his arms and swings me around.

'We're rich,' he shouts.

'Well, I don't know about rich.' I laugh and choose not to remind him of all the debts we probably still won't be able to pay off. Will handles all of that side though, so I will leave that to him.

Within seconds, Will gets a notification on his phone from his bank that there has been a deposit into the business account.

'They've paid right away,' says Will.

He might be fifty-two, but as he grins at me, I see that image of him from when we first met at a nightclub all that time ago. I am forever grateful to my best friend, Amanda, for dragging me out to the club in Penally that night. If it wasn't for Amanda, Will and I may never have met. As I was dancing with her, Will joined us on the dancefloor and knew all the moves. I fell for him instantly. Most of the lads just stood around ogling the girls and cradling a pint, but Will was different. He put himself out there and was brave enough to get on the dancefloor and let himself go. When I was twenty-five, that was all it took to impress me.

Here we are twenty-five years later, and that infectious smile never fails to remind me of that night. It is a sign that deep down he is still that same person, even though he may have lost a little of his *joie de vivre* over the years, following grief and difficulties with the shop. So this new online business will hopefully build up his self-esteem a little. It is exactly what he needs.

'Shall I pop the kettle on to celebrate?' I ask.

'No, you stay right there. I'm *popping* to the shops,' says Will.

'Well, don't spend too much,' I say.

I do hope he will be sensible with the money. We can't get carried away just yet. All I ask is that this helps pay off any outstanding creditors.

We don't have any customers whilst Will is out, so I amuse myself with a book on marketing. Reading this, I think I could become quite the entrepreneur myself.

Perhaps I should even consider my own Etsy store. I have always fancied making jewellery.

When I was at school, I would buy cheap bracelets, earrings and necklaces in Chelsea Girl or Snob, take them apart and make them into new, flashier pieces that I was always complimented on. I even took an Art A level in the hope that I could fulfil my creative side, but sadly the curriculum didn't cover jewellery-making. Instead, I had to paint works of art, and I wasn't so proficient at that and failed. I often regret not putting my creative talent to use over the years – although, I am not sure many would want the electric blue plastic earrings I used to make. Thank goodness fashion changes!

–

When Will finally returns an hour later, he is still on cloud nine. I cannot remember when I saw him smiling like this; it has been so long.

'Surprise,' he says. He throws a brochure down in front of me with a page open showing the Piazza San Marco.

'Venice?'

'Yes. Do you remember the promise I made that I would take you back for our twenty-fifth wedding anniversary?'

'Yes, of course.'

I thought he had long forgotten, so I am thrilled that he even remembers what he said all those years ago.

'Well, we're going back for our anniversary, just as I promised. Five nights in Venice, over Valentine's Day and the Carnevale.'

'Oh my goodness. Are you sure we can afford it though?'

I don't know why I even ask this question as I am pretty sure I know we can't.

'Of course we can. The doll's house has sold. It's only a matter of time before we sell everything else. We officially have a booming online business,' says Will.

Deep down, I can see Will getting swept away with this one big sale. It would be lovely to have a break though. For years we have sunk everything into the business, and a holiday away from it all has never sounded so appealing. I also know that this is Will's way of keeping the promise he made all that time ago. This will mean so much to him.

'Oh, how long has it been since we had a holiday?' I say.

'Not since the boys were small and we took them to Disneyland Paris,' remembers Will.

It is then that my mam instincts kick in.

'Dylan! He can't get time off A level college at such an important time.'

'He's eighteen, he's a big boy now. He'll be fine staying home on his own for a few days.'

'Oh, I don't know. I know he's a good lad, but you hear of friends persuading kids to have a party. What if they have a rave or something?'

'Don't be silly. Keagan will be the only one to come over, and you know how sensible he is.'

Keagan has been Dylan's best friend since nursery, and his parents are friends of ours, so Will is probably right.

'Besides, Ken and Patricia next door will tell us immediately if there is the slightest noise coming from the house,' says Will.

'Yes, very true. What about Monty and the shop?' I ask.

'I've already thought of that. We can ask Emily to look after Monty and the shop. She can bring him to work with her.'

'Wow, you have thought of everything, haven't you.'

'Not really. I just desperately want some alone time with you,' says Will, laughing.

'Oh, love. It will be so wonderful to get back there. That doll's house has brought us so much luck. Ooh, goodness, it's only a few weeks away. I'll have to check if our passports are in date. Do you remember if they are?'

'They should be. We can check tonight,' says Will.

'Oh, I'm going to have to ring Emily and tell her the exciting news. I hope she doesn't mind helping at the shop.'

'Well, she helped out before when you had your gall-bladder removed and I had to look after you. She didn't make too much of a mess of things. Secretly, I think she enjoyed being needed,' says Will.

I call my sister, hoping she picks up and hasn't booked herself into a health spa somewhere and not told me. It wouldn't be the first time I panicked when I couldn't get hold of her. Last time, she was at a Buddhist retreat in India and phones weren't allowed. I was an hour off calling the police when she finally updated Facebook with photos of her detoxing from all modern devices – that was until she realised how much she missed posting selfies. It's not that Emily intentionally keeps things from me; she is just spontaneous and decides on a whim to do things, forgetting to tell her worried sister.

Fortunately, she picks up her phone on the second ring.

'Libby, how lovely to hear from you. Don't tell me you're dying of boredom in that shop again. No customers?'

It stings as she says this. Her ex-husband, John, was a very successful investment banker and he paid her a generous divorce settlement. As much as I love her, she has this knack of making me feel inadequate at times. Sibling rivalry never ceases, even at this age.

'We're very busy, thank you. The business is doing extremely well,' I say. Sometimes I wish I didn't confide in her as much. 'In fact, I was ringing to ask if you could keep an eye on Dylan and look after Monty and the shop for us. Will is taking me away.'

'Taking you away? Ooh, where's he taking you? Let me guess... Saundersfoot?'

Now I am really starting to lose patience with her. Saundersfoot is a nearby village, and her sarcasm is met with indignation.

'Just because we've had our financial issues does not mean you have the right to mock my lovely Will. It isn't his fault half the customers have died,' I snap.

'All right, calm down. You need to get some Ayurvedic treatments, my love. I'll ask my practitioner the next time I see him what he recommends for a stressy sister.'

'I am not stressy. Look, can you help us whilst we're away over Valentine's Day, or not?'

'Sure. It's not like I'll be going off on a hot date,' says Emily.

Any resentment towards my sister diminishes as I hear that tone in her voice. I know that she will be alone for another Valentine's Day, just as she has been for the past five. She may have heaps of money and be able to flit off wherever she fancies, but she is incredibly lonely too. Since the divorce she hasn't been involved with anyone. Too hairy, too boring, too jovial – you name it, she has made excuses for any man who has crossed her path. I think she is secretly scared of getting hurt like she did with John, who left her for the skiing instructor he met in Courchevel.

'Thanks, sis. You're an angel,' I say.

'No worries, but it's on the condition that you have to let me plan an anniversary party for when you get back, okay? Only, you'll obviously have to do all the cooking.'

Typical Emily!

I agree, and with the arrangements for little Monty sorted, I rush straight to the safe we keep at home to make sure the passports don't need updating. I move the other bits that we keep in the safe, including my dad's precious watch, so that I can reach them at the back. Will stands eagerly beside me as I remove the passports and check the expiry dates.

'Any good?'

'We'll just about make it. Nine months left on both of them,' I say.

'Oh, phew. That's one less thing to sort then. Didn't even occur to me when I made the booking,' says Will.

'Well, it wouldn't be the first time,' I say, laughing.

We almost didn't make our honeymoon to Venice as Will hadn't thought to check his passport and had to make a mad dash down to the passport office in Newport at the last minute. I won't let him make the same mistake again.

I put the passports safely back in and take out Dad's precious watch so that I can take a look at it before I close the safe. I stroke it in my hand. I love touching it. It always makes me feel close to him. It's all I have left of him since he passed away five years ago. The watch was a wedding present from my mum who died many years earlier. Dad didn't have much money when he died, but he left the most sentimental of his belongings to his

31

youngest grandchild. As Emily never had children, this meant it was to be handed down to Dylan on his twenty-first birthday. Only a few more years until I am to pass it down to him. It is going to be very emotional handing it over. I like knowing it is close to me in the safe that we keep in the bedroom.

'Beautiful watch, isn't it?' says Will.

'It is. I always loved it on Dad. So many memories. He wore it the day of our wedding, Ewan's and Dylan's christenings… He always wore it at every special occasion.'

I look at the gold strap and the diamonds that have lost their shine a little over the years. I should probably take it somewhere to get it polished before I give it to Dylan. It needs a new battery too.

'It's a very good designer that. Italian,' says Will.

'I believe so. But I don't care who designed it, or what it's worth. It's so sentimental it could be worth a million pounds and I wouldn't let this family part with it,' I say.

I'm talking to myself though as Will is already making his way downstairs.

'Right, I'm making tea tonight. What shall we have?' he shouts.

I give the watch a kiss and place it back in carefully and close the safe.

'Oh, I think there's only one thing for it. How about pasta? It'll put us right in the mood for Venice,' I say.

Chapter Four

As if I wasn't already in the best mood ever, Ewan has called to say that he is coming home for the weekend and to expect a visitor with him. I love a full house and rush around throwing the bedsheets and spare towels in the wash. I feel like a mother hen as my boy comes home to roost. Albeit for a weekend.

With the washing machine going at full speed, I excitedly look through my recipe books for something special to prepare for dinner. Ewan won't tell me who the visitor is so it could be anyone. However, he has promised me that there are no dietary requirements which is always good to know before you start planning a three-course meal. I do hope whoever it is enjoys Scrabble.

For starters, I find a recipe for a halloumi, pomegranate and walnut salad. I hope this should suit most guests. I then decide on beef bourguignon and celeriac mash for the main course. I tell Will that I am taking the day off from the shop to prepare everything, including my late mother's family favourite pavlova recipe. Ewan will have such a lovely surprise to find that on the menu.

Dylan has hinted that Ewan is bringing a girl home. I can't imagine that he is right – Ewan never brings girls home, let alone for a weekend – so I have the spare room ready, as I am sure it will be one of his mates who wants to visit Tenby for the weekend.

Dylan is right though. When Ewan arrives, he walks through the door with a girl. A girl! I almost faint! This is highly unlike my rugby-mad Ewan.

'This is Nia,' says Ewan.

'Hello,' she says quietly. She looks lovely. Still, I never imagined him bringing a girl home; it feels so odd.

'Hi, I'm Libby. This is Will,' I say.

'Hi,' she says quietly.

'Well, umm, let me take your coat, Nia,' I say with a smile.

She stands around looking slightly uncomfortable. I remember the first time I met Will's parents and how scary they seemed, so I do sympathise. I hope I don't come across as scary as Will's mum, Janice. She was a bit of a battle axe, if I'm honest. We had many a clash over the years about how I should bring the boys up.

'Go and sit down. Food won't be long,' I say.

'Smells lush, Mam,' says Ewan.

I hurry into the kitchen to get everything prepared. I am still in shock. I know Ewan and Dylan tried to warn me, but still.

'It must be serious. Our little boy brought a girl home,' I whisper to Will in the kitchen.

'He's hardly our little boy, Libby. He's twenty-bleeding-one!'

'I know, but sometimes I find it so weird. It feels like only the other day I was taking the boys to nursery and now there's universities and girlfriends.'

'You need a life, Libby,' says Will, laughing.

'What on earth do you mean?'

'Well, you've spent so long with the boys trying to prove you can be the best mother, you've forgotten how to enjoy yourself,' he says.

I feel slightly offended by his comment. Does he know how inadequate I always felt with his family? I worked so hard to prove to that mother of his that I was worthy of him. I don't think she liked me until the day she died though. Nothing I did would make any difference. No woman would ever have been good enough for her precious son. I promise myself not to be like that with Nia or any other girl in the future that either of the boys bring home.

Will pours the Chianti that he picked up especially for tonight and hands me a glass as we chat in the kitchen.

'The boys don't need us as much as they once did. It's time for us now. To us and our future,' says Will, making a toast.

He clinks the crystal glass against mine. I made sure the best wine glasses were out and polished for tonight's special guest.

I gulp down the wine. I know that I need to face a future of not being needed as much, but it still takes some adjusting. The thought of designing jewellery comes to my mind again. Jewellery-making classes, perhaps that is what I need to do. I hate not keeping busy.

'We need to make a bucket list of things we're going to do once Ewan leaves,' says Will, as if reading my mind.

'Skydiving?' I say hopefully. It is wildly different to anything I would ordinarily do, but I have always had this desire to do something a little riskier one day. I saw a programme on skydiving once and was mesmerised. The crazy freedom of it... I envied the skydivers' bravery to just jump out of a plane like that. As we talk about our future hopes, this dream comes back to me again.

'Anything but skydiving,' he says.

'Sit at home and watch TV all night then? Would that be better for you?' I say. I can't help but get snarky with Will tonight. What is wrong with skydiving? Why can't we have some adventure in our lives now that the boys are growing up? For one day, I could be like Super Mam instead of Dependable Mam. Thinking about it, perhaps I have had too much wine for one night.

'What's wrong with you and me snuggled up in front of the fire, after one of your lovely home-cooked meals, watching a documentary on birds?' says Will.

'Birds! And you know, sometimes, it would be nice to go out for dinner and have someone else cook for a change,' I say. Will and I seldom argue, but since his comment about me getting a life, he has really wound me up. Just because I am primarily a happy wife and mum doesn't mean that it wouldn't be nice to have some of the pampering that Will used to shower on me when we first got married.

'You enjoy your cooking,' he says.

'I know I do, but it would be nice to have a treat every now and then.'

'Come on now, you know things have been tight. Anyway, there'll be no cooking in Venice,' says Will.

'Sorry, you're right. I just get a bit emotional as I think of the future. Fear of the unknown. I suppose I have to find myself again.'

Will gives me a big *cwch* in the kitchen when Dylan walks in.

'Mam! Dad! Get off each other, will you? Can't you argue like normal parents and stop being so soppy,' says Dylan. Maybe he would have preferred to have seen us a few moments ago.

We both laugh, and Will ruffles Dylan's hair.

'You wait, boy. Your turn next,' says Will.

'No chance. Never getting married,' says Dylan.

'I said that too, but look. Almost twenty-five years now.'

'You said you'd never marry?' I look at Will, astonished. That's the first I have heard of that.

'Only when I was his age. Not after I set eyes on you,' says Will, smiling.

'Oh, Dad. Stop being so cringe. I'm going to be sick now. What with them two in the living room and you, I can't escape this crap tonight.'

'Oi, don't use the word crap, please. It's not allowed in this house,' says Will.

'Come on, you can help me take in the salads for that.' I hand Dylan two colourful salad plates. The handy thing about selling antiques is that I have a dish for every eventuality and every dinner party.

'And you can take these.'

I give Will another two plates, I take one, and we all head into the dining room with the starters. We set the plates down on the antique mahogany dining table that has already been laid out carefully. This table was also another perk of the job.

'This looks nice,' says Nia politely.

'Thanks. Tuck in,' I say.

I don't know why, but I almost feel too nervous to eat. Sometimes, when I prepare dinner for guests, I am so busy making sure everything is perfect that I don't have the energy to eat it myself by the time I sit down. Tonight, I am more worried that Nia enjoys my cooking. Fortunately, it seems that I have nothing to worry about.

'This is stunning. My mum could never cook like this,' she says as she gobbles down the beef bourguignon. A wave of satisfaction rushes over me.

'Oh, I'm sure she can,' I say.

'Oh no, we grew up on steak and kidney pies in a tin, and even then, Mum would leave the saucepan to boil dry,' she says, laughing.

'Oh, there's a lot to be said for a pie in a tin… if cooked properly,' I say.

I can see that I will get along well with Nia if she is to be a regular visitor. In some ways, she reminds me of how I wanted to be when I was younger. She is studying business, which I would have loved to have done instead of going to secretarial college. People like me didn't really study business at that time though; the only jobs around were in offices helping with the typing or doing accounts. As I have dyscalculia, accounting would never have worked out well for anyone. Of course, Emily had to be different. She joined a casino as a croupier when she was twenty-one. She thought she would sashay about the place in a ballgown, like in some glamorous movie. She was devastated when the casino gave her a little waistcoat and trousers to wear as a uniform instead. She stuck at it though and that is where she met John when he and some high rollers walked in.

'So, what do you do when you're not studying?' I ask Nia.

'A bit of this and that, isn't it, Ewan?' she says.

'Yeah, she's doing a skydive for charity next week, aren't you?' says Ewan.

'No way. I've always fancied skydiving. I was just reminding Will of that. The thought of being free as a 'bird is so appealing,' I say. I notice Will roll his eyes as he listens to what he has heard so many times before.

'You should come down. I'm a member of a club near uni. They're all ages there. One lady jumped last week, and she was eighty.'

Eighty? How old does she think I am?

'Not that I am saying you're eighty. I mean, anyone can jump… You know.'

'It's okay. I know what you mean. I'll have a think about it. It is something I would love to do.'

Nia tells us about her dad who had prostate cancer and why this jump and the money she will raise is so important to her. I look at her and think how proud her dad would be. She is a genuinely lovely girl, and my heart swells with pride that Ewan has chosen such a nice person to bring home.

'We'll make sure to give you a donation, won't we, Will?' I say.

'That's so kind of you. My mum gave me two hundred pounds, but whatever you can give will be greatly appreciated. I'm four hundred pounds off my target,' she says.

Will looks at me in shock and mouths, *Two hundred pounds!*

I wonder if she thinks we are wealthy. I look around at the dining room with its antique grandfather clock and Victorian framed prints. It probably does look as though we have more money than we do to an outsider.

'We'll see what we can do,' I say. I was initially thinking twenty pounds, but it is difficult to say that after her mother's donation.

'Right. Anyone for dessert then?' I ask.

I clear all the dishes and bring out the pavlova.

'Oh my god, Mam! You made my fave,' says Ewan.

'Only the best for my boys,' I say.

'Thanks, Mam!'

I watch as everyone tucks in around the table and feel at peace with the world. Despite my little hissy fit in the kitchen earlier, I have the best husband ever, and I am grateful for my family every single day. Marriage isn't all chocolates and flowers. Sometimes, it is sitting in front of the TV with nothing exciting to watch, dealing with your financial struggles or arguing over the silliest of things. But then there are glorious moments like this. Moments that you want to capture in your memory forever because, luckily, you don't know what is around the corner.

Chapter Five

We don't go away often, but when we do, I always like to be organised. It's just a thing. I have to pack everything at least forty-eight hours in advance, and so I have already taken down my vanity case from the top of the wardrobe. Nobody really travels with a vanity case any longer. I think that is a great shame. I love mine as it keeps everything safe, including our passports and the tube of Fruit Pastilles I always make sure I carry to stop our ears from popping on the plane. With my handy vanity case, there is no need to fumble about and rummage in my bottomless pit of a handbag for passports. I just open the zip and don't have to delay everyone in the queue as I panic that I can't find the passports. Will says it is all about control. I do like to be in control, so he is probably right. I can't control things from tumbling to the bottom of my bag and joining the mints that are stuck to the lining.

Will suggests that we stay the night near the airport before we fly out early morning. So we have booked a little motel-type place nearby. After we say goodbye to Dylan and Monty – I tried so hard not to cry in front of them – we make our way up the M4 towards Bristol. I don't know whether I am excited or nervous as we head off on our first holiday alone in all this time. Nervous is probably the stronger of the emotions right now. It is the thought of leaving Dylan at home, and I already miss him and Monty. It's so silly. We are only away for five days, yet I feel as though I won't see them again. What if something happens to us on our travels and the boys end up orphans? I stop myself from stressing out, and I don't know why I think such awful thoughts. I wonder if other mams think like this or if it is just me.

I don't know what I fear, as everything is running smoothly so far. Not too much traffic on the M4, and it is as though there is some patron saint of travel who is helping us along the way. There is not a single hold-up.

In fact, we get to the motel earlier than we imagined, and as we check in, the welcoming receptionist asks if we want a reservation for dinner. We hadn't wanted to book before in case we were late, so we are delighted we can unwind a bit before our early morning flight.

We take our bags and hurry off to the room, where Will gives me a kiss.

'Isn't this gorgeous? Just the two of us?' Will grins and then pulls me close to him. He has that look. The knowing look means he wants a bit of nookie. I am not really in the mood after the long car journey. I also usually need a glass of wine before any of that nowadays to help me relax. We have been best friends for so long that over the past few years I have started to feel a little self-conscious about that sort of thing. I don't know what it is exactly. Perhaps it is because, after two kids and a gall-bladder operation, I am not confident being seen naked. Keyhole surgery is available now, and maybe I wouldn't be so self-conscious had I been given that option. To be fair, Will doesn't seem to care, but I do.

Don't get me wrong, it is nice to be alone with Will, but I still feel a bit strange with it being just us two when we have been surrounded by children and dogs for so many years. Things were so different before they all came along. We used to be much more spontaneous and couldn't keep our hands off each other. Over the years, I hate to say it, but sex has become a bit of a chore, and there are certain days when the washing up, or mowing the lawn, are more appealing.

'Look, I'd better freshen up.' I pull myself away from Will and start unzipping my luggage. 'Why don't you check to see if we've any more sales on the online shop thing? I'll text Emily to see how things are going there.'

'You've only just left. You're not already checking in with her?' says Will.

'I want to make sure she's given Monty his kibble.'

'If I didn't know better, I'd say you're making any excuse not to have sex with me,' says Will.

'Oh my gosh, Will. What a thing to say! Anyway, I'm not having sex here, the walls are too thin. Look.'

I knock the wall beside us and someone shouts 'Hello'.

'See. Maybe in Venice, okay?'

Will looks a bit sulky, but hopefully, that means I have avoided the inevitable for a bit longer, and I skulk off to the bathroom.

'So, any sales then?' I shout in between brushing my teeth.

'Just checking. Lots of people watching stuff. The Royal Doulton china set I put on hasn't sold. I did put it on for a bit too much. I just thought after the doll's house…'

'You can't get greedy just because of one big sale. I know that pricing items is your job but maybe you should check what other shops are selling things for. You can't overprice your pieces. I was reading in my marketing book that…'

'Marketing! Ha. My dad never read marketing books and he did all right.'

He left debts, I want to say. We were very fortunate many of them were cleared by his death, but not all of them. I stop myself. That would be a pretty mean thing to say. Will worshipped his dad, Nigel. He wasn't a bad man, to be fair, and he probably had to put up with a lot from his wife, Janice. Nigel had inherited the business from his own dad, Will's grandad. He had died before I met Will, so Nigel was already running the shop for as long as I have known the family.

I pull out a sparkly dress from my luggage for dinner. I was saving it for Venice, but decide to wear it tonight as I am starting to feel the holiday vibe.

'You look gorgeous,' says Will when I have changed.

Those eyes are starting to give me that look again. It is the same puppy-eyed look that Monty gives me when he smells lamb chops. Oh gosh, Will is really in the mood tonight.

'Thank you. Thin walls, remember,' I say.

Will looks disappointed again, and it does make me feel a little bit sorry for him. I feel terrible for having rejected him twice in ten minutes.

'Come on, let's get a drink before dinner. I quite fancy a cocktail,' I say, trying to cheer him up.

As we close the hotel room door, the couple in the next room to us are leaving at the same time. I thank my lucky stars that I didn't give in to Will. It would be mortifying to have to bump into them if they had heard us having sex!

The couple look as though they are in their early thirties.

'Hiya,' the young woman says.

'Hi,' I say, smiling.

We don't speak any further, but it is one of those embarrassing moments where we are all walking at the same speed and reach the door to the bar at the same time.

The bar, it seems, is where most of the holidaymakers spend the evening drinking too much before they have to face their fear of flying early the next morning. I am lucky that I like flying, despite my morbid views about not seeing my family again. However, Will isn't so keen. Well, it is more the take-offs and landings that he doesn't like.

The bar is full of people either starting their holiday as they mean to go on (with too much alcohol) or trying to numb their pre-flying nerves. There is only one table left in the whole bar and so I rush over to it. It seems our next-door neighbours at the motel have the same idea and so the woman puts her handbag down to claim the table at the exact same time I put mine down. *Awkward*, as Dylan would say.

'Oh, shall we just share the table?' she says.

'That would be the fairest thing to do,' I reply.

'I'm Claire and this is Ethan,' she says, introducing us to her partner.

'Libby and Will,' I say.

Ethan and Will start talking about rugby and I try to think of something to say to Claire.

'Where are you off on holiday?' I ask.

'Prague,' says Claire.

'How gorgeous. I've always fancied Prague. My sister, Emily, has been. She said it was brilliant. She went on some medieval dining experience and didn't stop talking about it for months.'

'Oh, yeah. We've booked that. I'm so excited. It's our honeymoon, see,' says Claire.

I look down at her sparkling wedding ring and notice Ethan has a matching one. I should have realised they were newlyweds as Ethan keeps stroking Claire's leg under the table. That will stop after a few years, I think to myself.

'And you guys. Where are you off to?' asks Claire.

'Venice. We're celebrating our twenty-fifth wedding anniversary.'

'That's so awesome. I hope we last twenty-five years. My mum and dad didn't manage anything like that. Six years, that was it. Ethan's parents got divorced last year.'

'Oh, what a shame.'

'It's all right. My mum is so much happier now. My dad, not so much. But anyway, if you've been together for so long, you must have some tips. How do you manage to have such a long marriage?'

I think about Will and me. Even though we have different interests and probably different sex drives nowadays, we were made for each other, so that probably helps. We have the same views about almost everything. Although I'm not sure if that is because we were always so similar, or if we grew to be alike over the years. We are one of those couples who even dress the same at times. We both love our polo shirts and jeans.

'You know, I think the main thing is trust. I have always felt like the one thing I cannot stand is secrets. I've always said to Will, I'd rather have the truth, even if it hurts, than have someone lie to me. I can't abide by lies. It's something I'm really funny about. We've never kept anything from each other. I think that's one of the reasons we're still so happy together.'

'Wow. So no lies, yeah? But I mean, when you buy, like, a new dress or something, surely you have to lie about the price? I mean, we all knock a few noughts off if your other half asks how much it cost, right?'

'No, I'd always tell Will how much things cost. No secrets, no lies.'

'Goodness. I'm amazed you're still married then,' says Claire, laughing.

Will overhears the conversation.

'Yup, she told me that on our wedding day. There's to be no secrets or lies ever between us. It seems to have worked.'

Will puts his arm around me and I lean into his neck. I think the last sip of the Blue Moon cocktail is starting to make me chill a bit.

'Another cocktail?' asks Will.

'Are you trying to get me tipsy, Mr Jones?'

'Well, a little Sex on the Beach would be good for you, don't you think?'

The innuendos that Will has always been full of used to make me giggle. Now all I can think is that I hope we won't be near any beaches in Venice.

'Will, they hardly know us. Don't be cheeky.' I blush at him saying such a thing in front of Ethan and Claire. 'On that note, it might be best to skip that cocktail and head for our dinner reservation next door, don't you think?'

'Aw, well, it's been so lovely meeting you. I hope we're like you when we're your age. You two are made for each other,' says Claire.

'We are indeed,' says Will.

He taps my bottom as we leave the table, and I decide there and then to make sure he has plenty of alcohol at dinner. That will make sure he falls asleep as soon as we get back to the room.

Chapter Six

Will still has a bit of a sore head by the time we land in Venice. I do feel terrible for encouraging him to drink so much. But at least he had a good sleep, which I witnessed by listening to him snoring all through the night. I forgive him for that though. After all, arriving at Marco Polo Airport would make anyone forget they were exhausted. Just seeing the airport signs in Italian is already getting me in the mood for this Venetian city break.

I assumed that we would get a bus from the airport and then a shared water taxi to the hotel, but Will leads me to a desk at arrivals and seems to have something up his sleeve.

'Reservation for Mr and Mrs Jones,' he says to the Italian man behind the counter.

'Yes, the boat is waiting for you,' he says.

Did Will truly remember everything? He promised me that when we came back, we would travel from the airport by private water taxi.

We walk in the direction of the private transfers and the boat is ready and waiting. I feel like a movie star!

'Oh, Will. I can't believe you've arranged this!' I kiss him on the lips in my excitement. This is going to be the best holiday ever.

I make a conscious effort this time not to struggle to get on the boat and step on graciously, remembering the lady I saw last time. All I need is a straw hat and I would be just like her. I wonder what happened to her.

I sit down on the boat's cream leather seat and look around at the open canal in front of us. The sunlight is glinting down on the water as the panorama of Venice lies ahead. This makes a welcome change from doing my sudoku puzzles as I wait for customers to walk into the shop. The driver starts the gleaming wooden speedboat up and we leave the mooring. He starts off slowly and then speeds up until it feels like we are flying through the canal. My hair is blowing in the cold February wind, and it feels refreshing after all the travelling.

'How amazing is this?' I say.

Will doesn't seem quite as enthusiastic as I am. He looks a little green if I am honest. It is probably the combination of the alcohol last night and the speed at which the hull is hitting the wake. Other boats pass us, making it even rockier. It is certainly a very busy waterway.

I look at Will to make sure he is okay, but he doesn't speak and instead gives me a thumbs up. I feel awful for plying him with so much alcohol before our travels.

As the journey progresses, the palazzos in the centre of Venice finally come into view.

Will has booked us a hotel right on the edge of Rialto Bridge, so when I see it getting closer, I know we are nearing the end of our journey. What a shame. I could have been ferried around like a princess on this all day.

We moor right outside the hotel, and the driver helps remove our bags from his boat.

'Thanks so much. That was amazing. Ta-ra,' I say.

He waves us goodbye with one hand and reverses his beautiful boat back out into the canal.

'Ooh, I want to do that again.'

'I'm not sure I can afford it twice,' Will says, laughing. He hasn't told me exactly how much it cost, but I can imagine it wasn't cheap.

'Oh, gosh, no, of course. We don't want to spend too much.'

We check into our hotel with its old-fashioned reception and room keys stored in compartments on the wall behind. I can imagine Will mentally adding up how much some of the antiques that are scattered around reception are worth. Sometimes, it feels that going on holiday with an antique and curiosities dealer is a bit of a busman's holiday.

The receptionist leans behind him and gives us a key.

'Suite 101,' he says. We take the key from him and make our way in the lift.

'Suite?' I say.

'Oh, I think they call all the rooms a suite. Don't get excited,' says Will.

'Oh, I wondered if they'd upgraded us for our anniversary then.'

The room might be one of the smallest of the rooms the hotel has, but it is still absolutely glorious. There are long red velvet curtains, and drapes that swish over the headboard. It is all so dramatic.

'Isn't this gorgeous, Will.'

'I'm glad you like it,' he says, putting his bag down.

'Come here.'

I give Will a big hug.

'Thank you for arranging all of this.' I fiddle with the top button on his shirt. 'You know, this is quite romantic, don't you think?'

Perhaps it is the small bottle of cheap plonk I had on the plane, but, finally, I am feeling quite amorous.

'Yeah, sure. Look, sorry, I've still got a bit of a headache,' says Will, pulling away from me. I get a taste of my own medicine and the rejection that Will must have felt last night hurts a little.

'No, of course. I shouldn't have encouraged you to have that extra pint last night. Do you want to get a walk?'

'Yeah. And maybe a bite to eat.'

We are lucky that there is a cafe near the hotel. The window display of pizza entices us to walk in without hesitation. I am surprised to see that you can get so many different types of pizza toppings, including chips. I don't remember pizzas like this the last time we were here. Perhaps I didn't notice then, but now I think of Dylan. How he would love to have a pizza with chips as a topping!

Will takes some photos of the various pizzas to send back to Dylan and simultaneously let them all know at home that we have arrived safely.

Following the most gorgeous ham and mushroom pizzas we have ever had, Will starts to look a lot more human, and so we head for a walk along to San Marco. Will takes my hand as we walk down the narrow passageways lined with all sorts of shops that lead to the square. The shops are a beguiling mix. Some sell jewellery, others have souvenirs, and many sell Venetian masks. As it is Carnivale time in Venice, I can't resist stopping to have a look at one shop that has a colourful collection of Venetian masks. They are so beautiful. There are so many different types of masks in the window. Some have bright harlequin patterns, others look like cats, and there are even plague doctor masks. However, one eye mask with feathers stands out from everything else.

'Oh, Will. Look at that! I have never seen anything more beautiful.'

It is a blue and gold eye mask, with a gold band around it to keep it in place. Popping out of the top left-hand side of it is an assemblage of the most spectacular deep blue feathers. The gold sparkles from the mask and catches the light. I can't stop swooning over it.

'Gosh, it is very well put together, isn't it? I love the craftsmanship in Venice,' Will says.

'Me too,' I agree.

'Do you want to get it?'

'No, we couldn't afford something like that,' I say.

'How do you know? Come on, let's go in and check how much it is.'

The shop is like a cave full of treasure, unlike ours back home. There are masks hanging all over the walls. I wish our shop looked more like this, but there probably isn't a market in Tenby for Venetian masks.

A serious-looking shop owner greets us at the counter as we enquire about the price of the beautiful blue mask.

'It is hand-designed. Very good quality. One hundred euros,' he says.

Will asks me again if I want it, but I refuse. One hundred euros could possibly pay for a couple of meals if we are careful about where we eat.

So we head back into the alleyway and continue our way towards the square.

However, the next set of shops are too tempting not to stop at.

'Look at this beautiful jeweller's,' says Will, pulling me to the other side of the alleyway.

One side of the window is full of watches. Will looks at them whilst I look at the other window, which has a display of rings. They are stunning, with all sorts of diamonds, sapphires and topaz stones. There are also cheaper rings with gemstones, which makes me think again about how much I would love to design jewellery. A sign on the door says that they sell gemstones, so I decide to pop in to see if I can find some little stones that I could start my new hobby with. I think how I could start by making necklaces and earrings and carefully go through a basket in the shop that has some of the cheapest gemstones. I am excited as I hunt through the basket. It is my first step in finding something new to do once Dylan has left home. I find exactly what I am looking for and happily pay forty euros for the gems that are like a little piece of Venetian magic that I can take home with me. I don't mind the cost since I figure this is my first-ever business investment. I don't take much notice of the man who is serving on the other counter as he tries to sell Will a watch. I am too excited about my gemstones to listen to his sales talk. I notice from the corner of my eye that he gives Will his business card in an attempt to get our repeat custom. When there are so many shops down these little alleyways, it is probably quite sensible of the shopkeepers to give out business cards to ensure tourists can find them again.

By the time we finally reach San Marco and find somewhere to sit down, my feet are aching. As we wait for our eye-wateringly priced lattes, I look again at my gemstones.

'I really don't understand what you want them for. Why don't you just sell them in the shop?' says Will.

'I've told you a few times I want to make jewellery,' I remind him. That is the other thing that happens after twenty-five years; you sometimes forget to listen to each other's dreams.

'I'm not sure why. You have a job in the shop. You don't need anything else to do,' he says.

I sip angrily at my latte. How dare he! This is my dream. I support him by working in the shop. Is it too much to ask that he gives me a little encouragement for my jewellery business?

'Anyway, talking of the shop, I'd better check the app. Are you sure Emily will be okay with posting all the orders out?' says Will.

'She's not stupid,' I snap. Even though I have my moments with my sister, I won't let Will be condescending towards her. I feel like adding that there won't be many sales for her to send out anyhow! However, I bite my lip as I realise that I feel resentful towards the business, not necessarily Will.

It might be a family legacy to him, but to me, it is a sheer liability. It is like a burden always hanging around our necks and there is never a day we can escape it. Even here in Venice when we should be able to have a holiday without a care in the world, Will is thinking of his stock.

'No sales and the shop rent is due,' he says, looking at the app.

Will puts his phone down beside the coffee that we now definitely can't afford and he looks towards the gondolas that are just about in eyeshot.

'Sorry. I know it's a tough time. We'll get through it,' I say.

It seems appropriate that we visit the Bridge of Sighs next, especially since Will hasn't stopped sighing since he checked the app.

'You do know there's a reason it's called the Bridge of Sighs, don't you?' I say as we walk across it.

'Because they are sighs of passion and love. Venice is all about romance, isn't it?' says Will.

'No, don't you remember the last time we were here? What the guide told us? Were you not listening as usual?'

'I usually have stuff on my mind,' he moans.

'Well, I'll teach you. It's actually a very sad story about how the prisoners would sigh with despair when they crossed this bridge as they knew they wouldn't get out alive and this was the end for them,' I say.

'Oh, that's not very nice.'

'I know, it's terribly sad. There's so much history here. I'm surprised you didn't remember that one.'

Will sighs once more.

'Look, think about this bridge. I know you are down about the business, but there are always worse things to happen in life.'

I suddenly get a shiver down my spine as we reach the other side. The things this bridge must have witnessed.

'Prisoners get fed and don't have bills though,' says Will.

'Oh, I hate it when you're in one of these moods. Come on, we're on holiday. Cheer up. Besides, I'm going to sell my handmade jewellery and make more than the shop ever did.'

'It's not right. You know I'm old school. I'm a proud man. I believe in supporting my family, just like my father did.'

Do I remind him that his dad didn't make that look easy? If debts mean supporting a family, then I guess he managed that bit.

'I had one job, and that was to make a go of the business and support my family. Look at me.'

'It's fine. We have the online shop. It's only early days.' I know he is worried, but at least I am trying to get us out of this mess. If only Will would quit the business, we wouldn't be in this situation at all.

'But what if it fails? I spent all this money on a holiday trying to pretend that everything was okay, but it's not. It's not okay at all.'

'What do you mean, it's not okay, Will?'

'Oh, fuck it. I'm not in the mood for this.'

Will swore! The first time I have heard him swear in twenty-five years! Then he storms off. I try to catch him up as he leaves the building, but he runs ahead of me in the direction of St Mark's Basilica.

'Will, wait,' I shout.

But it is no good. The crowds have gathered around Piazza San Marco and Will is quickly becoming a dot in front of St Mark's Basilica. Until, finally, I can barely see those familiar long legs.

The tourists are stopping everywhere to take photos and they are making it impossible to get through the crowds to reach Will.

In all our years of marriage, this is the first time he has sworn or stormed off and left me alone. I know he is worried about things, but this is truly out of character. To just leave me like this in the middle of a busy square in Venice alone. I look at the other couples near me. Arm in arm, holding hands, kissing. They all have one thing in common – they are all so in love and happy. Then there is me. My chin is quivering, and I desperately try not to burst into tears in front of so many people, but I can't help it. As I make my way towards the windy alleyways back towards the hotel, I have tears running down my cheeks. Suddenly I start to feel the February chill. I had been immune to it up until now. The clouds darken over the Venice sky and the earlier sunshine vanishes. I start to shiver as I head back to the hotel alone.

What happened to the couple who were full of excitement and dreams the last time we were here? Look at us now. It is Valentine's Day tomorrow, and I don't think I have ever felt so alone as I do right now.

Chapter Seven

When I get back to the room, I begin to worry. There is no sign of Will. I assumed he would be here apologising by the time I arrived back. I can't work out if he has come back here and gone out again, or what he has done. But I am sure I didn't see the empty foil for his painkillers on the dressing table when we left. I must be mistaken. I decide to pop down to reception to ask if they have seen him. But the man at reception doesn't understand my description and just says, 'No see.' I walk outside the hotel door and look up and down the street, but I don't see Will and decide it might be best to wait in the room in case he has calmed down and tries to call or something.

I try calling Will, but it goes straight to voicemail. I think he might be in an area of bad reception, so I send a message, but it doesn't go through. His WhatsApp is showing one little tick, and I watch and watch, praying for another tick to appear. It doesn't. I tell myself that he must need some time to cool down. Perhaps he has switched off his phone as he needs some space. But I can't help but worry that something has happened to him. What if he has had an accident in his temper and fallen into a canal and into the oncoming path of a gondola full of tourists? What if I am wrong about the foil wrapper and he's taken one too many painkillers? I pace up and down and try to take deep breaths to calm myself.

I look at the phone again. One tick. Where could he be?

Surely, if something had happened, there would be some sort of commotion. Wouldn't someone eventually come and find me?

I realise that I can only stay in panic mode for so long. I am tired from travelling, and so I lay on the bed. Eventually, I must doze off as I wake up to hear the hotel room door. At first, I can't make out if it is someone knocking or trying to get in.

I sit upright and rub my eyes. What if it's the police at the door?

Then I see Will's familiar face as he walks in and closes the door behind him.

I breathe a sigh of relief.

'Will, I was so worried. Where on earth have you been?'

He looks so much calmer than when he stormed off.

'I'm sorry. I didn't mean to worry you.'

'Well, you did. I was thinking all sorts. How could you just storm off and leave me like that? I looked like a right muppet wandering around on my own in tears when everyone else was enjoying themselves.'

'I just needed some time on my own. Sorry, I didn't mean to worry or upset you.'

'Well, you didn't do a very good job of that!'

'I'm so, so sorry. I'm taking my problems out on you, but everything will be fine now because guess what?'

'What?'

Will is smiling now. It's like he has had a total transformation from earlier. 'We just had a big sale whilst I was out, and believe me, I am feeling so much better after that!'

'Oh, wow, what sold?'

'There were a few bits, so it all mounted up. In fact, I've just been having a word with the concierge, and we've enough money to attend the Saint Valentine's Masquerade Ball tomorrow.'

'Never mind spending money on a ball. What about the shop rent?'

'Plenty left over for the shop rent. Don't worry about that. Let's just enjoy the rest of the holiday. Our problems are over.' Will grabs hold of me and lifts me up.

He is so excited that I can't help but soften. He knows it was always my dream to go to a Venetian ball. He must have remembered that from when I told him about them on our honeymoon all those years back.

'Don't do your back in. You're not the same age as the last time you did that in Venice,' I tease. 'But wait. I still don't quite get how everything has been sorted with just a few sales.'

'Do you trust me or not? Just believe me. Our worries are over.'

I am quite shocked how one minute he is sighing and the next our troubles are over, but take his word for it. Perhaps he has miraculously sold lots on the online shop as he says he has and I am not giving him, or his stock, enough credit.

'I'd better let Emily know then. She'll need to start getting some stuff packed up.'

'Ah, it's already sorted. Don't worry. I'll be delivering it all personally when we get back. Anyway, it's time for you to start thinking about what you're going to wear because you have a ball to go to tomorrow.'

'Oh, good grief, tomorrow? I don't have anything to wear to a Venetian ball.'

I hadn't taken much notice of the carrier bag that Will had been holding. He puts it down on the bed and removes something.

'You do now,' he says.

Will pulls out the beautiful blue and gold eye mask with the feathers that we saw in the shop down the alleyway.

'Oh, Will. You remembered the one I liked! It's stunning. But we really can't afford this,' I say.

Will puts his finger to my lips. 'Sshh, Libby. Just enjoy it.'

I hold the eye mask up to my face. My gosh, it is magical! I feel like a Venetian aristocrat. 'What about you? Did you get something for yourself?' I ask.

Will pulls another half mask from the bag and shows me his purchase. It is red and gold and has a long nose. Personally, I think there is a risk he could look like Pinocchio.

'I'll sell it on in the shop once I've finished with it,' he says, sensing my hesitation. He puts it on and grins. What a difference to earlier! I am so glad we have made up.

Will chases me around the room in his mask and we laugh, just the way we did on our honeymoon.

'Oh, Will. I do love you.'

'I love you too, Mrs Jones.'

'Now take that mask off so I can give you a kiss,' I say.

We have a big hug and a kiss and put everything behind us.

'I still don't know what I'm going to wear to the ball though,' I say.

'Ah, well, when I picked up the mask, I noticed costume rental shops. Shall we see if they have anything available to rent? Let's make the most of the experience. I quite fancy dressing up in an eighteenth-century costume.

Unless they wear those merkin things. I draw the line at wearing one of those,' he laughs.

This is much more like my old Will.

'Yup. I'd leave that for those crazy rugby boys back at the club!' I say, laughing.

Will always used to dress up when he was younger. Fancy dress parties, or rugby tours, he was constantly looking for a costume that would make him the centre of attention. He dressed as a baby once on a stag night. He walked around all night wearing a nappy and only took his dummy out to sip on a pint. This costume will hopefully be a lot more stylish.

As the ball is tomorrow, Will suggests that we should probably go straight to the costume shop before they have nothing left. He shows me the ticket for the ball just as we are leaving and that is when I notice the price. Six hundred euros! I knew they weren't cheap but that is €1,200 for both of us. I nearly fall on the floor. Then there is the cost of the rental for the costumes.

'Will, we can't spend this much on a night out. We really can't!'

'Yes, we can. It's our big anniversary and Valentine's Day. We've had a tough time the past few years with everything. We deserve this.'

He pulls his phone out of his pocket and shows me the business account.

'Look. Nothing to worry about.'

I am shocked when I see that rather than being overdrawn, which it normally is, it is showing a balance of £25,000.

'Still. We can't whittle through it all,' I remind him.

'For one night, let's live a dream in Venice. You don't know what tomorrow holds.' Will takes my hands and looks into my eyes.

'Exactly. That's what worries me.'

'Look, there's still plenty more stock to sell. I told you. Things are on the up. Let's not worry about anything this holiday.'

I was always brought up to be careful with money. So I am uncomfortable with this level of spending and hesitant about going to the costume store. I really feel we should get a refund on the tickets, but Will reminds me that it is too late now. We either go or lose the money.

I know that Will is trying to make all my dreams come true, and I am grateful, but I do wish he had checked with me first before spending this much money.

Persuaded that it is now too late to change anything, I go along with it, and I am not disappointed. The costume store is just glorious and as soon as I walk in and see all the wonderful gowns, I forget any earlier reservations I had. Just like when I chose my wedding dress, I know immediately the outfit I will choose. It is blue and gold, perfectly matching my eye mask. There is the most enormous six-ring petticoat underneath it. It puffs out so much that, when I move, I need at least two metres' space, or I would bang into everything. The bodice cinches in my waist and pushes up my chest. I haven't seen my breasts that high up for years! I feel beautiful. In this dress, I am a glamorous aristocrat, and it feels fantastic. I look at myself in the mirror and absolutely love what I see.

'Oh, look at you! My beautiful wife. You suit eighteenth-century costume. You were made for it,' says Will when I step out of the changing room.

'I know, but three hundred and fifty euros? For a rental?'

'What did I say? Stop it and enjoy this moment. Don't worry about the future. I've got it covered. I won't listen to you worry about our finances again. I promised you I'd spoil you. Let me just do that, okay?'

I feel another argument may come on if I say anything. I try to tell myself that I am being a bit too cautious, as I always am. I have seen for myself there is a decent sum in the account. I must try not to worry... but it is *so* much money.

'Okay. I'll take the dress.'

Will chooses one of the golden nobleman costumes and pulls at the waistband of his trousers.

'What do you reckon?'

'Ooh, very handsome,' I say.

He is a good-looking guy, my Will. There has always been something quite distinctive about him, and dressed like this, he looks positively gorgeous.

'I could almost... You know?'

'You could almost what?' says Will.

'Ravish you,' I say, laughing.

'Ravish?' Will is laughing now, too, and everything we have been through today slips far from my mind.

He tries to get closer to me, but my petticoat gets in the way.

'It's like contraception, this thing,' says Will, pulling on my skirt.

We manage to give each other a kiss, and Will strokes my hand. This is more like it. I feel incredibly happy. It is beginning to feel like our honeymoon again, all those years ago when we couldn't take our eyes, or our hands, off each other. We still even make each other laugh.

'You do look funny in those shoes,' I say, giggling.

He looks down at the black shoes with gold buckles he is wearing. So different to his usual boating shoes.

'Just wait till the boys back home see this,' he says, taking a selfie in the mirror and laughing.

'They definitely won't recognise you once you've got that mask on, that's for sure.'

We take our costumes and head for a bite to eat near the hotel on the opposite side of Rialto Bridge. Even though it is quite cold, we sit outside to watch the world go by. Despite the patio heaters being on full blast, I can feel the cold air, and I huddle under a blanket that the lovely Italian waiter passes me.

As usual, Will and I choose the same thing from the menu and both opt for lasagne.

'This is lovely. Now I've stopped thinking about the cost, I can't wait for the ball. What a thing to do on Valentine's Day! Emily will be so jealous when she finds out what a fabulous time we've been having.'

Emily has always thought she is the only one of us to have nice experiences. I won't gloat, of course. But it will be nice for *me* to finally have a glamorous story to tell.

'She's always been jealous of you,' says Will.

'No she hasn't. I've always been the underdog.'

'You've always been the one with a family and kids. That's what she wants more than anything.' I never thought of this before. I am quite surprised that Will feels this of Emily.

'No, she couldn't cope with kids. Remember when Dylan was sick in the back of her convertible? She was livid.'

'Yeah, maybe. It's different when they're your own though.' I begin to wonder if Will is right.

We sit and watch the gondolas go past as we wait for our meals and chat about everything, from the boys to where we should go on holiday next. I fancy Greece; Will fancies Tenerife. The one thing we don't mention is the business, which I am immensely glad of.

We are lucky that we never run out of things to say. An older couple beside us seem to have nothing to talk about as they stare out into the distance. I don't think a word has passed their lips all night. I wonder what they are thinking about.

By the time we finish our lasagne and drinks, we are exhausted and head back to our room for an early night. It isn't surprising really when we have had such an eventful day. We have flown in, done a bit of sightseeing, then had a tiff, which ended up with surprise Venetian ball tickets. What a day!

We snuggle up together in bed and kiss each other good night. Unlike our normal bedtime routine, we don't turn our backs on each other and instead I spoon into him. Will is asleep in minutes, but I have to uncurl myself from his body, as I toss and turn and toss some more. I stare up and memorise every detail of the Italian Renaissance mural of a cupid on the ceiling. Cupid looks like a chubby little toddler, just like Dylan and Ewan were all those years back. But no matter how hard I look at the mural, I can't fall asleep.

The more I think about today's events and our new financial status, the more worried I become. Something doesn't feel right about it, and it is really troubling me. I can't get it out of my head, and I certainly can't sleep.

Chapter Eight

After a fitful night's sleep, I wake up to find that Will has already made me a cup of tea and left it on my bedside table.

'Happy Valentine's Day and happy anniversary, my love,' says Will as I open one eye.

'Happy anniversary.'

I rub my tired eyes and tell myself that I won't mention anything about money today. Not on Valentine's Day and our anniversary.

I take a quick sip of my tea before going into my suitcase where I hid Will's anniversary card.

'Sorry, love, I know it's customary to give silver for a twenty-fifth wedding anniversary, but I thought you had enough of that in the shop. All those candelabras and things,' I say as I hand him the gift that I carefully chose for him.

'Well, as you know, this trip and the Valentine's ball are your presents, so I'm sorry you don't have anything to unwrap,' says Will.

'Oh, that's more than enough. You've been far too generous.'

Far too generous! The thought of the huge sum of money comes to the forefront of my mind again. I force myself to say nothing so I don't spoil the mood.

I watch as Will unwraps the Welsh wooden love spoon carved with our initials that I had made for him.

'That's lovely. I'll always treasure it.' Will strokes the love spoon, exactly as he does with his antiques. He is smiling and his eyes sparkle.

We kiss with so much love between us before getting ready for breakfast at the hotel.

Today, we have decided to take a gondola ride and see inside St Mark's Basilica. I had originally thought we could take the cruise down to the islands of Murano and Burano and see the Murano glass workshops, but I don't want to stay out all day as I imagine it will take me hours to get myself into the costume I hired for tonight's ball as I want to look my best. We both agree that we might need to keep some stamina for a late-evening event. I may even try to squeeze in a 'nana nap' if I can. That is what Ewan calls them when I say I'm going to have a midday nap at the weekend and now I have adopted the term. There is nothing quite like a nana nap.

Shopkeepers are still setting up when we leave the hotel after breakfast. I find it fascinating that boats are used for delivering goods. Our local Co-op has a huge truck, but here, deliveries are by water to the shops on the front. It is quite wonderful to watch the traders unload the goods as they pass them along from canal to shore. There are boxes of foodstuff and drinks which are delivered to nearby cafes for the day ahead. As their doors open to receive the goods, I can smell delicious herbs that are being prepared in dishes, which tells me they are busy behind the scenes.

Some moored gondolas wobble about as a police boat whizzes by under a bridge. I wonder what the emergency can be. I can never get enough of watching the sights of Venice. In fact, I may have to get a hot chocolate once we do our sightseeing and plonk myself down in a cafe and do a spot of people-watching before I have my nana nap.

I am already making my way to the alleyway we went down yesterday when Will insists we should walk another way to St Mark's Basilica. He says that we should explore things and try different routes. I was hoping to have another look in the gem shop, but I figure there is plenty more time for that. After all, today is about Will and me and not my burgeoning jewellery business.

He leads me by the hand down a neighbouring alleyway and we see more shops that I would have missed had we not explored this route. Similar to the other alleyway, there are shops selling yet more masks, and I am delighted to see a couple of women pass us in their full eighteenth-century Carnivale costumes. One of the ladies is wearing a huge red hat and coordinating dress with a skirt that billows out thanks to a hoop petticoat, just like the one I hired for this evening. A mask covers her whole face. The plain white mask makes her look as though she has the face of a china doll. What a place this is! Where else would you see ladies parading the streets in period costumes on a Monday morning?

'Oh, I love Venice, Will.'

'Me too. It's fab, isn't it?'

'This is definitely the best holiday ever.' I take Will's arm and link mine into his.

'I thought our honeymoon was the best holiday ever,' he says.

'No, I think this is. We have everything now. The boys, we've been together so long and are each comfortable in our own skin. Everything is just perfect. Especially now you've sorted the business problems out.'

I raise my head up and give him a kiss. 'Twenty-five years, hey? And you kept your promise to me all that time. I'm impressed.'

We carry on walking until we reach a dead end. I love how a dead end in Venice means nearly walking into the canal. After a few drinks down some of these alleyways with their little streetside bars, I can imagine a number of mishaps. If you take a left, you could end up over a little bridge, but take a right turn, and you could find yourself plopping straight into the canal. It can be a bit of a gamble if you don't know your way around.

We pass a *pasticceria*, and the smell of espresso and sweet cakes wafts out. I begin to regret indulging in my hotel breakfast. I overheard someone this morning talking about how tasty the *fritelle* were, and I quite fancy trying one before we leave. The man said they were like little doughnut balls, only made during Carnivale season. They sounded scrumptious, and I stop to look in the window of the *pasticceria* to see if I can spot any. However, there is only an empty tray where they should be, which is probably just as well.

I enjoy the rest of the walk to St Mark's Basilica and stop every now and then to window-shop. But we pick up speed as it starts to rain as we are approaching the cathedral, and we rush for its shelter.

St Mark's Basilica is just as impressive as Will keeping his promise. With its gold-domed ceilings and mosaic inscriptions depicting Old and New Testament stories, it is absolutely fascinating. Hundreds of grand columns support so much history in one place.

When we have seen all of St Mark's Basilica, Will insists we take a gondola ride just like the last time. I am getting quite used to jumping on and off them now, so I don't hesitate as I confidently step on board. We huddle together on the seat of the black and gold gondola, and the driver starts to sing in Italian. I don't know what he is singing, and the words could mean anything. But whatever it is, it sounds like the epitome of romance. I am pretty sure no couple could ever have a falling out on a gondola. Perhaps I should have done this with Will sooner.

As we drift down the canals, under the bridges and past the palazzos, all our worries seem to have drifted away too.

'I think we should come here for our fiftieth anniversary, too, don't you?' I say.

'Do you think you'll manage the gondolas in your seventies?'

'Of course I will! I'm getting on them easier now than when I was in my twenties,' I retort, laughing.

'We'll see, but we'll definitely come back again. I promise. Even if we have to skip this part,' laughs Will.

When our time is up on the gondola, we decide to head back to the hotel. After all, it's the night of the big party. I can't remember the last late night we had. We are normally in bed by ten at the latest. However, tonight's tickets are for the latter part of the Valentine's party as, unbelievably, those were a bit cheaper. I found out that tickets for the full party were almost double the price and I thank my lucky stars that Will didn't splurge on those!

Later in the evening, it takes me over an hour to get ready. I never realised how much effort is needed for these ladies who walk around Venice in such fineries. When I tried the costume on in the shop, the lady there helped me into it, so now I have to depend on Will to pull me in and assist me into my petticoat.

'You look so hot in that,' says Will as I stand there in the six-ring petticoat.

'Get off, will you? I'd feel more comfortable in a Marks and Spencer petticoat, I can tell you,' I say, laughing.

Will helps me get the costume over my head and zips me up and ties me in.

'Ouch, I don't think I can breathe,' I say.

Will unties me a little so that I am a bit more comfortable. As I catch sight of myself in the mirror, I notice my cheeks are a little flushed from all the puffing and panting of getting into the outfit. Although that is probably a good thing as my rosy complexion now looks the part with my dress. Despite my ribcage being squashed, the outfit does look fabulous. I put my hands on my waist and look at myself in the mirror. The gold brocade swirls almost twinkle in the lighting of our room. I smooth down the skirt with its different layers and a blue flash of colour peeps out from underneath my gold dress coat. This has to be the most incredible dress I have ever worn; it is even more beautiful than my wedding dress. I feel like a princess.

Will steps beside me and admires my outfit.

'You look so beautiful.'

'Thank you. We do make a fine couple, don't we?'

'Maybe we should just stay in the room,' says Will, stroking my arm.

I look at him with mock sternness.

'With the price of those tickets, I don't think so. Cinderella will go to the ball!'

I can only just about manage to get out of the hotel room door with my big skirt, but soon get the hang of walking in it by the time we reach the end of the corridor.

At first I feel a little self-conscious when we get to reception, but thankfully, there are two other couples dressed in eighteenth-century gear too. I remind myself that this is Venice, and this is what people do here, especially at this time of year.

The palazzo is within walking distance of the hotel, and when we reach the venue it is every bit as extraordinary as I could have imagined. Everything is straight out of the eighteenth century, and I feel as though I am in a magical fairy tale. A jester juggles under the crystal chandeliers and couples dance a minuet together, reminding me of a Jane Austen television adaptation.

Everyone is so extraordinarily glamorous here. If I didn't know better, it could be mistaken for a movie set. This has to be the most beautiful party I have ever attended. From the gold woven tablecloths to the gilt stucco columns of this beautiful palazzo, everything is just perfect. Gold is certainly the colour scheme, and I am glad that we chose these costumes and now complement the décor.

I watch the handsome couples dance together in their exquisite costumes and envy their expert moves. Will can obviously see how mesmerised I am by them and holds his hand out for me to dance with him.

'Oh, I can't. I'd never be able to do that. I just enjoy watching them,' I say.

'Yes, you can. Watch what everyone else is doing. Come on, be a sport,' says Will.

Reluctantly, I take his hand and head to the dance floor and join the crowds. I feel a bit silly at first, but then I ease into it after a few steps. I still don't find the minuet an easy dance though. It's not like bopping about on the dance floor like I used to in my disco days, but it is certainly something different and a fun experience. Still, I am glad to sit down and rest my feet when the music changes and a violinist starts playing. As I sip at my glass of Prosecco,

I persuade myself that I am Venetian royalty. I think I may have been born in the wrong era! By the end of the evening we have heard everything from classical music to opera singers.

Will was right that this is a once-in-a-lifetime thing to do, and I hate to admit it but maybe he did the right thing spending a small fortune, because this is something that I will never forget as long as I live.

By two a.m. we can no longer take the pace and decide to head back to the hotel. As we leave, Will turns to me and puts his arm around my shoulder.

'Well, that was amazing. I've had the time of my life,' he says.

'Yes, me too,' I say.

It has certainly been one of the most spectacular evenings we have ever had. It was as though we were in a spell with its magical, bewitching atmosphere. However, when we step outside everything feels different.

I am dizzy as the air hits me, and I can't help but feel a sense of unease. It is like a sixth sense. Perhaps I have had too much of that Prosecco, or it could be the sight of all the plague doctor masks. Maybe it is the full moon and the fog that is starting to close in around us. My mother always said that fog and a full moon meant something bad was on the horizon. I can't help but get this terrible feeling in the pit of my stomach that she might well be right. It is like there is some kind of ominous cloud hanging over us as we leave the palazzo and I can't quite figure out why I feel this way. We have just had the most amazing experience, so why do I suddenly have this sense of impending doom?

Chapter Nine

Will has another of his headaches when we wake up. He did get carried away at the ball last night, but then again, it was the event of a lifetime.

'You shouldn't have had that last gin and tonic,' I remind him.

'I know, but it felt good at the time.'

I realise that Will has been drinking much more than normal recently. Two headaches in as many days is quite unusual for him. I suppose we haven't had a holiday in so long that he could be enjoying himself a bit too much, but I must make sure he stops drinking like this when we get back home. Perhaps that is the ominous feeling I still have in the pit of my stomach. Will's drinking is getting out of hand.

Will takes a couple more of the painkillers that he seems to be surviving on, and we head to the costume shop to return last night's outfits and get our deposits refunded before we have to leave for a tour of the islands of Murano and Burano. I am so relieved that they are in one piece and that I didn't manage to rip anything; I couldn't bear to lose our deposit. Although I am sad saying goodbye to them.

Once the costumes are safely dropped off, we make our way to the pick-up point for our tour. I am so excited that we will finally see the islands. This is something I have always wanted to do, but we didn't have the money for excursions last time. However, I notice now that the price is certainly nowhere near that of hiring a gondola.

'Are you sure you're okay to go on the boat ride?' I ask.

'Yeah, I'm fine. The tablets have kicked in now,' says Will.

I am so glad he is okay as I would have hated having to cancel this trip.

The motorboat ride to the islands is quite fast, and once again, Will is looking slightly off-colour. Fortunately, the boat ride isn't long, but he really must stop doing this to himself.

Our first stop from the boat is at a glass-blowing factory. For a moment I wonder how interesting it will be when I see all the heavy machinery and ovens. It's like any type of industrial place. Then a glassblower starts working away, and the whole tour group watches in awe as he sculpts a huge blob of glass and creates it into a magnificent stallion.

'That's amazing, isn't it?' I say.

'Maybe we should start selling Murano glass in the shop,' Will replies.

'Goodness. Why would people in Tenby want souvenirs of Venice?'

'Well, you never know.'

After the glass-blowing exhibition, Will seems quite mopey. His moods seem so up and down right now. But then I did snap at him for bringing the shop into conversation again. It's just that we are viewing something magnificent here. I am so happy, and all he can think about is the business again.

We visit the San Pietro Martire church, followed by the Basilica di Santa Maria e Donato, but despite their magnificence, Will still seems quite forlorn throughout the trip. Nothing seems to get him enthusiastic.

It is only when we get back to Venice in the early evening and we are doing our usual walk across Rialto Bridge that he perks up a bit.

'Look, a rose seller,' says Will.

'Oh no, not this trick again,' I say.

I attempt to walk in a different direction on the bridge so that I don't have to deal with the embarrassment of haggling over a rose, but it is too late.

'Please, take a rose,' the rose seller says.

'No, I'm fine. Thank you very much.'

'No, please. Take the rose.'

I keep walking and pretend not to listen to him as I know he won't take no for an answer.

'I'll take one,' says Will.

'No, it's fine. I don't need one,' I insist.

'Come on, you didn't have one last time. This time I'm giving my Libby a rose. It's what you deserve.'

Will hands some money to the rose seller and I accept the rose.

'Thank you,' I say to the rose seller.

'I'm sure it can't be easy making money selling roses, so I guess you did the right thing, Will. At least he had a sale tonight.'

'Yeah, I did feel sorry for him. Hey, that looks good.' Will points across to a trendy-looking bar.

It is the type of place we probably wouldn't frequent at home. Far too modern and busy. Here on holiday though, it looks like great fun with the singer in the window and all the people enjoying themselves inside. However, I worry about Will and feel that he probably needs some caffeine, rather than alcohol.

'Are you sure you fancy alcohol and not a hot chocolate?' I ask Will.

'Yeah. It might shift the rest of this headache. You know what they say about hair of the dog,' says Will.

Hesitantly, I agree. Although I do wish he would order a soft drink. Instead, he orders a pint and I opt for a glass of wine. The bar is lovely though and the singer is belting out the type of familiar songs you hear on the radio but couldn't say who sang them. We start to relax and enjoy ourselves. I can see that Will is definitely in a much better mood. Perhaps it is because the hair of the dog made him feel better.

We start chatting with the barman, who is a super-friendly Italian guy. I tell him how much I love Venice and how envious I am that he gets to live and work here.

He is so kind that he offers us some Limoncello to sample. The fresh lemon flavour hits my tastebuds as I take a sip.

'Oh, that is delicious,' I say.

I don't remember sampling it the last time we were here. I would have remembered this gorgeous taste on my tongue.

'You want more?' he asks.

I look over to Will and he eagerly nods his head.

'Yeah, definitely. Gorgeous stuff. We'll take two more,' he says. 'Just running to the Gents first, back in a sec.'

As the barman is serving someone, I look out of the window whilst I wait for Will to return. I can see our hotel across the way. I can't believe we hadn't noticed this bar was so close to us before. Unfortunately, it is our last night, so we won't be able to return here again. If we ever come back, on another anniversary, this will be the first place I'll come for a Limoncello. Even if I am in my seventies or eighties!

The barman puts down the two shot glasses of Limoncello as Will returns.

'Good timing,' I say, smiling.

Will doesn't smile back. 'Look, I'm sorry, but my headache just got worse. I'm going to have to go back to the hotel,' he says.

'You do suddenly look a little pale. Never mind, I'll pay for these drinks and we can just leave them.'

'No, no. You stay. Have my Limoncello. I'll be fine. Need a lie-down, that's all. Please don't leave the drinks. You know the prices they charge in these places. Now that would be a waste of money.'

I try to protest, but Will insists I finish the drinks. We both hate wastage, so I do feel terrible to leave them, but I can't help but worry whether he will be okay going back to the hotel alone with such a headache. What if it's a brain haemorrhage and he collapses on the bridge? I decide to drink up as quickly as possible so that I can get back to the room.

I finish the first drink, which burns my throat as I try to gulp it down so fast. I am about to start on the second when an Italian man comes up to me. He gestures to Will's chair.

'Hi, can I sit here?' he says.

Good grief, am I about to be hit on by some Italian stud muffin? I look around and notice there are no spare seats left. The bar is packed, so perhaps he isn't hitting on me after all and genuinely wants to rest his legs. I move the rose we bought earlier closer towards me.

'Sure,' I say.

I turn my attention back to my drink, which I must finish to escape this stranger's glances. I don't know why he keeps looking at me as though he is itching for a conversation.

I take a sip of my Limoncello and soon realise that he does indeed want to talk to me.

'Hey, I know you,' he says.

'I don't think so.' What a strange man. How could I possibly know anyone in Venice?

'Yes, you are on holiday with your husband, right? Where did he go?'

'My husband?'

'Yes, I saw him just now and he disappeared. Where is he? I was going to say hello.'

I am unsure what I should tell a complete stranger in a bar about my husband, so I stay quiet for a moment.

'Sorry, you know my husband?' I ask eventually.

'Yes, I know him.'

'I don't think you know Will,' I say. I instantly admonish myself for saying his name. Now the dodgy stranger will have even more information about him.

'Yes, I knew it was him right away. I recognised the pointy ears, even from the toilets, and then I saw you,' he says.

'His pointy ears?'

My Will doesn't have pointy ears. It is obviously a case of mistaken identity, or this stranger is completely bananas.

I pick my phone up to show the man the screensaver photo of Will and me at a dinner party quite a while ago. I mean, we have both aged since this was taken, but at least he can see that he has the wrong person. Then perhaps he will leave me alone. I hold the phone up for this mysterious man to take a good look. 'I think you're mistaken. This is my husband,' I say.

'Yes, you see. Pointy ears man.'

He jabs a finger at Will's ears on my phone. Come to think of it, his bald head makes them look pointier than I have ever noticed before. In all these years of marriage, I had never noticed that Will had pointy ears until this evening. How did I not notice his funny little elf-like ears before? They make me even fonder of him now. Bless, they're so cute.

'How can you know us?' I ask.

'You came to my shop. You bought some gems and then pointy ear man, sorry, your husband, he gave me something very nice,' he says.

'He gave you something?'

'Yes, it's a beautiful piece,' he says.

'Wait? What's a beautiful piece?'

'The watch,' he says.

'The watch?' I repeat.

'Yes, you know... The watch he sold.'

For a moment I can't quite compute what he is saying.

'Which watch?' I ask.

'Ah. You don't know,' he says.

'No, I don't know.'

'Ah, then I'm sorry. I never give away a man's secrets. I made a mistake.' He gets up to leave and walks out of the bar.

I chase after him, completely forgetting about the untouched Limoncello I still had in front of me and leaving behind my precious rose.

'Wait. Please, I have a right to know. Why would he give you a watch?'

'Look, I was only trying to be friendly and say hello because you gave me custom. I don't want any trouble.'

'So you bought a watch from my husband. Is that what you're saying?'

'No, no. I said too much. I have to go now,' he says.

'No, please. What did it look like?'

'I have to go now. You speak with your husband. Not me, sorry,' he says.

The man dashes away as fast as he appeared in the bar and I watch him go out of sight. I walk back across the bridge to the hotel and try to gather all the thoughts that are spinning around in my head.

Will has never worn a watch. He always hated having any kind of constraint around his wrist. Even when we would go to an event that required a wristband, he would be desperate to tear it off. He would never manage at one of those fully inclusive places in Benidorm. I know for certain that he doesn't have a watch to sell.

There has to be some mistake. When would he have met the man to give him a watch anyhow? The only time he has been on his own was when we had the row on the bridge. I think back to his mood and how it changed when he got back. Suddenly, the business had been saved and his mood ameliorated. It had to be to do with the meeting of this man. Will has made money from a watch. But the question is, whose watch is it? The only watch we have is Dad's. But that's securely at home in the safe, or at least as far as I know. Surely Will wouldn't go as low as selling my dad's watch to save his family business, would he? However much I try, this most awful thought will not go away.

Chapter Ten

I practically burst into our room when I get back to the hotel. I am desperate to confront Will about my strange encounter, but he is fast asleep, or at least he pretends to be. I shove at his shoulder to try and disturb him in the bed. I could poke his pointy ears, I am so desperate for him to wake up right now.

'Will! Wake up,' I say.

He groans and says he is tired under his breath. I feel like I could shake him and make him wake up! Instead, I go to the bathroom and lean over the sink. *Think, Libby. What should you do?*

Will is obviously in no mood to talk, and we have an early morning flight to catch. As much as I demand answers right now, I decide to calm down a little. I am too emotional to think straight. I will get to the bottom of this in the morning over our breakfast before we leave for the airport. He can't avoid any questions when we are face to face over our coffees in the middle of a packed breakfast room. I also need some time to think. It doesn't matter what Will says – that man definitely had the right person as he even knew about the gems I bought. It looks as though he was undoubtedly sold a watch by Will.

I toss and turn all night, and when the alarm goes off, I feel absolutely dreadful. It must have been the last Limoncello I had, as it is my turn to suffer from an awful headache. When I remember the man from last night, my head hurts even more. No matter how groggy I am feeling, I need to clear the air.

'Good morning, sweetheart,' says Will when he finally wakes up.

I feel like shouting at him and saying 'Don't you sweetheart me!' But I don't know what is going on yet, so I try to control my anger.

I jump in the shower and throw the last of my bits into the suitcase. We take them downstairs and hand back our room key before going to the dining room for breakfast. It is then that I am ready for the confrontation.

'I'll miss these croissants every morning,' says Will.

'Yeah, they're nice,' I say.

I take a sip of the strong black coffee and start.

'You know, after you left last night, a guy came up to me in the bar.'

'A guy hit on you?' says Will.

'No. I wasn't sure at first what he wanted. Then he said he knew you. I think he was just trying to be friendly.'

'A guy knew me?' says Will.

'Yes, he knew you.'

'That's preposterous. Who would I know in Venice?'

I take another sip of the coffee. My gosh, I need this. 'The man you sold the watch to.' I look him straight in the eye and watch his reaction.

His feet shuffle under the table and he smacks his foot into mine, but his face doesn't show any emotion.

'Watch? I don't wear a watch,' he says.

I might have known he would say that.

'Look, he recognised you in the toilets and said that you gave him "a beautiful piece". He seemed very pleased with it.'

'I'm sorry, but I really don't have a clue what you're talking about. I don't know anything about any watch, or any man here in Venice. You've completely lost me now.'

'The shop where the gems were. The man in there.'

Will puts his napkin down on the table. 'Want any more toast?' he asks.

'No. I don't. I just want answers,' I say. How can this man think about breakfast when he is so obviously lying?

I let him get his toast before I start again. 'Will! You have to tell me the truth. This man knew you. He recognised you.' I look at his ears and am reminded again that they are incredibly pointy. So pointy that he could easily be a character in an Enid Blyton book.

'So, we went into his shop. But I don't know about any watch.' Will shrugs his shoulders. 'Look, who are you going to believe? The husband you've known forever or some sleazy guy in a bar? If I say I don't know about any watch, I don't. He's obviously just some weirdo.'

'Well, he looked quite smart to me. A proper businessman.'

'I certainly don't do any business in Venice. I wish I did so that we could come here more often. I don't want to leave now, do you?'

'Don't change the subject,' I say.

'But there's nothing more to say, Libs.'

He always calls me Libs when he wants to shut me up and refuses to discuss something further.

I bite at the skin around my nail in frustration. Will must know what the man is talking about, even if he isn't giving anything away. This husband of mine has got to be lying. I would trust Will with my life, I always have, but none of this makes any sense. A stranger like that has no reason to lie to me. He was only trying to be friendly, and it seemed as though he just let something slip that he shouldn't have.

I feel sick at the thought that Will might be sitting there in front of me lying to my face. Surely he wouldn't do that?

My phone starts to ring and I see that it is Emily. I worry it might be something to do with Monty or Dylan.

'Hey,' I answer.

'Hi Libby, how's it going? You still having the most amazing time?' she asks.

I look across at Will, who is shovelling a pastry down his throat. 'Yeah, one of us is,' I say.

'What does that mean?'

'Oh, it's just Will here enjoying his breakfast before we leave. Anyway, what's up?'

'Just to say that everything's fine here. Your boys are looking forward to having you back. Just wanted to check if you'd like me to tell the butcher to keep a joint to one side for tomorrow.'

'For tomorrow?' I say.

'Yes, for your anniversary party. You haven't forgotten, have you?' says Emily.

'No, of course I haven't. That would be great. A beef joint, please,' I say. With so many things on my mind, this hadn't even occurred to me. Right now, I am not sure I want a party. I can't tell an excited Emily that though.

'Fab. Really looking forward to it. Will be nice to have an anniversary party for you both. I can't wait to celebrate such an achievement.'

I look at Will again. He wipes his mouth with his napkin and it immediately annoys me. Not only has he pointy ears that have turned from being cute to annoying, but he dribbles, too, it seems.

'Yeah, I guess so. We'll pick Monty up from you around eight p.m. when we get home, okay?' I say.

'Brill. Safe flight then. See you in a bit,' says Emily.

I don't know what to say to Will when I put the phone down. He won't discuss the man in the bar any further, and we have a flight to catch. The only thing I can do is run to the safe when we get home and make sure Dad's watch is safely in there.

We grab our bags and leave for the airport once again. Unlike on our arrival, we get one of the regular water ferries back to the airport and then a bus. I suppose we need to get back to ordinary life again. We have lived life a little too large in Venice and now it is definitely time to get back to normality and curb the spending. Especially since I have more questions than ever before about where the windfall has come from.

Upon arriving at the airport, we are informed our flight is slightly delayed. How typical when I am desperate to get home. Will tells me to chill as it is only an hour. Little does he realise that every hour counts right now. I try to calm myself down by popping into duty-free to pick up a couple of souvenirs. I decide on a bottle of Limoncello for Emily as I know she will love the stuff. I search for something for Dylan who is more difficult to choose for. He is at that age where things are either too young or too old for him. However, as I still consider him to be my little boy, I can't resist picking up a small wooden Pinocchio for him. It reminds me of Will's mask. I know Dylan is far too old for this, but it is incredibly cute with its long wooden nose, red and white striped body and yellow hat. Plus, it says 'Venezia' across it. I am pretty sure he will hide it from his mates, but it will hopefully bring a smile to his face whilst also reminding him of our family rule of no lies. Right now, I am thinking I need to buy one for Will as a reminder too! However, I tell myself that I mustn't jump the gun here. I won't know who the true liar is until we get home and I open that safe. Is it the stranger or my husband? The flight home is full of worry that my life is about to fall apart as I discover that Will has done the cardinal of all sins and lied to me. As for Dad's watch not being there, I can't begin to imagine how I would cope. It is so precious that I don't want to even contemplate it.

We end up arriving back in the UK two hours later than scheduled and hurry to pick up the car in the hope that we will avoid the customary Friday traffic that heads down to West Wales. However, the delay means that we do hit rush hour. I have never been so desperate to get home, and yet everything seems to be hampering our journey. I message Emily and Dylan to tell them that it looks like we will be home much later than expected. This is so frustrating, and the whole journey back is so opposite to the excitement we had on the way out. Now we are squabbling about which lane to go in to get home the fastest.

'Look, that lane is definitely moving faster,' I say.

'We're fine where we are,' says Will.

'Move out. I'm telling you, that lane's faster.'

'Libs! Who's driving here? Me or you?'

Libs! There, he's told me. End of discussion.

I give out a big, frustrated sigh and Will turns up the radio.

'Mr Blue Sky' by ELO is on, but the sky certainly isn't looking very blue from where I'm sitting. In fact, it is looking positively gloomy.

Will starts tapping his hand against the steering wheel and this annoys me further. I could almost grab the steering wheel from him.

'Concentrate on your driving,' I say.

'What? We're not even moving.'

Everything he is doing is driving me potty. But then he starts singing! As if it couldn't get any worse. Will always thought he should be in some male voice choir but didn't quite have the ability to join one. As he sings in the car, it reminds me why that dream didn't quite work out for him. He doesn't sing that often since his rejection from the choir and then a local singing group. It tends only to be when he is stressed or overtired. I try to work out which he is right now. Of course, he could be stressed because we are stuck in traffic, or overtired because we have been travelling. Or he could be stressed because he knows that in precisely two hours' time, I will be putting the passports back into the safe and looking for Dad's watch.

'Did you want to stop for a bite to eat on the way home?' asks Will.

'No, just want to get straight home.'

'Don't you fancy some chips or something? I'm starved.'

Everything he says makes me think he has an ulterior motive. Is he trying to delay our inevitable return home? Or is he genuinely hungry?

'Let's just get home first, hey. You can always drop me off and pop out for some chips after.'

'Yeah, I might just do that.'

I breathe a sigh of relief.

After a tense drive home, we finally see the sight of the signpost that welcomes us to Pembrokeshire. My stomach jumps a little. It is so good to be safely back in our home county with Dylan and Monty, but it also means that I am about to find out if my husband is one big Pinocchio or an innocent man.

Firstly though, we have to stop by Emily's to pick up Monty.

'Come in, come in,' she says.

'No, we have to rush. It's been a long drive. We'll catch up at the party tomorrow, okay,' I say.

'Okay, but at least tell me how the holiday was.'

'Oh, it was fabulous. Sorry, I'm so tired, and it's been a long day. Thank you so much for looking after Monty so well. He looks well fed.'

I don't mean to be rude to her, but I can't think of anything else other than getting home and opening the safe. We pop Monty in the car and head home.

Dylan is not quite as excited as Monty was to see us, but I give him a big hug and tell him how much I missed him the second he opens the door.

Luckily, he is in the middle of some online game, so he doesn't stop me to ask questions about how Venice was, unlike Emily. I can't hold off a moment longer as I am desperate to get up those stairs. I can't concentrate on anything but what I will find in the safe when I unlock it.

Will puts the kettle on in the kitchen as I run upstairs. I lock the bedroom door so that I am not interrupted and walk towards the safe.

My hands start to shake as I dial in the combination. Please let the stranger in Venice be wrong. Please tell me that there was no watch sold, or if there was, it wasn't Dad's, and it was all a genuine mistake. The door of the safe springs open and I shuffle my hand around in the darkness inside. There is nothing that feels like a watch. Absolutely nothing. The only thing in there is the box that I keep Dylan and Ewan's baby teeth in. I don't know why I keep them in there; it is just a thing I did a very long time ago. Even though I can feel that Dad's watch is missing, I put the torch of my phone on to double-check. Have I somehow missed that familiar feeling of the gold strap? I bend down and peer in, shining the torch into every crevice.

It is not there. Dad's watch is definitely missing from the safe.

I sit down on the edge of the bed in shock. Dad's beautiful watch is *gone*. For a moment, my mind wants to give Will the benefit of the doubt again. A silly thing to do, but I question myself in the shock of everything. Did I take it out and place it somewhere else and forget? Have I taken it to a jeweller for a new battery and left it somewhere? But whilst my heart is desperate for a more palatable explanation, I have to face the truth. There is no way it could be missing other than Will having physically removed it. He is the only other person who knows the combination.

The liar was my husband and certainly not the Venetian stranger. So it seems that I can trust the word of a complete stranger before my husband's. I put my head into my hands and take a deep breath before my heart is completely out of control. The realisation that my husband has lied to me is quite probably one of the biggest shocks I have ever had. My body feels warm, then cold. I feel like my whole body is short-circuiting. But I know that I have to pull myself together and deal with this.

I shout downstairs for Will, but there is no response. I practically scream his name.

'Will, come here!' There is nothing. No answer: just silence.

I run down the stairs and twist my ankle on the last step in my hurry. I fall down to the ground, and when I look up, I notice that Will's coat is missing from the banister.

'Mam, are you okay?' says Dylan.

I cradle my ankle and then wince in pain as I try to get up.

'I'm okay. I shouldn't have rushed down the stairs so fast. You see, this is why I always told you boys not to run up and down the stairs. I need to speak to Dad. Where is he?'

'He went to get chips but said he might stop for a pint on the way back. He said you didn't want any chips. Did you?'

'No, I don't. But I do need to speak to him. I'll ring him now.'

I manage to get up and hobble into the kitchen to find my phone to call Will. However, as soon as it starts to ring out, I hear his ringtone nearby. I should have guessed he would leave his phone at home in such circumstances. He never leaves his phone at home. This reiterates that he knew full well what he was doing.

'Is everything okay, Mam?'

'Yeah, fine,' I say.

'You don't look like everything's okay. You look hurt,' says Dylan.

He has no idea quite how hurt I am, but it isn't my ankle that the pain is coming from. I can't believe Will would do this. He has stolen my dad's beautiful watch from the safe, lied about the man in Venice and now run off knowing I have found out.

How on earth could he do such a terrible thing to his wife of twenty-five years?

Chapter Eleven

Once Dylan has gone to bed, I sneak my duvet down-stairs and lay it on the sofa. I have decided to sleep in the living room so that I can catch Will the moment he walks through the door. Like a cat waiting to pounce on a mouse, I don't want him to escape my confrontation.

I plump up the cushion under my head and attempt to read a book as I wait for Will. I can't concentrate on the pages and keep reading the same page over and over. I keep thinking about what I am going to say to Will when he walks in. I can't stop myself from having a virtual argument in my head. Then the startling chime of the grandfather clock striking midnight reminds me that there is still no sign of him.

Again, at one a.m., the chime startles me as I realise Will is nowhere to be found. At two a.m., I am wondering if he is okay. But then I tell myself, he is probably just avoiding me. At two thirty a.m., my stomach is getting butterflies. What if something has happened to him? What if he has fallen under a bus? Do buses run at this time in the night? Should I pop the local radio on just in case?

At two forty-five a.m., I get that sick feeling again. How long is someone supposed to wait before they call the police and report a missing person? This reminds me of the exact same uneasiness I had in Venice.

Then, finally, just after the clock has struck three a.m., I hear the front door. I listen to the sound of that familiar drag of the rug as it gets stuck under the door. Will is pushing against it. Now that I know he is safe, part of me wishes I had well and truly wedged it against the door so he would have to sleep on the doorstep.

I squint my eyes as I watch him tiptoe in the darkness towards me. I notice he is trying to be as quiet as he can. He probably thinks he will get away with our conversation for another evening if only I don't know he is home.

Unfortunately for Will though, he doesn't notice my legs stretched out in the darkness under the duvet on the sofa and plonks himself down right on my shins.

'Ouch!' I shout.

My ankle is still throbbing from earlier; now my shins have joined in.

'Holy shit. Who's there?' says Will.

'Who do you think it is? And don't swear.'

I reach for the table lamp beside me, and Will stares straight at me.

'Why aren't you in bed?'

'Why do you think, Will?' I almost spit my words out.

'Couldn't sleep?'

'Of course I couldn't sleep. Not until I know where Dad's watch is.'

'Oh, not this again.'

His nonchalance is making me even angrier.

'Yes, this a-flipping-gain!'

'Right, listen. It's really late and I need some sleep. I've been driving and travelling. Aren't you tired, too, Libs? Let's talk about this in the morning.'

'I want to talk about it now, Will. Besides, it already is morning.'

'Yeah, look, after the party then. I promise I will explain, but after the party.'

'I'm cancelling the anniversary party.'

'You can't cancel our party. It's too late now. Look, we have a small problem we need to sort out. That's all. I promise you, if you can just stay calm and get through the party, I will explain everything.'

I sigh, unsure if he will ever tell me what is going on in his head. I begin to wonder if torture is the only way he will talk. I try to think what brutal police officers in movies do to get their criminals to confess, but of course, I couldn't use any of those methods.

'I mean, you don't want Emily to know that we have a bit of conflict going on here, do you?'

Emily. How is she going to react when she finds out? She is going to kill him. I don't think I need to worry about having to torture him.

'Conflict? I think we have more than that going on here. You've stolen from me.'

'No, Libs. Honest. I haven't stolen from you. I've had to do something temporary for the sake of our family, but I haven't stolen from you. We have a bit of a misunderstanding going on, that's all.'

'A misunderstanding? Have I *misunderstood* that my daddy's watch is missing?' I can't help but raise my voice now. In fact, I am positively shouty.

'It's safe. I know where it is, okay?'

'It's not safe. It's with some stranger in Venice. How can it be safe?'

I hear the stairs creak and realise I have disturbed Dylan.

'Mam, what's going on? Why are you shouting?' Dylan rubs his eyes and I feel terrible that I have woken him up.

'Sorry. It's just something me and Dad were talking about. I'm just a bit emotional. You get back to bed.'

'Yes, Mam's a bit overtired. You need some sleep too. We've all got a big day tomorrow. It's party time.' Will smiles and touches my arm.

Mam's a bit overtired? Now I really want to torture him. My skin crawls at his touch, but I try not to show Dylan how bad things are.

One of the house rules we have is that we don't argue in front of the family. Not even snide comments. Although this rule is getting more difficult to stick to recently.

'Yes, I think we all need some sleep.'

It comes out like I'm some kind of zombie as I try not to let the emotion I am feeling slip.

I grab my duvet and drag it back up the stairs. As soon as I reach our bedroom door, I close it fast behind me and lock it. There is no way Will is sleeping in here tonight. I listen to the stairs to make sure I can't hear him but realise that even Will knows to stay away.

I am so relieved. Not only has he taken the only possession I really care about, but he has lied to my face, avoided me, patronised me in front of Dylan and is now pretending it is all no big deal. Right now, I don't ever want to see that man again.

Unfortunately though, there is just the small problem of having to fake my way through a party with him tomorrow for the sake of the family.

Chapter Twelve

How I regret agreeing to the anniversary party. Had I known that my husband was such a liar, I most certainly wouldn't have.

Will sits there smiling at Nia whilst I try and look as though things are normal. When Ewan and Nia arrived this morning, full of excitement about tonight's dinner party, I didn't have the heart to tell them that I desperately wanted to call it off.

All day I have had to pretend that nothing untoward is going on. I haven't even been able to confront Will further as he seems to have taken the cowardly route and makes sure that every time we cross paths, someone else is in the room. He knows I wouldn't dare make a scene in front of my beloved family.

So that is how we are sat here now, with fifteen guests around the table and me trying to serve up a sumptuous beef Wellington with all the trimmings when all I want to do is cry into the gravy.

'So how did you enjoy Venice, Libby?' asks Robert, one of Will's friends from his rugby playing days. I suspect that is whom he was having a pint or five with last night before he finally came home. His third wife, Natasha, is sat beside him. She smiles at me, undoubtedly waiting for me to tell them both how wonderful it was.

'Didn't Will tell you when he was sat drinking with all of you last night?' I say.

It comes out sharper than I intended. I don't want Nia, as an outsider, to pick up on the tension and anger that is bubbling away behind the scenes. She isn't to blame for any of this. So I try to grit my teeth and tell all our guests what a wonderful holiday we had. Even though I can't bear this, I twist things a little to protect everyone.

'I'll have to show you the beautiful mask Will bought me. It was just the perfect break,' I say, smiling. I begin to realise that Will's lies are now making me into a liar, and I am utterly disgusted with myself.

'Yeah, we went to an amazing ball, didn't we?' says Will.

I nod my head without looking in his direction and take a huge swig of wine to stop myself from saying something I may regret. I try to swallow all the things I truly want to say and feel as though I am choking.

'Well, I think we should have a toast to you both. As best man at the wedding all those years ago, I'd say I'm the right man for the job,' says Robert.

I try to smile, but the last thing I want is a toast right now. I can barely look at Will, let alone toast the man! How can I possibly go along with this evening and let everyone think how lucky I am to be married to such an honest, caring man?

Robert starts speaking and I almost want to roll my eyes. Since I confronted Will in the early hours of this morning, I have gone through feelings of shock, anger and sadness. The anger is currently winning as Will sits there smiling away like nothing is wrong. So far, it is as if he is in denial and seems to think that by selling the watch he was somehow helping the family. From what I can see, Will seems to think that he actually did us all a favour.

Will reaches out to touch my hand as Robert starts his toast and I could honestly smack it away in front of everyone. I think of those who are sat here celebrating around us though and so I simply move my hand away quietly rather than making a big scene.

'These two are a match made in heaven,' starts Robert.

I find myself being unable to look up at everyone. Instead, I stare at the tapestry placemat in front of me that I carefully selected for this evening. I pull on the edge that is starting to loosen. I fear it may unravel, just like my marriage, but I still can't help pulling at it. My cheeks redden as Robert goes on saying what a terrific bloke I married.

'So all I'm saying is that Libby is a lucky woman. She married my best mate. What more can I say? To Libby and Will, who have stood the test of time. Bloody made for each other, they are. Cheers.' Thankfully, Robert finally sits down, and I attempt to smile as everyone congratulates us.

'Thanks, Robert. I struck lucky the day I met our Libby,' says Will.

A noise comes from my throat that didn't mean to come out and I kind of grunt at him. I grab my wine glass and down it in one go as I once again try to drown all the things that I truthfully want to say.

I pick up the bottle of wine on the table to refill my glass but there is only a drop left.

'Oh, the bottle's finished. Excuse me, I'll just get some more,' I say.

I am relieved to get away from all the prying eyes watching me around the table. Staying quiet is proving to be the hardest thing I have ever done.

Whilst I am in the kitchen leaning down to get another bottle of Sauvignon out of the wine fridge, Emily startles me.

'Ooh, where did you spring from?' I ask.

'Didn't you hear me call after you?'

'Um, no.'

'Listen, are you okay? You've not been yourself all evening. You're doing that thing when you clench your jaw,' says Emily.

'What on earth do you mean? I don't clench my jaw.'

'You're doing it now. You've done it since you were twelve. It's this thing you do when you don't like something.'

Emily lowers her voice.

'Are you not keen on Ewan's girlfriend or something? She seems lovely.'

'Of course I like her. I gave her a donation for her skydiving jump thing,' I say.

'Oh, you should ask if you can do a tandem jump with her. You've always wanted to do that, haven't you?'

Emily takes a sip of her wine and puts her glass down on the kitchen table. Then she looks directly at me.

'So, what is it then, sis? Something's troubling you. Was it the holiday? Is it money?'

How do you tell your sister that your husband has stolen your dad's watch from the safe and flogged it to some man in Venice? It is part of her family heritage too. She will be devastated if she finds out it has gone. But she is also the only other person in the world who would understand how I am feeling right now. I think for a moment about how I can begin to tell her. She is much more confrontational than I am, so I am worried that she will go straight up to Will and have it out with him in front of everyone. Her protective side came in handy when I was her little sister at school and someone pinched my sweets, but at a dinner party, with all our family and friends around, I fear this might be detrimental.

'It's nothing,' I say.

'You're a bad liar. I know you better than this. Something's on your mind.'

'No, I promise. I'm fine, and you know I never lie. Maybe I'm a bit tired after the travelling yesterday. In hindsight, it probably wasn't the best idea to have a party the minute we got back,' I say.

'It's not that. I can tell when you're tired. Don't forget I had to babysit you as a kid when Mam and Dad went out. You'd have this stare, like a spaced-out look when you needed bed. Now you look upset. You can't pull the wool over my eyes. I know you better than anyone.'

'Look, please, just leave it, okay.'

This isn't the right time for such a discussion, and Emily is starting to annoy me.

'You do know that I'll get it out of you by the end of the evening,' she says.

'We'll see,' I say.

When we get back to the dinner table, I listen carefully as the boys tell everyone about their respective universities. Ewan has got his finals in a few months, and Dylan is delighted as he tells everyone how his predicted grades will hopefully get him into his first choice of uni.

Natasha tells us how proud we must be and what a good job we have done as parents to bring up such polite and well-rounded boys. I think to myself how I may have married a thief but at least our boys turned out well. I thank her and tell everyone I will fetch the dessert. I don't know how much longer I can take this and I need to hurry along the evening. I want this night to end so that I can finally talk properly to Will and decide what I am going to do next. Since this is such a huge lie, it makes me wonder if I know him at all. I would never have believed such a thing could happen. To think that I couldn't trust my own husband with the combination of the safe is just too much. I don't see a way forward from this. I feel like an observer as I look around the table at everyone chatting happily and celebrating with us. It simply doesn't feel like this is the husband I know and love. I always trusted Will with my life.

What everyone around the table has no idea of is the fact that I foresee this to be the last anniversary party we will ever have. I don't think we can get over this. If I can't trust him with my only family heirloom, something he knows I care so deeply about, how can I trust him with anything? This party should be so special. Everyone I care for is here around us and yet I am sitting here absolutely crushed. What is even harder is the fact that I can't confide in anyone.

I put down the bowls of homemade rice pudding that I made earlier and sit down with a sense of relief. The charade is almost over. Hopefully, I can get everyone out within the next hour.

'Bon appetite,' I say.

'I love Mam's rice pudding,' says Ewan.

'Aw, thanks, love.'

I watch impatiently as everyone clears their bowls. Our dinner parties usually end with liqueurs in the living room, but tonight I decide not to give our guests that option.

The second the last person has put their spoon down, I start to clear the bowls.

'You want a hand with those?' asks Emily.

'No, I can manage,' I say. However, Emily is once again her insistent, pushy self and follows me through to the kitchen with two bowls in her hands.

'Come on, spill. You can't wait to get rid of us all. I'm not stupid.'

'Look, you don't want to know. Please stop it. Not now,' I say.

Emily grabs at my arm. 'I'm not leaving here until you tell me what the heck is going on.'

I don't want to tell her like this, but she isn't leaving me much choice.

'You're getting me worried. What if it's, like, a medical diagnosis and you're not telling me? I'm your sister. I want to be there for you.'

'Please don't push this,' I say.

'Just tell me. I won't tell anyone. I promise.'

'No, I can't.'

'Was it something in Venice? Did something happen?'

'Nothing. Please, leave it.'

'Tell me now before I go and ask Will or the boys what's wrong with you.'

'Oh, for goodness' sake. If you really must know, Will stole Dad's watch. Happy now?'

I hear the chatter in the dining room stop and pray they didn't hear me.

'I told you not to push me to say anything.'

'Hang on. What do you mean, Will stole Dad's watch?'

'He took it from the safe and sold it, for quite a bit of money, I suspect. I think he sold it to a jeweller in Venice.'

'Oh my god. Are you saying that Dad's watch is gone?' she says.

'I'm so sorry.' I start to cry now. I can't bear to see Emily's shocked face. It is almost like losing Dad again. It feels as if we are both back at the hospital as the doctor told us that he wasn't going to make it.

'I'm so sorry,' I repeat.

'It's not you who should be sorry. It's that *thief* of a husband who needs to be sorry,' shouts Emily.

'Shh, not now. Let the guests leave, please. What will Nia think of us?' I whisper.

But it is too late as everyone has obviously heard what is going on. Robert and Natasha pop their heads around the kitchen door and announce they are leaving.

'Thanks for a great evening,' says Natasha. She smiles with her head to one side as if in sympathy as she leaves.

'Now look what's happened,' I say.

'Well, if Will has done such a terrible thing, they deserve to know. Where the hell is he, anyway? I want to speak to him.'

'I'm here,' says Will, standing behind Emily. 'Please keep your voices down. We have guests.'

This makes Emily louder and madder.

'Don't you even dare tell me to keep my voice down after what you've done. How could you do this to us? It wasn't yours to sell,' says Emily.

'I had to take it to save my family business, okay? It was the most valuable thing we had, and my dad's business was going down the tubes. I wasn't going to be the one in the family to lose it. My grandad set that business up in 1959.'

'But it was okay to lose our dad's legacy?'

'A watch isn't really a legacy, is it? It's just a possession,' says Will.

I look at him incredulously.

'Just an *item*?' I shout.

'How could you marry such a man, Libby? To steal from your own family. What a waster.'

'I wasn't stealing. I was borrowing. In business, it's called diversifying.'

'Diversifying!'

I am practically screaming at him now. Yet again, I have broken another of the family rules because of Will's behaviour and shown myself up in front of them.

'Whatever I say is going to sound terrible. I'm sorry. I just didn't have any other option. But look, your dad's watch has helped us save my dad's business. I did it for us. For the family.'

'Oh my goodness. You just don't see it, do you? So your side of the family is more important than ours now?' I say.

I grab Emily's arm for support. I feel so much shame as my big sister has discovered such a dreadful thing and all because of my husband.

'How could you do this to us?' says Emily. She unlatches herself from my arm and jabs a finger in Will's face. 'You're an absolute disgrace. I wish my sister had never set eyes on you.'

It is at this moment that I decide that I don't ever want to see Will again. Not only am I truly devastated and angry but it is also the loss of face. The shame in front of Emily.

'We're done,' I say, looking at him.

'What do you mean, we're done?' he asks.

In the heat of the moment I had forgotten that there are still a few friends left in the dining room, as well as Nia, Ewan and Dylan. In the scale of things though, none of it seems to matter any more. They are all about to find out that I am throwing Will out.

'What I just said. We're done. Our marriage is over. I want nothing more to do with you. Pack your bags and get out!'

'Now, come on, Libs.'

'Don't even try talking me out of this, Will. You're just making me angrier. I want a divorce.'

'What? Now, come on. Don't do anything rash here,' says Will.

I have never been one to forgive and forget. Will knows this. In fact, it is probably my biggest weakness. I still won't look at a girl I went to school with who I sometimes pass in the street because she used to mock the second-hand shoes I had to wear when my parents went through a financially challenging time. If I am ever wronged, I will hold that grudge until the day I die.

'It isn't rash. I've been thinking about it all night. Get out. What you've done is truly unforgivable. You know I never forgive and forget those who have wronged me. *Ever.*'

'No, she never forgives; none of us do. It's a family thing,' says Emily.

'But…' says Will.

'I'd get out now if I were you before I call the police. Do you want everyone to know that you have stolen an expensive watch?' says Emily.

Dylan and Ewan walk in. They look so shocked and upset. It is clear that they have heard every word.

'Mam, can we all sit down as a family and have a chat?' says Ewan.

'No, love. I'll explain everything when I feel a bit better. But right now, Dad has to leave. It's for the best for everyone.'

'Yeah, it's okay, Ewan. It is best I leave. Mam needs some space for a bit.'

When Will finally walks out, I start crying. I don't know how I've possibly held it together since that night in the bar in Venice. In my heart, I knew that stranger was telling me the truth.

I hear the front door slam, and Will eventually walks out with the last of the guests. I don't know where he is going, and right now, I really don't care. Emily puts her arm around me to console me.

'Don't worry, sis. We'll get our revenge on him. Nobody does the dirty on our family.'

'He's still the boys' father. I don't want to do anything to hurt him,' I say.

'Oh, we'll get him right where it hurts. He should have thought of that earlier. Now, you leave it all to your big sis. Nobody messes with my Libby. That man won't know what hit him.'

Chapter Thirteen

We arranged over text message that I would leave the house on Sunday afternoon so that Will could come back for more of his stuff. How different things are between us already that we now only communicate via text with not even a kiss at the end of each message. He has given up trying to convince me to forgive him after the last ten messages he sent me this morning begging for us to talk. As far as I am concerned there is nothing to say. No excuse or story is going to make this better. It's a waste of his energy trying to convince me otherwise. If I give him a chance, he may even lie further to me, and I don't want to hear another fib.

He should count himself lucky. If I was someone else, I could have been all dramatic and thrown his stuff out of the window and screamed obscenities at him. But I don't want Ken and Patricia to hear me swear. I would love to be the type of person who would pack his stuff up in a suitcase and smash it all over the pavement outside so he'd have to clamber around picking things up, as you see in the best movies. But I think of the neighbours and all the gossip. I would never live it down. Besides, Nia is staying all weekend and I need to show some decorum. So instead I cook Nia and the boys a full Welsh breakfast with laverbread and cockles, then paint on a fake smile. Something I am forcing myself to become more adept at.

'What a fab breakfast. Are you sure you're okay though?' says Nia at the kitchen table. I have been whizzing about like one of my trusty kitchen appliances until now. I was hoping that nobody would ask if I was actually okay.

Thankfully, no one has discussed what happened last night, until now. The boys just look a bit shell-shocked. They have never seen their parents in such a fight. For that, I am remorseful. If Emily hadn't forced it all out of me, then I could have perhaps kept it out of earshot. However, the one thing I do not feel remorseful about is telling Will to leave the family home. I know I have done the right thing. I will never abide by liars and cheats and am not forgiving of such behaviour.

'Yes, I'm fine. I'm just sorry you had to witness that last night. It is quite embarrassing.'

'Don't be silly. You should have seen my mum when she found out her ex was cheating. I thought she was going to murder him. At least you didn't do anything like that. You didn't shred his clothes like my mum did.'

'Oh goodness. No. I can't bear things being destroyed or being wasteful. I couldn't do that to someone, no matter what.'

I might sometimes wish I was more vengeful, but I couldn't really do anything like that.

I attempt to change the subject and keep myself busy by offering more tea and cleaning out the toaster crumbs. Toaster crumbs! This is what my life has come to. But I will do anything not to get into a big conversation at the breakfast table. However, Dylan takes after his aunty and demands answers.

'Is it true Dad stole my watch from the safe?'

I think carefully before answering. Ultimately, it is Dylan's watch, and his dad has effectively stolen from him. As much as I hate Will right now, I must still try and protect the boys.

'I think he had some financial difficulties. Perhaps more than he ever shared with us. You know what Dad's like. He keeps things to himself until they blow up and get too big to handle. Remember when he kept ignoring the oil light on the car and we broke down on a bend on the way to Aberystwyth? I think this is a bit like that.'

'So why were you shouting in the kitchen about getting a divorce if it's something that just got out of hand?' asks Dylan.

'It's the principle of the thing. You know how I've always told you boys there are to be no lies. He lied to me about the situation, so I'm very mad at him.'

'But divorce? Why don't you just separate for a while? See if you can cool things down a bit. Maybe you're being a bit hot-headed,' says Dylan.

'We'll see,' I say. Dylan is such a wise boy for his age. He could be a peacekeeper with his diplomacy skills. However, right now I can't ever imagine forgiving Will even if it already feels strange without him. It doesn't help that Monty keeps sniffing and standing by the door waiting for his dad. I wish I could explain to him why his daddy isn't here.

'Both of you are so stubborn,' says Ewan.

'I'm not stubborn. Your dad's more stubborn than I am,' I say firmly.

'You're very stubborn, Mam,' says Dylan.

I try to change the subject to something lighter.

'Anyway, what are your plans when you get back to Cardiff, Nia? Have you a lot of studies to get on with?'

'It's not too bad at the moment. I've some study leave Thursday so I'm sneaking off and doing a skydive. Well, if the weather's okay.'

'Oh, how lovely. I'll keep my fingers crossed the weather holds out then.'

How I envy Nia's freedom. I smile wistfully.

'Do you want me to ask about booking a skydive for you whilst I'm there? Didn't you say you fancied doing one?'

Nia is such a perceptive young lady. I certainly need something to cheer myself up, and what could be more thrilling than jumping out of a plane? Surely all my pent-up anger could be released with something that physical.

'Oh Nia. You remembered. Well, that does sound like a lovely idea. Let me think about it. Although, on second thoughts, there's certainly no harm in enquiring about a booking.'

'It's a deal then. I'll have a word with them.'

When everyone finishes breakfast, I get myself ready to go out. Despite Will saying he wouldn't be here until midday, I am not taking any chances of bumping into him when he arrives from Robert and Natasha's. I hope he doesn't expect to stay on their sofa for too long. I am sure he could afford to stay in one of the many guest houses in town with the money he got for the watch, I think, bitterly.

I decide to head to Emily's for the afternoon where she adds further fuel to the fire.

'I just can't believe he'd do this to us,' says Emily.

'I know,' I agree.

'Well, I know a bloody brilliant lawyer. Tomorrow morning, if you don't call them, I'm calling for you,' says Emily.

'About that… I think the boys want me to think things through properly before rushing in with lawyers.'

'Nonsense. You have to file first. Honestly, it's so important. You can't mess this up or you'll lose your home as well as the watch.'

The thought of losing the home that we brought the boys up in would kill me. We have lost enough to the business as it is. Over a bottle of red wine with Emily, I agree to speak to the lawyers in the morning.

When I arrive home, I am feeling certain that I am doing the right thing. I remind myself that I am merely safeguarding the boys and my future. We can't recover from this, even if I do feel utterly devastated when I see many of Will's familiar things missing from the house. The first thing that strikes me when I open the front door is that the man bag Will carries to the shop is gone from the side. Even the big black and white umbrella that he keeps in the brolly stand is missing. When I go to the bedroom, it is even worse. I open his side of the wardrobe to see that the loud shirts he loves to wear are all gone. I open a drawer to find it empty. No pants or socks. He has taken everything, just as I asked. My heart sinks, even though I know that I have no choice but to do this. He listened to me and took almost everything.

When Ewan and Nia leave to head back to Cardiff in the evening, the house that I enjoy having full of loved ones feels empty. It is only me, Dylan and Monty left now.

When I wake up alone in the middle of the night, I desperately want to get Monty from the kitchen to keep me company. He has always slept in his basket in the kitchen, though, and I know I mustn't encourage him. However, sleeping without Will feels alien. Even though I slept alone last night, it seems different tonight. Last night it felt as though we had simply had a tiff and he was sleeping in the other room. Now, there is not even the alarm clock he keeps on the bedside table to keep me company. It is just me and my things. It is as though Will has never been in here, even though I can still smell his aftershave on the pillow. It smells of that musky scent I always loved. I turn around in the bed and face the other side to move away from his lingering aroma.

The first thing I do in the morning is strip the bed and put the sheets in the wash. I can't bear to smell him again tonight.

The next thing I do is phone the number that Emily gave me. My heart thuds as I dial the number of a lawyer I have never heard of before. This feels so sudden, final and terrifying. Last week we were celebrating our anniversary and a divorce was the last thing on my mind so I can't get my head around any of this. I don't want to rush into anything, and it all seems so absurd, but Emily's warning about losing the house next is all it took. I am determined that I will never let him steal anything else from under me. So I continue dialling the number and try not to let my voice give away the nerves I am feeling when I resolutely announce that I am looking for a divorce lawyer. As the words are said out loud, my decision seems to become more final in my head.

I have always kept a little bit of money aside for a rainy day, but I don't think it will enable me to pay the legal fees. Knowing how the shop was struggling for the past few years, I worried that we wouldn't be able to pay our utility bills. Thus, I had shaved a small amount off grocery bills where I could and put that money into a small account offering a reasonable interest rate. It is amazing how coupons, loyalty points and interest on what I saved added up over the years. However, as I hear how much the initial appointment will cost, I realise that it is nowhere close to a divorce fund and I may have to turn to Emily for help. She will only be too happy to help after what Will has done. I still feel that I am moving too fast with all of this, but every time I have the slightest wobble, I think of Emily's words.

I can't quite believe that Will had the barefaced cheek to think that saving his failing family business was more important than my memories of my dad. I can't ever imagine getting over it. This will show him what a terrible thing he has done.

After arranging my lawyer's appointment, I take Monty out for a walk to clear my head. The other odd thing about all of this is that I have nowhere to go. It's not like I am going to walk into the shop and work for Will all day. Not that I did much work unless that involved tea-making.

Monty and I have a lovely walk along the beach, and as the wind blows through my hair, I feel like everything will be okay. I have always thought of myself as a strong woman. Someone who can cope with what is thrown at her. I never imagined this, but I can get through it. I have always been determined; plus it is amazing what the sea air can do for your mental health.

With a clear head, I think of how we will survive this financially. Food, electricity, gas and council tax don't come cheap. I will naturally look for a job right away, but I also need something more. February isn't the best time of year for employment in a seaside town. So I think again about my dream of making jewellery. It could be a little side hustle.

By the time I get home, I am more positive than I have been all day. I search on the internet for videos about making jewellery and decide that I am going to start the Etsy shop that I always wanted. If I am not working for the business any longer, then it is time for me to become my own entrepreneur in between searching for full-time employment.

I run upstairs, open the drawer I keep for knick-knacks and take out the gemstones I bought in the shop in Venice. They are still safely tucked in the plain blue wrapping from the shop. The same shop Dad's watch is in. No doubt it will be on a shelf now with a huge price tag. I may have a little money tucked away, but nothing like the amount that the watch would cost to get back. If only I had a thriving business though, then who knows, maybe I could buy it? I laugh at myself as I realise how ridiculous I am being. However, I can't help but dream that I could get that watch back somehow. It's going to take a lot more than a few beaded necklaces and earrings though. I remind myself that everyone has to start somewhere, so, with nothing better to do, I start creating my online store and proudly name it Libby's Gems. I won't put it live until I have made something I can put on there, but at least I have a storefront. As I step back and admire what I have created, the storefront is my beacon of hope that I can go it alone and create a new beginning. The next thing I do is enrol myself in some jewellery-making classes at the local college. I notice that classes start after Easter, which is only a month or two away. It feels as though it is meant to be and it makes me wonder if I might one day become more successful than Will. That would be nice revenge. No cutting up clothes, no throwing his suitcase out, but success. *My* success. He always ran the show and didn't include me in his business deals, and where did it get him?

It is my turn to show him how to run a business. He will soon see what I can achieve without him. I just need to speak to the lawyers first.

Chapter Fourteen

As I walk into the lawyer's office for our meeting a week later, I feel sick. It is as though I am signing myself up for a big flashy tattoo that I may regret in the future, but there will be no option of lasering this off. I will be stuck with this decision forever. I begin to get cold feet but when I start talking to the lawyer who specialises in divorces, a friendly lady called Nikki, my nerves settle down again. It also helps that they offer a choice of teas, including calming chamomile and lavender. This decision to offer such a variety of relaxing beverages promotes my confidence in the law firm immensely. Perhaps that is why Emily recommended them.

'So tell me what the reason is for the divorce?' says Nikki.

'My husband stole an expensive watch from me,' I say.

'Oh, so do you want to press charges? This could be a criminal case,' says Nikki, putting her pen down.

'No, it's okay. I don't want to press charges. He's the boys' dad at the end of the day. Though my sister, Emily, would if she could. I just want a quick and easy divorce,' I say.

'Okay, I get that. Irreconcilable differences, then. Although we can do a no-fault divorce nowadays. I must warn you though, not many of the divorces I arrange are quick and easy,' says Nikki, picking her pen back up.

'Will doesn't have much. We only really have the house and probably a lot of debt, so hopefully it won't be too messy,' I say.

'Okay, well, let's see. You'd be surprised what comes out in the wash sometimes,' says Nikki.

'Oh, no. I really don't think Will has anything hidden,' I explain.

We go through lots of legal jargon and questions, and finally, Nikki has everything she needs. She asks where she should send the divorce petition. I give her Robert and Natasha's address and walk out, leaving all the carnage to begin. I don't think Will is expecting me to move this soon to the next stage. He might even think I have been calling his bluff. Will he even care when he receives the papers? Or will he care more about the business? I try to work out what his reaction will be when he receives the petition, but I really don't know.

It is two days later that I find out how he reacts when Dylan has a phone call from Will asking him if he knew that I'd already filed for a divorce. This makes me even angrier with Will since I always make an effort to protect the boys from any disputes and lessen anything they know. I hadn't even told Dylan that I had been to the lawyers as I didn't want him to worry after him asking me not to rush into things.

Apparently, Will phoned Dylan distraught and said that he wouldn't agree to any divorce and that I would have to wait two years of being separated if I wanted one.

However, what he doesn't realise is that the lawyer told me the law has changed and I could have the no-fault divorce she mentioned, so I know that is incorrect. Fortunately, Nikki was very thorough.

I had blocked Will's phone number for a few days, so perhaps that is why he called Dylan instead of me, but I remain resolute. I decide to unblock Will to message him to tell him that he needs to get himself a lawyer.

He messages back right away.

> How could you do this to me? And I don't have money for a lawyer.

This incenses me further as I wonder if he has already managed to splurge the money for Dad's watch.

You had plenty of money in Venice when you sold my dad's watch, I write.

> Look, I'm sorry. Can we talk? How can I explain everything and make things better when you won't talk to me?

> I told you. There's nothing to say!

> Oh, Libs. Please. It was a stupid thing to do. I'm sorry. I'd love to talk this out with you.

Nope. I throw my phone down. Has he already forgotten how much I detest liars? How can I even trust him to talk things out with me when he tried to palm this whole incident off as no big deal? I can't trust a word.

> Look, at least let me see Monty. Can I take him for a walk?

I look at Monty, who still keeps peeping at the front door, and immediately agree. It is clear that he is missing Will terribly. Within twenty minutes, Will is at the door. I thought perhaps he might try to use the key, but he knocks on the door of his former home like a cold-calling stranger would.

Monty goes bonkers when he sees Will and tries to jump all over him. I feel immensely guilty for keeping them apart for a few days. If only I could explain.

Will grabs Monty's lead to take him for a walk. As he walks out of the door, he leans into me and says, 'I won't sign any paperwork, you know.'

'You will,' I say.

'You want a bet? Let's see who wins.' Will looks at me with sheer determination.

'You don't want to do this. You've always been a poor loser,' I say.

'I know in my heart that I will never allow you to divorce me because of one silly mistake. Look, I'm sorry.'

Every time Will tries to apologise, he makes me madder.

'A silly mistake! You call stealing someone's family heirloom a *silly mistake*?' I say.

Monty pulls at the lead as he waits impatiently for his dad to walk him, and so they both leave, just in time for Will to escape the confrontation. Monty happily wags his tail whilst Will looks upset. If he had a tail, it would certainly be between his legs.

For a moment, even I feel sympathy for him. But then, like a flashback, I see myself opening that safe and the shock of the watch not being in there. I think of the man in Venice who must have thought what a fool I was not to know that my husband had just sold him a very unique and wonderful watch. What must he have thought of me? Another person that Will has made me look stupid in front of with his lies.

I am unsettled as Will walks Monty and so, with the house empty, I find myself walking around from room to room. This house holds so many lovely memories of being such a happy family home. Sure, we have had our troubled moments with finances, or when Dylan broke his wrist at rugby, and when Ewan didn't get his first choice of uni, and he ranted for a few weeks, but generally we have been lucky as a family. We always had each other's backs, until now. No matter what happened in the world around us, we were one team. Now that team has been destroyed.

I try to take my mind off our fractured family by sitting down with a jewellery-making kit I ordered from the internet after enrolling on the course. Now I can add the gemstones I bought to the pieces of silver that come with the kit. Even though I am still waiting to begin the course, it is fun to have a go and see how far I can get. At least then I won't be completely clueless in front of the other students if I get some practice in.

I read the instructions that come with the kit and try to memorise the names of the items. There is even some type of cement. This is a whole new world to me, and I am pleased that I decided on a head start.

As I bend some silver thread to put a delicate gemstone on, I feel excited about my humble little venture, something that I haven't felt in years. I feel fulfilled as I finish off the necklace with the gemstone on. I am holding it up proudly when Will returns with Monty.

'What's that? Been treating yourself to some new jewellery already?' says Will as he notices the necklace.

'Not that it is anything to do with you, but I made it,' I say.

'Really? That's fabulous. I could sell it in the shop,' he says.

'I have my own shop now. I don't need yours,' I say. Immediately I realise that I sound like a nasty ex-wife already.

'You have your own shop?' says Will.

'Yes, I'm not *just* a housewife helping you out in your shop. Sometimes I wonder if you ever knew the person I am inside. I had dreams, too, you know.'

'Like what?' says Will.

'You know full well about the skydiving one,' I say.

'Well, that's just silly though, isn't it? Why would anyone want to do that for fun?' says Will.

Once again, he winds me up. I always listened to him when he used to say how he dreamed of sailing around Corsica, or perhaps it was Croatia. I don't remember the exact details. But still, I know his dream was to hire a sailing boat and go around Europe somewhere. He has always dismissed my dreams, and I put everything aside to support him and the boys.

'I think it's time you left now, Will.'

'I don't want to, but I will, because I know you want me to. I am trying here, Libby. It feels so weird leaving my own home to stay at my mate's.'

'You'll be fine. Go and enjoy a few pints or something,' I say. I feel like a harridan but remind myself that I have got to stay strong. The more he hangs around here, the more risk there is that I could change my mind. 'You should have thought of the consequences before nabbing Dad's watch. What did you honestly expect to happen when I found out?'

'All right, all right. I get the hint. I don't want to talk about it. Can I come and see Monty again tomorrow?'

As much as he is now starting to completely provoke me, I could never keep a dog and his master apart.

'You can come when I'm not here. I'll be out tomorrow evening. You can come then,' I say.

'Out?'

'Yes, out.'

'So you're going on nights out and you're making jewellery. You're a quick worker. What next? A date with someone?'

The thought of a date with someone is absurd. However, at this moment I want to hurt him just as much as he has hurt me. So I find myself not lying, but making up a fictitious story one word at a time. I don't even know where it comes from. It is just pure spite.

'You know what? I am thinking I may go out with someone, actually. I've met a lovely man in the park who…'

I ignore the hurt in his eyes and continue.

'He was very kind to me, and he asked me to visit his farm. You know how much I love animals…'

'Don't. Just stop. How could you do that when my bed isn't even cold? Perhaps you're not the woman I thought you were. You say that you didn't know me, but it sounds like I didn't know you either. Your family always came first and now look at you. Going out, fancy jewellery, a date with another man. Oh my god. I've heard enough. If you want that divorce then go ahead. Bring it on, Libs.'

I snap completely at his words.

'Going on a night out isn't exactly a sin, you narrow-minded little man. Get that lawyer sorted so we can do this as quickly and cheaply as possible,' I say.

As Will turns on his heel, Dylan walks through the front door from his rugby practice.

'Hiya, Dad. You're back. I knew you two wouldn't argue for long,' he says.

'Sorry, but Dad was just leaving,' I say.

'Did you know about the date she's going on with a farmer? Have you seen a man here in our home?' says Will to Dylan.

Poor Dylan looks like he is about to faint. He has had enough surprises these past few days.

I want to say it isn't true, but I also want to hurt Will as badly as I can.

'It's a long story, Dylan. It's not as bad as it sounds, I promise. I'll explain in a bit.'

'A farmer of all things! You're always complaining about the smell of manure when they do the fields. And you get road rage whenever a tractor's in front of you holding you up. How could you date a farmer?' says Dylan.

'Look, I'm not. Oh my gosh, this is getting out of hand. Will, it's time you left, and Dylan, I promise to explain.'

The three of us stand in the hallway looking at each other exasperated. How on earth have we ended up like this? The only one who is oblivious to this mess is Monty. He stands in between us all, looking up and wagging his tail.

Oh, Monty, life is so much easier being a dog.

Chapter Fifteen

By the time Easter comes around, I have made lots of different pieces of jewellery, including one piece I save especially for Emily as a thank you gift for being so supportive following all the fights with Will. This break-up may have fractured my relationship with Will, but it has only strengthened my relationship with Emily. We have had our moments in the past, but this whole debacle has proved that blood is thicker than water and both me and Emily have lost something of great importance.

I have also made a pendant with a star for Nia because she really is a superstar. Whenever she comes to stay with Ewan, her positive vibe shines bright, so when I saw this in my jewellery kit, I knew it was perfect for her.

With Ewan and Nia on their Easter break, we arrange a family lunch. For once I am not cooking and we have a special roast at a lovely local hotel with a big open fire. I would have loved to have everyone at mine, but without Will being present and all the drama at the moment, it was better that we went somewhere different. There are too many memories of dinners at home, and it would feel odd with one empty chair.

Dylan and Ewan sit by each other, and the women sit on the other side of the table. I hand over the special heart pendant to Emily first and then the star to Nia. I carefully wrapped both of them in tissue paper and tied a bow around them. I have learned from my marketing books that packaging can make all the difference, so I wanted to experiment and judge their reaction.

'I didn't think you'd appreciate an Easter egg as I know you try to stay off chocolate, so here's something I made for you. It's also to say thank you for all your support,' I say to Emily. 'And Nia, this is something that reminded me of you.'

As Emily looks at the package, I suddenly feel nervous at handing over the necklace. She is so fussy that I begin to regret my decision. What if she hates it?

'Oh, Libby, you shouldn't have. You were there for me when John left. It's only natural I am there for you now.'

I think back to when John left her, and Emily would call me up in tears. I wonder if I really was that good to her. After all, I had the boys and my husband, and it makes me realise how absorbed I was in their lives. Did I give her the time she deserved? If I am honest with myself, I know that she deserved more support. I was always rushing here and there and don't know that I was the best listener. Perhaps I haven't always been as good a sister as I could have been.

Emily eagerly rips open the tissue paper. She never was any good at waiting to open presents. She used to be the same at Christmas when we were small. She'd rip everything open with no patience as she was desperate to see what was inside.

She takes the necklace from the packaging and holds it up to look at it.

'Wow, it's beautiful.'

'I'm so happy you like it. Are you sure you're not just saying it though?'

'No, I absolutely love it. It's so delicate and pretty.' Emily touches the little pink heart and admires it for a moment. The light shines right through and gives off different hues as though it is a luminous pearl. 'Gosh, it's stunning. Where did you find it? I hope it didn't cost you too much. You need to save your money.'

My heart swells with pride. She thinks I bought it somewhere! I haven't told Emily or Nia about my mission to launch a shop or that I am starting my first jewellery-making class later. I should have probably confided in Emily, but I was afraid she would laugh at me. As my big sister, her approval means everything to me, even at this age. She is hugely encouraging though when I tell her.

'Are you sure you even need lessons? My goodness, Libby. You're obviously a natural. This is absolutely terrific. You could very easily sell these.'

Nia is touching her necklace and asks Ewan to help put it on.

'Oh, Libby. I love this. It's so thoughtful and beautiful,' she says.

I feel myself blush slightly. They both approve!

'Well, my dream is to put a few bits online to sell.'

'No way. You're a dark horse. Why didn't you tell me? You know I could model for you. I've always wanted to model,' says Emily.

'That has crossed my mind. I just felt a bit embarrassed that I thought I could try and make money from a hobby.'

'Oh, darling girl. This is not a hobby. You have a gift. I hope you're going to continue with this.'

'Yes, this is awesome. You have some serious talent,' says Nia.

'Thank you, both.'

'I'm so happy for you. I wish I'd done something like that when John and I split up instead of moping about and crying all the time,' says Emily.

I get that guilty feeling again about not being there for her as much as I should have been. I will never make that same mistake again.

'I'm so proud of you for sticking to your guns, you know that. You're doing the right thing,' says Emily.

'Yeah, you're doing amazing. Oh, and I forgot to tell you. I've opened a Just Giving account for your skydive. Now all you have to do is book the date and choose your charity,' says Nia.

'Oh, it has to be for Dad's hospital. What do you think?' says Emily. She seems thrilled at the thought of doing something for the hospital, even though she would never do anything as audacious herself, so I gladly agree.

'Definitely. That would be fantastic. At least then I'll feel as though I am doing something for Dad after losing his lovely watch.'

Emily squeezes my hand, and this comforts me, making me more determined than ever that I have to carry on with the divorce. Will has to be taught that he can't get away with doing such a terrible thing.

–

By seven p.m., I am excited as I open the door to the community centre and get ready for my first jewellery-making class.

There are only six of us, which I am pleased about. I have never been one to make small talk with big groups of people. This is just about the right size for me to handle.

The tutor introduces himself as Giles, and he is a very charming man indeed. If I was ever ready for a relationship, I would probably be blushing every time he came over to help me with my soldering iron. I regret not bringing Emily along with me; she might have hit it off with him. I can see now why old agony aunt columns used to recommend evening classes as a way of meeting people.

For our first lesson, we are introduced to the tools we will need. There is some serious stuff here such as an enamelling kiln and a gas torch which I fear will allow me to set fire to the curtains near the window. I am probably the type of person who could set fire to a hundred-year-old community centre, so I will make sure that I use that with caution.

I am paired up with a lady called Judy. As we work together, sharing materials and equipment, she tells me about her husband and how he plays darts every Tuesday night. That's why she felt it was time for her to find a hobby. She doesn't seem as serious as I am about making the jewellery though and I realise there and then how much this means to me. There is no plan B. This enterprise has got to work. So I hang on to every single word that Giles says and make notes as I go along.

Just before the end of the class, I have managed to design a small pair of earrings. I am surprised when Giles comes up and shows my classmates my work.

'These are incredible,' says Giles, holding them up for the class to see.

I feel so immensely proud that I have managed to impress my new tutor. This never happened to me in school, or anywhere else.

'You see how Libby has designed the swirls and shape of these. Very creative. Very sinuous. You seem to have a natural flair. Maybe next week, we can be a little more ambitious than I was planning.'

I feel like the school swot! Perhaps I will bring an apple for the teacher next week.

By the time I say goodbye to Giles and the other new classmates, I leave the centre feeling on top of the world.

As I walk down the street, I hold my head up high with my newfound confidence.

Libby Jones, I do believe you have finally found something you are good at, and even Emily agrees!

Chapter Sixteen

The satisfaction of finding a new passion leaves me feeling quite upbeat about my life. However, that all changes when I receive a very formal letter from Will's lawyer two weeks later.

Will is asking for the house to be sold, since it is all that he has. He desperately needs somewhere to stay as he can't sofa surf much longer. I suppose even his best friend can't put him up forever.

There are no assets, only debts and this four-bedroom house, which luckily has no mortgage on it since we bought it so many years ago. When I receive the letter, I feel the shock that Will must have had when he received the divorce petition. Even I can see that we are two people playing a silly game that is spiralling out of control, lawyer's letter by lawyer's letter.

I break down in tears as I realise the enormity of all of this. Until now I have been relatively staunch about everything. But I am beginning to realise that before too long, we could be forced to sell up the family home, the one constant we have had in our lives since before we married. Will has sent me a message saying that since Dylan will be heading to uni in a couple of months' time, there is no need for us to keep the family home and that by selling up, we can both have a home. I ring Emily in despair.

'I told you he'd do that, didn't I?' she says.

'Oh, Emily, this is all going too far now. I don't know what to do.'

'Look, you'll just have to leave the lawyers to sort it out. That's their job. They do it every day.'

'I know, but this house is just as much Will's as it is mine. It's going to have to be divided between us.'

I pause for a moment as I think about it all.

'We're going to have to sell it. I just know it. All this fighting and neither of us will end up living there. What a mess.'

'I know, divorces are messy. But you can't let a man get away with stealing our dad's watch. You have to be strong now, Libby. Don't forget that I've been through all of this myself. It's not fun, but I promise that you'll come out the other side. Six months to a year from now and things will be so much better.'

I remind myself of Emily's advice as I go about my daily routine of making jewellery that I hope will impress Giles. I have only done a couple of classes, but I dread the thought of them ending in a few weeks. It is funny how much I need Giles's validation; perhaps it is because then I can see that at least one part of my life is turning out well.

However, looking at this letter, it doesn't seem to matter how well I am doing in class. I am about to lose my home because of a lie my husband told me.

I try to remember that this time will pass. There will surely be a day when there won't be threatening legal letters coming through the door and calm will be restored. I dream of the day when I shall have a jewellery empire and can finally show Will what I am capable of. I daydream of a jewellery exhibition with Giles at my side, telling everyone how wonderful I am. Then Monty needs a wee, and this brings me right back down to earth.

As soon as Monty is back in, I continue with my creations. I have decided that it is better for my health not to have a free moment. From when I wake up in the morning to the minute I go to bed, I choose to stay busy, and the bags under my eyes are proof. Making all of this jewellery gives me something to focus on whilst Will and I pointlessly fight over plates, wedding presents we forgot we had, the car and, sadly, our home.

If I stop for one second, I remember that Dad's watch is missing from the safe and Will is to blame. It is all too much to think about. Although, there is a positive side to this nervous energy that I am emitting and I have managed to make three pairs of earrings and one necklace in a couple of hours this morning. With Emily's, Nia's and Giles's belief in me, I am confident enough to open the shop online.

I take photos of the items on a white furry cushion I have and post them on the Etsy site and wait for my first-ever transaction. Finally, I have enough items to go live.

I decide that if I do sell anything, I will treat myself to fish and chips on the seafront, although I am going to look for a new bench. It wouldn't be the same sitting on 'our' bench without Will.

I have bought pretty pink tissue paper and little tags that say 'Made with love', so I am all set to package everything up if I do get that sale. The thought that I could fail hasn't really occurred to me.

For the remainder of the day, I continue making more stock. I start with a bracelet with some of the pretty coral gemstones from Venice. Then Will creeps back into my mind as I handle the gemstones. I was so happy that morning back then. I am glad I didn't know what was about to happen. I stop myself from thinking again. I must not worry about it all. I put Will back in that box I don't want to open that I keep in my head and carry on. I am almost in a trance as I design an ankle bracelet. With summer coming up I might be able to get a new trend going; who knows? I know anklets were huge when I was younger. Perhaps it's time to bring them back to the majorities. This thought excites me, so I start drawing out plans of how I could make a trendy range of ankle brace-lets. I was never that great at drawing, but I find some of Dylan's coloured felt pens that he needed for a geography project and start to draw and colour in my designs. I design one in amber and am pleased with the result. These could definitely work, although I would need to sell heaps of them to make any money. So I plan and plan. I sit there like a mad professor who is in the midst of creating a new invention.

I design ankle chains with initials and heart charms until I have a whole range. I could even ask the local traders if they would stock them. I am pretty sure tourists coming to Tenby would love these. They'd look so cute on the beach. Then I have a brain wave and consider designing hand jewellery as you would see at an Asian wedding. A little boho chic would work well. As all the marketing books I read have told me, I have to find my USP. I know there are other boho chic companies, but I have my own individual style. So I begin to design hand jewellery and will ask Emily to model for me once they are made. This can become something we do together as our relationship becomes closer now we are both going to be divorcees. I hope this will put an end to the sibling rivalry we have had at times over the years.

I am producing my first anklet when I get an alert telling me that someone has bought a necklace and matching earrings. My first sale and it is not just for one, but two items! I finish putting a charm on the anklet and then start to lovingly wrap my first sale. I pray that they love it and give me good feedback.

To celebrate, I take Monty with me to get fish and chips for tea after I have been to the post office to drop off my first package.

We search for somewhere to sit down and eat.

'Oh Monty, where shall we sit?' I ask. A pointless question but I am hoping that someone moves from all the busy benches. There is only one bench free, and it is 'our bench'. I can't possibly sit there, although Monty is already gravitating that way.

I look around, and nobody is budging. It will have to be that bench. Monty is much more pleased with the location than I am and happily wags his tail as he desperately waits for me to drop a chip. He eyes the ground with great precision.

'They're not good for you,' I remind him as I stuff them into my mouth.

I don't particularly care what they will do to me. I care more about Monty. He's twelve now, and I want him to live forever. I stuff the fish batter into my mouth. It tastes so good that I momentarily don't care what it does to my arteries. My heart is already broken anyhow.

An old lady stops and asks if anyone is sitting next to me.

'No, nobody,' I reply. I feel like telling this stranger why I am sitting here alone. Fortunately, I manage to stop myself. I think it is only because the cod tastes too good to stop for a moment to speak. But I could really do with confiding in someone and telling them what I am going through. Then I remind myself that I cannot open Pandora's box. I can't let myself think about my marriage because that is the moment I will crumble to flaky little pieces, just like the bits of cod I throw down at Monty. So I just keep quiet and smile like I don't have a care in the world. Then I offer the lady a chip as I can't possibly eat all of this by myself. I never realised quite how big the portions are at our favourite chippy until now.

She looks a little surprised and politely declines. I feel a bit silly now having asked a stranger if she wants to share my chips because I can't eat them all.

I get up and walk off with Monty and realise that this is how my new life will be. I no longer have anyone to share my chips on a bench with.

Chapter Seventeen

A few months after I've filed for divorce, Emily insists she fixes me up on a date. It is the last thing I want to do, but Will has been rather petty about an antique bookcase we both love, and so I do it out of spite more than actually wanting to go on a date. Of course, I do feel guilty for giving any false hope to my prospective date, but it is only an evening out.

Simon works for a hotel selling golf memberships. Apparently, Emily met him when she considered joining the local golf club to get her out of the house. Golf is not my thing at all, so I can't see what we have in common. However, Emily had kept in touch with him on Facebook, and when he complained he didn't have anyone to take to a concert, Emily said she knew the perfect person he could go with since he is definitely not her type. I am worried that she is palming off her unwanted admirers onto me though.

The concert is being held at a vineyard. As I do like my wine, I thought I would give it a go. That is how I find myself getting ready for something I never ever would have dreamed I would be doing. I put the final touches of my lipstick on and am ready for the date when I hear Will knocking on the door to take Monty out. Perfect timing.

'Where are you off to looking like that?' he says.

'What about hello, Libby?'

'Hello, Libby. Where are you off to looking like that?'

'On a date,' I say. He has that look again. That broken look, which almost makes me feel sorry for him. Even as I attempt to wind him up, I realise how out of hand this is all getting. It is like a game of cat and mouse, and neither of us will give in.

'Good for you,' he says.

My stomach hurts and I feel sick. I hadn't expected that reaction from the look on his face. My soon-to-be ex-husband is okay with me going on a date. I know in my heart that if he went on a date, I could possibly die crying. I almost want to fling myself into his arms and ask him what on earth we are doing to each other. I don't though. I remember the watch and how he cannot be trusted. The man I thought I knew is no more. So I leave him to come inside and play with Monty whilst I walk out of the door and off to my date with Simon. As I close the door on my past, I stride forward to move on to the next stage of getting my head around my upcoming divorce.

Simon is a tall, slim man. He is so different to Will and that dad bod I love so much. He is in better shape than Will is nowadays, but when I meet him, I don't feel the excitement I had with my husband.

'Hello, Emily's told me a lot about you,' he says.

'Oh goodness, I hope it was nothing bad,' I joke.

'All fantastic things. In fact, Mother can't wait to meet you.'

'Mother?'

'Yes, she gets so excited when I have a date.'

'Oh, right.' This is weird. Perhaps she is desperate to get rid of her bachelor son. 'How old is she?' I ask.

'Eighty-two. She still makes all the decisions. She's as fit as a fiddle.'

'Oh, great,' I say.

'Yes, if Mother doesn't like my date, then I don't go on a second,' he says.

'You take all your first dates to meet your mother? Is that what you're saying?'

'Yes, absolutely. You don't mind if we stop at my home on the way to the vineyard, do you?'

'Um, no,' I say. I want to get out of his car and run, but that wouldn't be polite. However, I am quickly becoming more and more unnerved about this date with a stranger.

I am glad that the road we travel on is all lit and in a busy area, so there is no chance of him kidnapping me in the car. I thought because Emily knew him online that he was okay. Now I am beginning to wish I had found out more about him from her. However, just because she sees his Facebook profile and he may post photos of cute cats, or whatever he does, doesn't mean that she truly knows him. Why did I let myself get talked into this?

When we arrive at Simon's home, the first thing that strikes me is the vast array of gnomes. Yes! Gnomes! I begin to wonder whether he thinks that gnomes keep the grass down like sheep or goats would. Because there are gnomes all over the front lawn. This evening is going from bad to worse. However, I soon realise that this is only the beginning.

'Mother, we're home,' says Simon as he opens the door.

He removes his shoes, and I start to walk in behind him.

'Shoes!' he almost barks at me.

'Oh, sorry, yes. I should have realised when you took your shoes off. How awful of me.' I remove the high, strappy black sandals that I carefully chose for this evening and suddenly realise quite how tall Simon is. My head only comes up to his chest.

'Mother, this is Libby,' says Simon.

I look in the living room, with its outdated fireplace with one of those old bar-type electric fires perfectly positioned in the middle. Gosh, this house feels even more ancient than the stuff in the shop.

'Hello,' I say to the lady on the leather-look sofa. She has grey wiry hair, with matching hairs coming from her chin. At least she looks cosy wrapped up in her Welsh woollen blanket. I expect they don't put the heating on in here as the old stone house feels cold, even though the evening is mild.

'Come here then,' says Simon's mother. For a moment, I wonder if she needs help with something. Did her blanket slip down and she needs help? Simon said she is fit as a fiddle.

I move closer towards her, and she grabs my cheeks.

'Let me look at you then.' She holds my head in her hands and inspects me as if she is a mother gorilla looking for fleas on her offspring.

'Mother's eyes aren't what they were,' explains Simon.

I want to step back and tell her to get off. But, again, politeness prevails, and I allow this complete stranger to look over me. I decide the minute I get out of here I shall feign a migraine. I don't care that a vineyard is my dream venue for a date; these two are off their trolley.

'Lovely, not bad at all, Simon,' she says.

I half wonder if they have some kind of cannibal pot in the kitchen waiting for me. I feel like a juicy peach in the greengrocer the way they are talking about me.

'Did you want a cuppa before we leave? I'm putting the kettle on for Mother,' says Simon.

I choose to decline. I don't trust anything in this weird house. Goodness knows what they could put in the tea. I also noticed the grime in the kitchen, and there is nothing whatsoever appealing about a cuppa from this house.

'I'm sorry, I think I'm getting one of my migraines,' I say.

'Give her some of my painkillers, Simon. She'll be right as rain,' says Mother.

'Oh, no, thank you. I'm okay. I just need a lie down in a dark room,' I say.

'Well, I don't normally allow young ladies into Simon's room. He should be married for that, but if you want a lie down in there, Simon can show you where it is,' says Mother. 'Simon, show your young lady friend to your room.'

Simon gets up, and I insist I am fine.

'No, it's okay. You know, maybe I need some fresh air. I'll go for a walk whilst you have your tea.'

'Do you want Simon to come with you? You can't be too sure at this time in the evening. There are some strange people out there.'

The only people I have seen who are strange tonight are you two, I think to myself. I feel as though I would be a lot safer outside than in here.

'No, honestly. You two have a little chat and a cuppa and I'll be back. Won't be a tick,' I say.

I grab my shoes from the hallway and put them on as quickly as possible. I hadn't planned on walking anywhere in them tonight, but I will do anything to get out of this mad house.

I open the door and am greeted by a gnome with his trousers down doing a moonie. What a night! I begin to wonder if the gnome and strange etiquette are all some type of prank that Simon does if he doesn't like his date when she turns up. I can't quite decide. Surely this is not their normal behaviour. Whatever is going on here, I need to get out as quickly as possible. Fortunately, I know the area. So I walk as fast as I can to the nearest bus stop and catch the number 59 bus back home. I have never been so relieved to sit on a bus.

Gangs of youngsters get on, all ready for a night out. I must be the only person on the bus who has finished their night out and is on their way back home. In fact, I get home way too early. As when I arrive home, Will is still there. This was definitely not part of my plan.

'Wasn't expecting you back so quickly. Is everything okay? You look a bit pale,' he says.

'Yeah, had a migraine,' I say.

'Oh no, let me get you some tea. Should I get you that ice pack you usually use on your neck too?'

I feel like confessing that I don't have a migraine at all, but that I just had the date from hell. I can't quite tell him how bad it was though. He may laugh at me.

'No, it's okay. I think it's passing now. I might have a glass of wine instead.'

'Unusual for you to have wine when you've got a migraine. You usually go straight to bed,' he says.

Once again Will reminds me how well we know each other. Even if he didn't always listen to my dreams and aspirations, we were familiar with each other in sickness and in health. Will pours us a glass of wine and I feel the calmest I have since all of this started. What if all we both needed was to calm down, communicate with each other and sit down and discuss everything over a bottle of wine?

Could we possibly put this behind us and be a family once again? For a second, I start to think that this could happen. So far, we are both the most civilised we have been to each other in what feels like a very long time.

'Cheers,' I say.

Will takes the drink but then turns to his phone.

'You seem engrossed in your phone tonight. Busy with the shop?'

'No. I'm just on Tinder. What do you reckon?' Will shows me a photo of a beautiful lady in her fifties. I feel a huge pang of jealousy, and bile rises from the pit of my stomach. This was not part of the plan. I should tell him to get off the dating site. That we need to talk. Maybe we can prevent this whole mess that we've found ourselves in. But I don't. I bite my tongue and say something I never thought I would dream of saying to my husband.

'She looks lovely. You should swipe, or whatever it is you do on that thing.'

Will looks surprised but then swipes across his phone with his finger. 'Well, you're not willing to make any effort to fix our marriage. I can't sit about begging you forever. Robert told me I need to get out and about a bit now. Get back on the bike, so to speak.'

His words make me so angry, and I am mad at Robert too. I don't want Will 'getting out and about'. As for getting 'back on the bike', please tell me I didn't just hear that. It makes me feel bitter again, and I remember why we are in the middle of a divorce. I return to spite mode.

'I don't need an app for my dates,' I say.

'Why do you always have to be so smug?' asks Will.

'I'm not smug.'

'Yes, you are. Look at you. You were smug at the motel we stayed in before Venice. When we met that couple on their honeymoon. You sounded so smug when you gave advice to… What was her name?'

'Claire,' I say.

'Yes, you were giving her advice on how to keep a marriage happy. Look at you. Didn't manage that very well, did you?'

Anger rises from within me. I don't know how we have managed to go from soulmates to enemies so quickly. I have never felt such conflict with anyone.

'I think you'd better leave,' I say.

'Yes, don't you worry. I am. Melinda on Tinder has swiped back. I've got a date to plan,' says Will. He slams down the glass of wine that he hasn't finished and storms out of the front door.

I pick his glass up and cradle it as I take it to the kitchen. I feel around the rim of the glass, where Will's familiar lips have been. The divorce is too far gone for any reconciliation. With Will on Tinder, maybe it is time for me to start considering relationships after all.

I wouldn't dare sign up for Tinder in case Will saw my profile. What if we matched?

So I find myself searching for a more traditional dating site online. If Will is to meet a gorgeous new woman, then it is time for me to stop hoping a miracle will happen and that we can get back to who we were. That life is behind us now, and I try to remember that as I build my dating profile, just as I built my Etsy shop, which is already going from strength to strength.

Let's hope this online venture will become just as successful.

Chapter Eighteen

I don't dare check the dating site until the end of the week. However, I am shocked that when I eventually log on, there are numerous messages. My goodness, I never knew there were so many single men out there. Although I suspect not all of them are unattached, like the guy who is clearly wearing a wedding ring. Thank goodness for the delete button.

A kind-looking chap with a nice smile who is called Terry has messaged, and he looks like someone you could chat to. As I am looking for someone to go for dinners and to concerts with, rather than the love of my life, I decide to contact him back. We end up chatting and get along immediately, so much so that we chat into the wee hours of Saturday morning. I actually find myself enjoying this stranger's company.

We get on so well online that we decide to meet up the following day. I ensure that we don't go to his house this time. I wouldn't risk that ever again after Simon. Although, that was completely unplanned. I make sure that we meet in town, somewhere with plenty of people around us. My previous experience has taught me that no matter how nice someone seems online, you still don't know them properly.

Since we have decided to go for a simple ice cream together, I wear my loose trousers and a casual sweatshirt.

I also decide on trainers, in case I have to run from him as I did with Simon. I won't make that mistake twice.

I am waiting outside the ice cream parlour when I see Terry approaching. He looks just like his photograph, which is great as he could have been some 'catfish', as Dylan calls some of these dodgy people online. I notice he has a carrier bag with him and am wondering if he has brought me a gift. What a sweet man!

When he approaches me, he gives me a kiss on the cheek. My nose bumps into his, and it isn't the easiest of starts. Still, I remain positive. After all, we got on so well online that I am sure there won't be any awkward silences between us.

As Terry sits down, he keeps the carrier bag on his lap, as if it is a precious jewel and he is scared someone will steal it. In the end, I have to ask him about it. The suspense is killing me. What could possibly be so important that you can't put it down?

'What's in the bag?' I ask.

'Ashes,' he says.

'Ashes?' I begin to wonder if I heard him incorrectly but then remember we are not that far away from the local crematorium.

'Oh, gosh. I'm so sorry. Did you just come from the crematorium?' I ask.

'No. Tommy died two years ago now.'

Now I am totally confused. Is Tommy his brother? Uncle? Surely if the ashes were his dad's he would call him 'Dad'?

'Can I ask who Tommy is?' I say.

'It hurts too much to talk about it. So I'd rather not. But Tommy was my tortoise. He lives on with me though. I take his ashes everywhere.'

'Everywhere?'

'Yes, we went on a cruise together last year, didn't we, Tommy?'

I notice the table next door look over and make faces. I am the biggest animal lover, but I also believe there is a time and place for carrying around your beloved pet's ashes. How on earth are you supposed to react to this? I say nothing. Again, in an awkward situation, I decide the best option is to remain polite.

'Oh, that's lovely. How nice for you both to have a holiday,' I say.

The waitress puts down our ice cream, and Terry starts telling his deceased tortoise about how nice his peach melba looks. I realise then that this date isn't going to work out, no matter how patient I try to be. I can't come between a man and his dead tortoise, although I am sure there is someone out there for this sweet man. So I eat my ice cream so fast that I get one of those massive shooting pains in my brain with the sudden chill of it all. I look at my phone and make an excuse that there is an emergency at home and delete the dating app the moment I walk out of the ice cream parlour.

By the time I return early from another disastrous date, Ewan and Nia are there. It is so nice to have them home again. Over the past few months, my superstar new friend Nia and I have grown so close she already feels like a daughter-in-law. I hope they last the course. It pleases me to see that she is still wearing the star necklace.

We discuss Tommy and the ashes over a glass of wine and have a bit of a giggle about my disastrous dates, not to mention Gnomegate. As I *cwch* into my favourite armchair, amongst their fabulous company, it makes me realise how much I love just sitting here in my cosy home.

Although, it won't be for much longer as we have a court hearing coming up next week. Again, I pop that into the box in my brain that I try not to think about.

As we laugh over the two dates I have had, I decide that I don't want to date anyone again in future. I am not interested, and that ship has well and truly sailed. I thought that I had a good marriage, and look how that turned out. I don't want to do this again and am happy with my jewellery-making, which I can hardly keep up with due to demand.

A pendant with a big amethyst stone that I made in my final class sold for forty-five pounds. It is a shame that the classes had to end, but we all promised each other we would meet up for drinks one day in future and exchanged numbers. Although Giles didn't give us his number – instead, he mentioned his partner countless times that night and how he probably wouldn't be able to go for drinks with the pupils, even at the end of term. I do hope he didn't get the wrong idea as I clung to his every word. Oh well, there goes my dream of him admiring my work at exhibitions.

At least I have my skydive booked. Emily and I eventually decided that there was no better day to book it than for Dad's birthday, which is next week. A bit sooner than I had planned, but Nia also felt it was a great idea to seize the day and not think too much about planning the jump. She was worried I would back out if I had too much time to think. So I am all confirmed, and the donations have already started rolling in. Hopefully, people can donate for a while after the jump, too, but I have left all of that bit to Nia. As she keeps telling me, all I have to do is focus on the skydive and she will do the rest.

As I think about next week's adventure, the doorbell rings. I open the door to find Will standing there. I forgot that he was due to pick up Monty. I don't particularly want to see him with our court date looming. So I let him in and then quickly leave him to chat with Ewan and Nia.

I hear Will's familiar voice, and the excited noises coming from Monty. I try not to listen to what Will is saying, but I can't help myself. I hear him asking Ewan how uni is going, and they talk about the latest Ospreys scores. Anyone would think that Will wasn't taking his son's mother to court and that there wasn't a possibility we could all lose our home.

I suppose we always were equally stubborn and each time I think of our lawyers and court visits, I am reminded of that. I dare not think about how he is paying his legal fees. I expect the house sale will end up covering them if it comes to that. Once again, I question myself about how we got here. Then I remember the reason.

When I finally hear Monty and Will leave, I head downstairs. I pour myself and Nia another glass of wine and chat about the skydive. We have already managed to raise £250. My target was £350 so I am very happy with that. Emily said she would also give me a donation on the day, so I am on track for my target. It is only when I think of Dad's birthday that I realise the skydive is booked for the day after the court hearing. This isn't ideal as I have no idea what frame of mind I will be in. I am beginning to wonder, if I lose the house, whether my parachute will protect me from the elements if I end up on the streets.

Later, when Ewan and Nia decide to head out for a walk, the house feels eerily quiet. I busy myself by making more jewellery for the Etsy shop. I am glad this keeps me busy and relieved that I have sold so much that I need to keep making more jewellery. At least it hasn't been a complete flop. I don't know what I would do without this business. It has made £300 this month, which has marginally helped towards an hour's legal fee.

If only Will had been honest with me from the start. None of this would have happened.

Every now and then I search for Venetian jewellers on the internet to see if I can find the shop and work out how much I would need to buy the watch back. However, I don't remember the name of the shop that Dad's watch is in, so I don't get very far. I would like to know if there would be any chance of getting it back, but for all I know, it could have been sold ages ago. Another thing I would like to know is how much the man gave Will for it. I know that there was £25,000 in the account when Will showed me the balance in Venice, but how much of that was the watch? I imagine it must have been most of the money in there. But this is something Will has never clarified. My only hope is that we get to see the business accounts in court. Maybe it was my lucky day when Nikki told me that the court date we had been given was much sooner than normal. Apparently, this is a good time of year to apply for a hearing. So I don't have to wait long until I can see how much was transferred from Venice and perhaps find out the name of the person it was transferred from.

If I try to look on the bright side of the court date, at least it might give me some of the missing answers that I need to find out.

So whilst I don't want to do any of this, I realise that I must now put on my big girl pants and get on with it. Although as I look at the radiator in the kitchen lined with drying underwear, I realise that this is one thing I am not in short supply of.

Chapter Nineteen

Monday mornings are most people's nemesis, but this one has to be the worst. I button up a plain black coat that looks business-like and professional. My buttons are tight and restraining. I want them to be tight as I get some comfort from the feeling that it is holding me together. As I walk into court, security goes through my bag and insists I take a sip of the bottle of water I have in there. I made sure I had one in case my mouth got dry. It always goes dry when I am scared, and I have never been more frightened in my life.

When there is an announcement over the tannoy calling for Jones in room three, I feel sick. For a moment, I begin to question why we are here. We were a team. What happened to us? I wish I could tell Nikki that I am calling this off and that I can't go through with it. But then I see her looking over a bank statement in front of her. It is for the business account. I see an amount of £25,000 that has been paid from 'something' Venezia. I can't make out the jeweller's name as I am reading it upside down, but there is clearly an amount of £25,000 paid in from an account in Venice. It's the money for Dad's watch. That is the amount Will showed me was in the company account. I notice that he didn't put it straight into the other business account with all the debts, because he knew most of it would have been gobbled up. Seeing this makes the anger boil up inside me again. It fills me with hate for Will that he would do this to us and now want our home too. So I stand tall as I walk into the room where the destiny of our family home is being decided. I will not back down.

Will sits at the other end of the bench, with both sets of lawyers between us. He doesn't look at me. I glance over from time to time to try and gauge his reaction, but he just stares straight ahead at the judge.

Nikki is asked to put my case forward first, and as she tells the judge how much I need the family home, Will baulks and makes so many noises that he is told off.

I am pleased someone has told him off. I look at the judge for signs that she is on my side. However, as we are herded into separate rooms for a break, I am reminded that there are no emotions in court. It is all evidence-based, and the evidence shows that Will has used up every penny of his money to save the business. As I discover when we head back into the courtroom, there is only one asset left between us, and that is the family home.

'It has to be sold and split fifty-fifty,' the judge says.

I feel sick, dizzy and everything in between. I have to take a sip of my water to stop myself from a coughing fit as my throat tightens. When I put my bottle down, the anger rises again.

'Do you want to be the one who tells Dylan?' I shout across the courtroom to Will.

All those words about Will spoiling me for the rest of my life come back into my head. What a load of baloney. If only I could have seen myself here in this courtroom, I would never have married him. I would never have believed that because of this man's actions, we would all have to lose our family home.

'Quiet please,' says the judge. She then packs up all the files in front of her, and the court is dismissed.

Fortunately, by the time I get outside, there is no sign of Will. He seems to have scarpered. That is a good thing, as I can't even imagine what I would say to him.

When I reach the car, I ring Emily to tell her the terrible news.

'I lost the home. How am I going to tell Dylan and Ewan? All those memories of growing up there will be gone,' I say, crying.

'I'm so sorry. I really thought you'd manage to keep it. I know it's no consolation, but those memories won't be gone. That's exactly what they are. Memories. Nobody can take those away from you,' she says.

'I know. But I always imagined our grandchildren visiting and the dining table getting crowded with daughters-in-law and children running around.'

I can't stop myself from sobbing at this stage.

'You can make memories wherever you are. Mum and Dad's house is long gone, but we still have those memories, don't we?'

'Yes, I suppose.'

'I mean, remember when Dad went red with anger in the driveway because he thought you'd scribbled all over the leather interior of his new car? He'd only just picked it up,' says Emily.

'Yes, except it was you who did it and not me and you let me take the rap for it. You always landed me in it.'

As I say this, I feel a sudden resentment for Emily. She has always landed me in trouble and made me do things that I didn't want to. I remember when she made me go on a waterslide in Tenby, which I certainly didn't want to do. She called me chicken and walked around making clucking noises until I went down the biggest waterslide I had ever seen. It was pure sibling pressure that made me do it. I ended up banging my head on the way down and needing five stitches above my eyebrow. You can still see the scar in the right light.

Now she has made me seek out a Rottweiler of a lawyer, who couldn't even win my case, before I can even think straight about my marriage. I can't help but worry that she has pushed me into this too. It won't be a small scar I am left with this time, but the biggest hole in my heart. I can't decide who I am angry with. Is it Will? Is it Emily or the judge? All I know is that I feel broken. The big girl pants I am wearing might be able to control my tummy, but not my emotions. I am utterly broken in two. I wonder if Will may even move in with that Tinder woman once he gets a share of the money. The thought of him living with someone else makes me feel nauseous. I drive home in floods of tears. I wish my eyeballs had windscreen wipers and could clear the waterworks away just as my car is managing with the rain that has started lashing down.

By the time I reach home, the realisation of selling up is sinking in. I look at the pink roses I planted in the garden as I walk towards the front door. The first time they bloomed filled me with so much joy. These are the things that have always made me happy. There will be no more picking fresh flowers in the garden. I may not even have a garden wherever I have to move. They have valued the house at £400,000. Split between the two of us it will leave us with £200,000 each, which will probably mean an apartment. I would never be able to get a mortgage simply from the earnings of my Etsy shop, but I am grateful for a roof over my head at least.

Whilst the Etsy shop is ticking along nicely, I realise that, as much as I thought I might be the next answer to a bohemian high street jeweller, I am not.

When I open the door and see Dylan nibbling on a piece of toast, I don't tell him off for not using a plate and dropping crumbs all over the hallway, like I usually do. Instead, I give him a hug and tell him that we will have to sell the house. His response surprises me.

'Yeah, I already spoke to Dad. It's okay. I'm off to uni anyway. It's you I'm more worried about. Will you be all right?'

'I don't know. I'll try my best to be.'

Seeing how Dylan deals with things gives me the strength to power on. I can't let Will think it is okay to behave the way he did. I have to set an example to the boys. If I let their dad get away with stealing a family heirloom, then what sort of mother am I? Everything I do is for the good of these boys – except now I have managed to lose our home.

I am glad to see Ewan and Nia arrive later in the evening. We are all going to drive in one car for the skydive tomorrow.

'So, how you feeling about tomorrow?' asks Nia. She is so enthusiastic from the moment she walks in. I love the energy this girl has. She is just who I need to be around right now.

'Nervous and excited, I suppose. I have wanted to do this forever.'

I think again about how Will always stopped me from doing it. When we went to Spain on holiday, I wanted to give it a go, but he made such a fuss. Now, finally, I can see if it was worth waiting for.

After a few much-needed wines together after a terrible day, we decide to have an early night. Before I close my eyes, I check the donations that have come in and see that I have smashed my goal and reached £375 for the hospital. I may not have saved Dad's watch, but I can hopefully provide a small token of funding for the local hospital so that other people can be saved.

Despite the fact that my marriage has fallen apart, I am about to lose my home, and I feel absolutely dreadful about my life, I take comfort that tomorrow is another day, and I am about to make a bucket list goal come true.

Chapter Twenty

The first thing I see when I arrive at the skydive centre is a very old-looking Cessna. Nia called it a caravan, but it certainly doesn't look like the type of thing you would want to stay in.

In fact, it doesn't look like the type of thing I would want to fly in either. Apparently, it can take sixteen of us, which is a little daunting as it appears as though it wouldn't take two of us up safely.

I am still eyeing up the Cessna nervously when we are greeted by an enthusiastic instructor called Martin, whom Nia seems to know. His confident demeanour should put me at ease slightly. I didn't think I would be nervous, as this has been my dream for so long, but now my knees are almost knocking. I think it was the sight of the old aircraft rather than the jump that made the nerves kick in.

It doesn't help matters when I am handed death-defying-sounding paperwork. I read over the words that basically say that if anything happens to me, the centre is not liable. My stomach lurches and the hairs on my scalp prickle. What about my boys? Who will feed Monty tonight? If something goes wrong, I would at least like them all to have some sort of compensation. Reluctantly, I sign my life away and move on to the next task, where we are given our short training.

There are fourteen of us doing tandem jumps today. They are mostly couples, although one man looks a lot older than the young lady he is with, and I try to work out their relationship. They even look slightly similar, so I think they might be related. I can't help looking at his left hand for any sign of a wedding ring. Then I tell myself off. The last thing I want is to meet someone else, even if Will is seeing Tinder Woman. The rugged, handsome man catches me looking and smiles. I feel my cheeks blush and turn away quickly.

Thankfully, Martin distracts us all as he starts our pre-jump orientation, telling us what we will need to know for our jump. He goes through the body positions for jumping out of the aircraft, and my nerves start to rise once again. I guess I thought that I would just jump out and not have to remember so many things in order to stay safe. What if I forget something crucial and take my instructor down with me on our tandem jump?

I am surprised that the class only takes around twenty minutes. Twenty minutes of training to be let loose and jump out of a plane! It feels far too soon to get kitted out with our parachute and all the paraphernalia that goes with it. I have questions to ask that I haven't even thought of yet!

With the assistance of one of the skydiving team, I don the bright red jumpsuit first. I begin to wonder if they have chosen a bright colour so that the emergency services can find us if we go splat on the ground like a grilled tomato.

Then I am handed goggles and told to wait for my instructor as I stand there realising that I am about to look like Biggles. Of course, this is the moment that I come face to face with the man with no wedding ring. I find myself

self-consciously playing with my helmet and pushing it off my face a little. How can this man possibly look so good with his gear on?

Nia has gone to the toilet, leaving me standing alone, and so I search in my bag that is still beside me for my phone. I need something to keep me occupied. My phone is like a modern-day comfort blanket to me. I notice there is a message from Will. We haven't spoken since court yesterday. I am surprised to see he has messaged. I open up the message and immediately tears spring into my eyes.

> I've booked the estate agent to come around and put the house on the market on Monday. Make sure you're home.

Again, there are no kisses like our messages used to have, although that is the least of my worries. If I had any nerves about today, they immediately subside. My home is being taken away from me. Jumping out of a plane is the least of my worries. I look up and see that the handsome man is looking in my direction. I try my best to smile, and he comes towards me with his hand outstretched.

'Hi, I'm Nick. This is my daughter, Jade,' he says.

'Hi. Libby,' I say.

'Your first jump?' he asks.

'Do I look that nervous?' I say with a smile.

'No, not at all. It just looks like there are a lot of people who know what they're doing and you looked a bit baffled by the pre-jump orientation, just like me,' he says.

'Oh, yes. I see.'

'Are you doing a charity jump?' he asks.

'Yes, for the local hospital. They were very good to my dad. You?'

'Yup. Charity jump in memory of my wife. She had motor neurone disease. It would have been her fifty-fifth birthday today.'

'Oh, gosh. I am sorry. It's my dad's birthday today too. He would have been eighty,' I say.

Suddenly, losing the house and Will taking Dad's watch pale into insignificance. They are all material things. Things that we have taken so seriously that they have driven us to the situation we are in. But truly, nothing matters. It is our health and family that count. Today should have been about birthdays to celebrate, but instead we are doing a charity jump in our loved ones' memories.

Will and I have strived all these years to keep the business going and have a nice house for the boys, but does any of that really matter when it comes down to it? What if we focused on the wrong thing? I only wish Will would understand that money isn't everything and sometimes you have to let go of something that is dragging you down.

I decide that once I finish my skydive, I am going to have a chat with him about money. Maybe if I tell him about Nick and his wife, Will might see what ultimately matters in life and how being a family is more important than anything else. For now though, it is time to focus on survival as I prepare to jump out of an aeroplane.

It turns out that the skydive is touch-and-go and it is almost called off when the cloud comes in low. I am incredibly disappointed at this news and realise how badly I want to do it. So when we are told it can go ahead after all, right at the last minute, I am delighted. The moment I have dreamed of has arrived, even if it is in a battered old Cessna.

I climb in and am sat beside Nia, with Nick and Jade on the other side of us. I feel as though I am a sardine, squashed into a can, but still, it is exciting as the plane climbs up to 10,000 feet. The engine makes noises I have never heard before, and I am grateful for the parachutes on board.

As soon as we reach the correct altitude, our names are called one by one. Nick and Jade are two of the first to jump, and I wish them luck. I watch as they lean over the edge, and in a flash, they are gone. Seeing them disappear so quickly is a little disconcerting, but I hope it looks worse than it is. I haven't heard any screams from down below, at least.

Another lady does a tandem jump with her instructor, and I begin to feel as though I am part of a team as those of us who are left in the plane cheer each person on.

Until, finally, it is my turn and I am standing on the edge waiting to jump. I can see the ground below and the fluffy white clouds that are dotted around the sky. This is the moment I always dreamed of and now I am terrified. Is it too late to back out? Although, the thought of having to stay on this plane for landing makes it a bit of a no-win situation. I think I would rather jump.

My instructor reassures me with a run-through of his hand signals one final time. I am not sure I am digesting any of them at this moment though.

Then he attaches himself to me and we are ready to jump. Oh my goodness, the moment has finally arrived. What if Will was right and it is a stupid, dangerous idea?

The instructor holds one finger up, two fingers and then three.

As we leave the edge of the aircraft, I scream at first, although nobody can hear me in the sky. Hopefully, I won't deafen my instructor or any birds hoping for a peaceful migration somewhere.

Then I begin to calm down a little. I remind myself that I have to make the most of every moment as we won't be up here for long.

Once I have relaxed, I can take in the beautiful surroundings as we float through the blue skies with the Welsh fields below. I can see sheep grazing nearby. I hope we don't land in their patch. I don't fancy being rammed up the bottom by an angry ewe.

Perhaps it is safer up here where I feel weightless and free. Then suddenly it all seems to go too fast as the ground gets closer and closer.

We come back down to earth with a bang and my knee jolts to the ground. What an experience! I am literally on cloud nine.

'Woohoo, I did it!' I shout.

Nia takes some pictures of me with my thumbs up, which I might make my new social media profile photo to prove to everyone that I did it. Then she rushes off to get a bottle of Prosecco ready for us to share.

She hugs me before handing me a glass of the celebratory fizz.

'You did amazing. I'm so proud of you.'

'I would never have done it if it wasn't for you, Nia. You've made a dream come true for me. Thank you.'

As we sip our Prosecco, Jade and Nick approach us to say goodbye.

'Oh, come on. Have a drink with us,' I say.

Nick looks at Jade and she nods her head and smiles.

'That would be lovely,' says Jade.

'Wasn't that exhilarating?' says Nick.

'It was. I wouldn't mind doing that again.'

After we chat about the best parts of the day, Nick and Jade have to leave.

'Here, if you ever fancy a jump,' he says, handing me his business card.

'Pardon?' says Nia, giggling.

'Another skydive,' he says.

'Thanks. We'll see,' I say.

'Well, if not a jump. Perhaps a drink so we can toast our loved ones for their birthdays?' he says.

I smile and take the card.

'Sure, I'll be in touch.'

I tuck the card into my bag and tell myself I'll think about it.

Chapter Twenty-One

Despite the fact that I plan on talking to Will about how life is too short for all this bickering and money grabbing, I am aware that I need to find the right time. So I go ahead with the estate agent's visit to take a look at the house and do all the things I am expected to as a future divorcee, such as tidying up, putting a fresh loaf I prepared earlier in the oven so that the homely smell wafts through from the kitchen and light some candles in the living room for effect. In fact, the house is positively perfect by the time the estate agent comes around to take the photos and confirm the valuation.

'We'll have no problem shifting this,' he reassures me. I get butterflies at the thought of another family living here and loving it as much as we did. Then I remind myself what I said about possessions. All we need is family.

I notice how excited the agent gets when he walks into our beautiful dining room. It's my favourite room, and he seems to agree.

'Well, this is stunning. Lovely size. New houses don't have this kind of space. I do like a proper dining room. Hard to find something like this nowadays,' he says.

His words make me shudder. There is no need to rub it in, Mr Estate Agent! Usually, when you try to sell something, people try to get you down on the price and tell you how rubbish it is.

When we go into my bedroom, he is thrilled with the way the light shines through my window. He peers through it and tells me what wonderful views I have to wake up to. He then pokes around my en suite bathroom, and I realise I have left my HRT patches on the top of the windowsill. I notice him glance over at them and turn his neck to read the packaging. Oh no, this is so deeply personal. Please tell me he has a menopausal wife and understands.

Downstairs, he pokes around my cloakroom. I pray I remembered to change the toilet roll. I sneak a look over his shoulder and realise that I did. I even managed to remember to fold the tissue into a V-shape. Phew!

As we stand in the hallway saying goodbye, my eyes are drawn to the painting Dylan did of us as a family in his last year of primary school. Still today, it hangs proudly on the wall. Where would I hang that in a new house? Both Will and I have always loved the fact that it is the first thing we see when we come home. It is a constant reminder of our family.

The second the agent walks out of the door, I message Will to tell him that the agent didn't think we would have any problem selling the home and ask if we can have a chat. It is going to take a lot of courage to have a heart-to-heart. But what if Will got sick tomorrow, like Nick's wife, and I never told him about how money doesn't matter to me and that we all need to get along? We must try and be a family, no matter what our circumstances, and perhaps it is time I heard him out.

So I ask if he can come around this evening for a quick chat. Although, I don't plan on making it quick at all. In fact, I put a lasagne in the oven and have already bought in his favourite red wine. Then I double-check that Dylan is out for the evening, and the stage is set. I pop on a favourite black dress of mine and some make-up, which I never do when just sitting at home. Instinctively, I want to look my best for this chat.

For some reason, I even put on my best underwear. I know that is a little needless, but it is just in case something shifts in both of us, and he decides to scoop me in his arms and take me to bed immediately. I would hate to reconcile in my favourite bloating day pants! I look in the mirror and am pleased with what I see.

As I watch the clock, I get nervous. The thought of talking to Will has to be way more nerve-racking than the skydive. He is due at six p.m., and by ten minutes to, I can feel my palms begin to sweat.

When the doorbell rings, Monty and I rush to greet Will.

'Come in, come in,' I say. Will plays with Monty as he jumps all over him.

'Can I get you a drink?'

'No, I'm in a bit of a rush,' says Will.

'Oh, nothing can be that important, surely? I've made your favourite lasagne.'

'I have a dinner reservation, actually. My friend's waiting in the car.'

'Your friend? Who?'

'Just a friend. You don't know her. Now, what was it you wanted to talk about?'

Her! My heart feels like it is going to explode. It must be Tinder Woman.

He has already moved on from his family.

'Oh, just the house,' I say.

'What about it?'

'That they think it will sell quickly.'

'Yes, you already told me that. Why did you need me to call around to say that?'

'Sorry. I forgot. I don't know why you needed to come here really. It was silly of me. I just thought we could talk about some things, but nothing that important. Let's forget it.'

'Okay. Well, I'll see you when I get Monty at the weekend then,' says Will.

'Yes, sure.'

I open the front door and look towards the car. A lady looks at me from the passenger seat of *our* car. Tinder Woman is sat in the seat that was reserved for me. She has filled my space.

When I close the door, I smell burning. My lasagne! I ignored the sound of the timer that was perfectly programmed to go just before Will was due to arrive. The kitchen fills with smoke as I open the oven door. My evening has gone from trying to salvage anything I can from my marriage to discovering a woman has taken my place and a burned lasagne. I pour myself a glass of Will's favourite wine and cry. I cry and cry until I think I will never stop.

Eventually, when there is no more wine or tears left, I search for Nick's card from yesterday. It says he is an auctioneer. I wonder if Will has heard of him. I start to write a message.

> Hello, it was so lovely to meet you yesterday. About that jump you fancied…

Then I press send and make myself a strong black coffee before I say anything further.

I haven't even finished my coffee when his reply arrives.

> How lovely to hear from you. Hope you've recovered from yesterday.

> I have indeed. What a great day it was.

> It was.

> So, do you have any plans next week?

> I'm off to a retreat in Goa actually. Only for a week. Perhaps we could get that drink when I get back?

A retreat in Goa! I know someone who would be perfect for Nick.

I get this strong feeling that we were meant to cross paths for a reason.

> Yes, fabulous! It wouldn't just be with me though. Would it be okay if I brought my sister, Emily? I think you two would get along very well.

> That sounds lovely. I'd like that very much.

I message Emily and check when she will be free. As long as she isn't planning some kind of mindfulness retreat, she should be available. Unless she is booked on the same retreat as Nick! Now that would be a coincidence.

I make arrangements to meet Nick in a bar and am quite pleased with myself. My life might be a mess, but sorting someone else's life out feels cathartic. After all, I have spent my life focusing on my family and making sure they are happy. So what difference should it make now? This time it is my sister who needs my help. I wasn't the best sister when she split up with John, but perhaps I can make that up to her now.

Two weeks later, we are sitting in Emily's favourite pub on the outskirts of Saundersfoot when Nick walks in. Emily is blissfully unaware that she is about to be set up and I have no idea how she will react. I didn't want to tell her we were meeting him as I worried she might get into a flap. She might look like she oozes confidence, but when it comes to dates, she is a bag of nerves. She still finds it hard to trust anyone after the shock of her husband leaving like that. However, her reaction to Nick, so far, is encouraging. As he walks towards us, I notice that she can't take her eyes off him.

'Gosh, who is that?' she giggles. Then she nonchalantly takes a sip of her cosmopolitan and almost falls off her bar stool as he approaches us. Her heel catches on the footrest of the bar stool, making a huge clanging noise. The noise drowns out Nick's introduction to her.

'You didn't tell me we were meeting someone,' she whispers when Nick goes to the bar to get us all a round in.

'Would you have come if I had told you?'

'No,' says Emily.

'Exactly. There you go then.'

'So is this nice man your date?' she asks.

'He's a date, but not for me.' I wink at Emily as Nick returns with the drinks.

'You two ladies look as though you're hatching a plan there,' says Nick, laughing.

'That's sisterly love you have just witnessed,' I say with a smile. Then Emily's heel slips on the footrest of the bar stool once again and makes another big clang.

'Oh, she's trouble, this one.' I laugh.

We all clink glasses, and I make an excuse to go to the bathroom. Even though Emily is a quivering wreck, I feel they need some time alone to get to know each other. In fact, I may even feign another of my migraines if they get on well enough. I have it all planned.

I take my time in the bathroom and touch up my lippy about four times, check my phone and search for any stray hairs on my chin. The light in these bathrooms is quite shocking. I didn't realise I had so many.

Then I finally head back to see Emily and Nick already hitting it off. My plan worked, and they seem to be getting on like a house on fire.

In fact, when I sit down with my drink, they hardly notice me. I don't mind one bit though, and when they do finally stop talking for a second, I tell them about my spurious migraine.

'Oh no, do we have to leave already? I was having fun,' says Emily.

'No, I don't mean for you to leave. You both stay here. I'm a big girl. I can get home alone, don't worry,' I say.

'I can't do that. I'll come with you,' says Emily.

This bit certainly wasn't part of the plan.

'No, seriously. I just need to be alone. You know what it's like when you have a migraine. I just want to lie down in a dark room. You two enjoy. Don't let me spoil the fun,' I say.

'Are you sure?' says Emily.

'A hundred per cent. Now you two enjoy.'

Nick runs after me as I reach the door and says thank you for arranging the evening.

'Your sister is delightful,' he says.

I don't say that she can be less delightful when she wants to be, but I am just glad I have made two people happy for the night.

I get home and sink into bed alone. I have to try and get some sleep as tomorrow morning there is a viewing arranged for the house, and I am absolutely dreading it.

Chapter Twenty-Two

I am not one to be spiteful, but now that I know Will is spending time with Tinder Woman, I don't feel so inclined to sell the house. I know I should be the good girl that everyone expects of me, to be nice and play by the rules, but I feel grouchy and a little mean, to be perfectly honest. So when the older married couple come to view the house, I can't help but deter them.

'What a beautiful garden,' says the wife as she walks in through the front door.

'Oh, we have the most awful problem with moles around here. In fact, I wouldn't be surprised if they've dug under our foundations. So rampant,' I say.

'Nothing I can't deal with,' says the lady.

'Elaine is a very keen gardener. No mole has ever defeated her yet,' explains the husband.

'That's right, Gerald.' She looks so smug as her husband backs up her proficiency with mole control.

I try my best not to roll my eyes in front of them and instead point them in the direction of the living room.

Someone from the estate agency that I haven't met before follows closely behind me.

'What a spacious living area,' says Gerald.

'I'd change the wallpaper. I don't like that at all,' says Elaine.

I bite my lip and lead them into the kitchen.

'I'd rip out the kitchen. You could do quite a bit with it with some imagination,' says Elaine.

I begin to wonder if they realise I am here and decide there and then that, no matter what they offer, Elaine will not be getting her green fingers on my precious home.

'It's so cluttered in here. It needs a larder,' says Elaine.

I look at the collection of colourful bottles that I have collected over the years that I decorate around the kitchen and the pots that hang from the kitchen ceiling rack. This is not clutter; this is years of love and memories.

My hackles rise until I can hardly contain myself. She is talking about my beautiful kitchen where I have lovingly prepared so many meals! Who does this woman think she is? 'There is a big plumbing issue with the pipes. You can't change the kitchen,' I blurt out.

'Gerald knows a great plumber. No plumbing problem is too big for him,' says Elaine.

I might have guessed.

I leave the three of them to go upstairs by themselves. I can't bear to hear what they will say about my lovely, cosy bedroom and the fitted units that cost a bomb all those years ago before the business took us down.

When the couple come downstairs again, the estate agent pulls out a measuring tape.

'Mrs Jones, you don't mind if we measure this bit of the kitchen, do you? We want to check if Elaine and Gerald's Aga will fit.'

All I can do is nod my head. An Aga! I want an Aga, but we haven't been able to afford one. Trust Elaine to have an Aga!

I watch as Elaine pokes her head into my kitchen cabinets. What a nosy woman! If she is going to rip out my units, surely she doesn't need to see what is inside them too.

'Excuse me,' I say. I grab her hand and remove it from the knob of the next cabinet she is about to look in. Elaine looks at me in disgust.

'Perhaps we should come back another time. Like, when you're not at home,' she says.

I could quite literally push her out of my house. I am so annoyed by her presence that a wicked idea springs into my head. So instead of dragging her out by her hair, which I would if I were that kind of person, I smile and tell her that it is fine. She is very welcome to look around a little more. Then I go to Dylan's bedroom and search for the stink bombs that he bought in a joke shop at an amusement park we went to a while back. I pray he still has some left.

I find the unused pack and laugh to myself. *Thank you, Dylan.*

'Good grief, what's that smell?' says Gerald.

'I think I'm going to be sick,' says Elaine.

'It's like a sulphuric smell. I'm sure there's a reasonable explanation,' says the agent.

I walk back into the kitchen, pretending not to have heard them.

'What's the smell?' says Elaine, looking right at me.

'Smell? Sorry, I can't smell anything,' I say.

'It stinks,' says Gerald.

I open the cloakroom door where I let off the stink bomb and put my head in. The smell hits my nostrils. As much as I am almost heaving, I have to play dumb.

'Oh, it's probably the drains. To be honest, when you've lived here this long, you get quite used to it. I don't even notice the smell myself,' I say. 'I'm sure it's nothing your fabulous plumber hasn't come across before.'

'I'm not very good with nasty smells,' says Elaine.

'Oh dear. Why don't you go out and get some fresh air with the moles then?' I say. I need them to leave quickly before the smell dissipates.

'We'll do that,' says the agent.

I close the front door on them as they walk around the front garden and laugh to myself. Let's hope my cunning plan worked.

They haven't even left the garden before I see a message on my phone from Will.

> How did the viewing go?

> Awful. They weren't very happy with the moles.

> What moles?

What moles indeed. It wasn't much fun digging up the lawn into mounds of earth from the vegetable patch at eight a.m. this morning, but it was entirely worth it.

> We seem to have an infestation. Nothing I can't deal with

> That's disappointing

It is indeed. I'm sure someone else will come along.

I put the phone down when I hear a knock on the door. Oh no, I hope they don't want to come back in, as the smell has already faded.

'Thank you for letting us have that look around. I think they'll be making an offer,' says the estate agent.

'Oh.'

'I'll give you a call when I get back to the office to discuss. They think their plumber can sort out the drains, but they may want to knock something off the price,' he says.

I switch my phone off as soon as I close the door. If the agent can't get hold of me then I can't accept any offers.

What I didn't account for was the fact that they had Will's phone number too. When I put my phone back on later that evening to see if Emily has messaged about the blind date she had been unwittingly set up on, I see five missed calls from the estate agent along with two voicemails. But the text message from Will explains all I need to know.

Agent's been trying to get hold of you. Moles didn't put them off! They made an offer and I've accepted on behalf of both of us. It wasn't a bad offer. At least this means we can move the divorce through quicker and I know that's what you want.

I throw my phone down on the sofa. No, that is not what I want at all. I do not want to sell my home. Least of all to

Elaine and her husband Gerald. I do not particularly want a divorce either. I want my family back together, that is what I want. But of course, with Tinder Woman on the scene and the mess we have created, I can't say any of this. So I sadly agree, and my heart breaks that little bit further again.

Chapter Twenty-Three

By ten thirty a.m., I have made three bracelets and one anklet. Today I am on a mission to earn as much money as I can. I put them on the shop listings as soon as they are made. Trying to earn something gives me a sense of control when I have none over the house being sold. If I could only earn enough to get a mortgage and buy Will out. Sadly, I know that will never happen though. It is as far-fetched as getting the watch back.

However, it doesn't stop me paying £20 for a couple of tickets for a draw I find online. It is to win a £5 million house which I would, of course, sell immediately and then fly to Venice and track down the jeweller and give him anything he wanted to get Dad's watch back. I assume that the advert has been targeted to me thanks to all the estate agent googling that I have been doing as I search for a new home. That and all the chats I have had with Emily about property.

I am quite sure that AI bots listen to my conversations from my phone. Anyhow, if they help me win a £5 million house, they can listen to whatever they want to. I don't exactly have the most riveting conversations nowadays. The past twenty-four hours have all been about moles and the price of Agas.

I look wistfully at the advert for a house in Cornwall. What a shame it isn't in Tenby. Perhaps that is what I should have done with our home. Auction it off in some kind of raffle and not let Will accept the first meagre offer he received. Of course, legally, I can argue that I won't accept the offer. After all, he accepted without my agreement, but then things are going to be even worse between us. I would like to think that if we are about to go our own ways in life that we can remain cordial for the sake of the boys.

As I make more pieces for the shop, I dream of winning the life-changing prize. Five million pounds! But, I realise with sadness, all the money in the world couldn't repair my fractured beautiful family.

I am glad of the distraction of lunch with Emily to take me out of all the overthinking I have been doing these past few weeks. When I see her at our favourite cafe that overlooks Tenby Harbour, she is beaming. Despite the regular facial treatments she has and her vast range of expensive night creams, her skin glows more today than it has in a long time. People who don't know her probably assume that it is the Botox around her eyes that makes her look so indifferent, but I know it's the heartache she suffered all those years ago. This is the first time I have seen Emily glow for a long time, and she is beautiful.

'So how have things been with Nick? I don't think I even need to ask. Look at you,' I say.

'What do you mean? Do I look different? Maybe it's the highlights I just had,' she says, playing with her hair self-consciously.

'No. You look… Well, happier, I guess.'

'Perhaps it's the Botox top-up I had,' she says coyly.

'Stop making excuses and spill the beans. I knew you two would get on.'

'Oh, he's lovely, Libby. But I am terrified, quite frankly. I don't want to get hurt again, but I could just imagine falling for Nick. It's as if we've known each other all our lives,' says Emily.

'I could see that. I knew you two were made for each other. I don't think you need to be scared. I know we don't really know much about him, but Nick and his daughter seem really genuine.'

'I think that too. He told me all about Jade. To be honest, having a stepdaughter would terrify me, but she sounds lovely. Anyway, what am I talking about stepdaughters for? It's only been a few weeks. My goodness. Now, come on, let's order that bowl of cawl.'

It is unlike Emily to share her vulnerability, so I don't ask any further questions as that was a quite lot for her to admit. Luckily, at that moment, the waitress comes over and checks that we are having our usual.

We always order the same thing every time we come here. Two bowls of cawl and two cappuccinos. I suppose Emily and I have similar tastes sometimes, at least when it comes to food.

The steaming hot broth arrives with a warm crusty roll on a side plate and a big chunk of Welsh cheese. There is nothing like a bowl of cawl filled with lamb, vegetables and so much goodness as we head towards the autumn season.

'Oh, delicious,' I say.

'Indeed. Although I'll need to watch my waistline. I know it's a bit soon, but Nick was talking about us going away for a weekend. He asked me if I fancy going to that place in Oxfordshire that's owned by Raymond Blanc,' she says.

'Le Manoir aux Quat'Saisons?' I say.

'That's the one. Only Nick pronounced it better than that. Did I tell you he's fluent in French? He used to own a gîte in Brittany.'

'No, you didn't, but that doesn't surprise me. He seems like a well-travelled man.'

'Oh, he is. He's led such an interesting life. I could listen to his stories for hours.'

'I'm so pleased,' I say. I am genuinely happy for Emily. We may have had our differences, but perhaps she has her reasons for behaving the way she does sometimes. She loved John more than anything and she never expected him to let her down so badly. Now I am beginning to understand how it feels.

'So, have you heard from Will?' asks Emily.

'Not much. He only messages when he has to collect Monty or needs to talk about the house. He's accepted an offer.'

'You've sold the house?'

'Well, kind of. I suppose. Will has accepted an offer, and I don't have much choice but to go along with it.'

'Oh, but you do. Fight it all the way. Don't let him win,' says Emily.

'No, it's just putting off the inevitable. When I heard about Nick's wife, I swore that I'd never be bothered about material possessions again. Except for Dad's watch, that's sentimental. But, still, this is my home.'

'Of course, darling. How can I help you? Can I do anything?'

'No. I have to move on. What do I need a big house for? Dylan's off to uni soon; it will just be me on my own rattling around with Monty, and he doesn't exactly take up much space.'

'Well, maybe it's a blessing in disguise. There must be some life lesson in there.'

'Maybe, but goodness knows what!'

'Oh, before I forget, I won't be able to come for cawl next week. Nick is taking me to London for a few days. We're going to see a show he's got tickets for.'

'Oh, how lovely.' I refrain from showing my disappointment, but secretly I feel a little left out.

When we have caught up on all the news and finished the lovely cawl, we bid farewell. I have a feeling I will be seeing a lot less of Emily now that she has hit it off with Nick. All these years I had a family and she was on her own, and now the tables have turned.

As I walk back to the car, I pass the estate agency. I look in the window and notice our home with an 'under offer' sticker on it. Like the prospective buyers, Elaine and Gerald, they didn't waste any time. I should look to see what else they have within my budget, but I can't face the thought of looking at decrepit properties in my price range. Everything seems so expensive.

I head back inside my empty home and am glad to see lovely Monty greet me. At least the dog cares.

I pop the kettle on and check the Etsy shop. Three sales. Enough for some more tea bags and a bottle of wine, but definitely not enough to save the house. Who was I kidding? I really need a full-time salary, but jobs are scarce, and employers don't seem to see the benefit in hiring women whose experience amounts to having looked after their children and helped the husband in the family business. If only they would realise the value of that work and that I have put in a lot more hours than any employee would do ordinarily. But, unless I can tick those specific boxes that an employer is looking for, it seems I have zero talents that they want. It also doesn't help that my boss is my future ex-husband. I can't exactly put him forward as a reference. Who is going to want me with no credentials for most of my working life?

I did enjoy working in the shop; some mornings I even miss it. I know there weren't many customers, or any customers, most days, but I liked the community feeling when the other shop owners would come in and say hello, or how I would pop out to pick up something at lunchtime and stop and have a chat with the other traders. I enjoyed doing the merchandising, trying out my marketing skills. But the one thing I don't miss is all the dusting and that musty smell the shop sometimes gave off.

I wonder if I have been the gossip of the town. Do the local shop owners all know why I am no longer in the shop happily popping the kettle on for a chat with them? I haven't been into any of their shops for my meat, not even to the bakery for my favourite sausage rolls since all of this happened. I just couldn't face the shame.

Fortunately, Dylan is a lot more perky than I'm feeling when he arrives home.

'Dad just called. He's got tickets for the match on Saturday,' he says, grinning.

'Oh, brilliant.'

'So, because we might not be back until late, he said we'd book a hotel and have a boys' weekend in Cardiff.'

'Fantastic,' I say. I remember when I would have gone along, too, for their boys' weekends. They would go to the match, and I would do a bit of shopping around Cardiff, and then we would meet for dinner afterwards. I suppose this is another adjustment that I need to get used to. I am no longer included in any plans.

Already, I begin to wonder what I will do for the weekend. Then I realise that I have a home of over twenty-five years to consider packing up. It is going to take forever to go through all the stuff in this house and with a definite downsizing on the cards, I suppose it is never too early to start, even if I dread the thought of a huge clear-out.

'Oh, and I don't know if I should tell you this, but Dad is bringing his friend,' says Dylan.

'Friend?' I say.

'Yes, apparently she's meeting us for dinner after the match.'

'Oh, is she now?' No matter how hard I try, I can't hide the hurt in my voice.

The thought of my beautiful son being introduced to another woman with his dad makes my stomach churn.

'I'm sure you'll have a lovely time,' I say.

Then I rush upstairs and burst into tears on my bed. The black mascara that runs from my lashes furrows into the threads of my lavender silk pillow. I pull the pillow from the side that Will used to sleep on and put it over my mouth. Then I scream and scream and scream and pray that Dylan doesn't hear me.

Chapter Twenty-Four

It is difficult to stay chirpy when your son is meeting his dad's new girlfriend for the very first time. However, I try not to think about what time they are meeting, or where they will be going for dinner and what they will eat. Instead, I focus on the task in front of me. Emptying a house that is packed full of all these memories.

As I open drawers full of mementos, I try to stay strong. I hoarded some silly things when I think about it. I even kept menus from planes we have been on. Why do I need to be reminded that British Airways served a couscous salad on a flight in the Nineties? There are pamphlets from funerals of acquaintances in the village that I didn't have the heart to throw out, and spare lenses from glasses I have replaced over the years. It is funny how these things seemed too important to discard at the time but, in the long term, pale into insignificance. Still, it makes me feel awfully guilty when I throw the funeral pamphlets into the blue recycling bag and see faces that have long since passed looking back at me.

I try to tackle the least important drawers first. I decide to leave the cupboard in the spare room until last. That is the one that still has my wedding dress and shoes in it. It also houses Dylan's and Ewan's christening outfits. I couldn't bear to part with any of it. Until now.

My wedding dress was a huge white meringue one. They were the fashion in those days. It has big puffy short silk sleeves and a huge skirt. I thought I was the bee's knees. I would have no chance of fitting this dress into the wardrobe of a small two-bedroom apartment like I am hoping to find, so I put it in the charity pile. Although I feel slightly sorry for any charity as I imagine they might be stuck with this for a long while. It is nothing like the elegant dresses brides wear nowadays. Funny how wedding dress fashions change so much. Even the fake fur shrug that I wore over it for our winter wedding looks dated. If I were married today, I would go for something much sleeker and less meringue-esque.

It is pointless hanging on to something that now means so little. Those marriage vows have been broken. Although I don't think there were any vows that were mentioned about stealing from each other, no matter how desperate one was to save the family business.

When I stumble upon the wedding album, I try so hard to resist a peek inside its white leatherbound cover. Then I find a copy of the wedding video. I am grateful that I am unable to watch it as I no longer have a video player in the house. But as much as I want to put the wedding album into a recycling bin right now, I don't. I put it in the 'keep' pile. I pick out a few more bits and keep turning my head to the album. I tell myself over and over again that I mustn't peek. What good would it do? Besides, I am in the middle of clearing out my cupboards. I can't spend valuable time looking over old photos. But then I realise that I have been doing this for two and a half hours now. What harm could it possibly do to take the album with me downstairs and look at some of the photos whilst I have a coffee break?

A lot of harm, it seems. As soon as I open the album, I see a photo of me and Dad as I am getting ready. Then I flick over the page, and my mum is there. Everyone is now gone and only left as memories in a photo album. I try not to cry, but when I see the photo of Will's reaction as I walk down the aisle, it is impossible not to. He looked so happy. Proud, even. Now it seems as though he looks at me with hatred in his eyes. I could never have predicted that from looking at this photo.

Emily is with John in the photos. Even they looked happy back then. Cousins are with ex-boyfriends and ex-girlfriends. It is funny how people come and go in your life and then you never speak to them again. Yet at the time they share such an important part of your life. I smile when I see a photo of Will's lovely gran. Iris was a kind lady. She would always welcome me into her home and put the kettle on, even though she was crippled with arthritis and struggled to get up. She would make homemade jams and send them home with me. I would politely ask for the recipe but know that with two little ones at home, I would never have the time to make them. Our cupboards ended up full of jam, but I didn't have the heart to tell her that we couldn't possibly get through it all. It made her happy to give her jams to friends and family and that is all that mattered. Then one day, there was no jam any longer. She was too ill, and another family tradition died along with Iris.

I look at the happy photos of Will and me driving off into the sunset in a borrowed Mercedes. We are waving goodbye to everyone as we go off on our own, looking forward to that wonderful honeymoon in Venice. The honeymoon photos are at the back of the album, and, as I see myself, I am quite surprised by how skinny I was.

Compared to today I am positively a beanpole! How I wished I had realised how slim I really was.

I hadn't remembered there was a photo of us that day on a gondola in the album. I don't know why I left it in there and didn't get it framed. Seeing these photos makes me hanker for a visit to Venice again. No matter what has happened, Venice is where I have spent one of the happiest times of my life. I need to go back there to revisit those times, even if it is just for closure. I want to go back as there are still so many things I want to see.

We didn't even get time to visit Caffè Florian or Harry's Bar for a Bellini, although I would probably need a bank loan first. There are still so many things left to explore in life. When the money comes through for the house sale, I have decided to put some of it aside to return, and I will also visit the jeweller's. I will make it my mission to at least speak to the man there. I want to tell him he was right and ask if he will give me every detail, even though I'll probably be torturing myself. I can't help it: I want to know what Will said. Did he tell the man how precious it was, or simply talk about the financial value? Did he at least ask him to look after such a special watch? I need to know. If the shop owner remembers after all this time, that is.

I head back upstairs to put the album back in the pile. That is enough of a trip down memory lane for one night. I look at my watch. Dylan and Will shall be having dinner soon with who I suspect is Tinder Woman. I probably should have arranged a night out myself, but now even my sister is coupled up. All my friends are also Will's friends. I never realised that when you get divorced, you lose a number of mutual friends too. They don't know what to say to you and they don't want to choose sides. I guess that is fair enough. So it is just me and Monty and a skip-load of bin bags on a Saturday night.

The only positive thing is that I have worked so hard all day that I sleep like a log. I even manage to forget that Dylan is in Cardiff until I wake up the next morning.

I stumble over a black bag as I make my way out of bed. I stub my toe on the bed, and everything comes back to me again. The clear-out, the house, and Dylan being in Cardiff to meet Will's new 'friend'.

I can't wait for Dylan to be home again. It makes me realise just how quiet the house will be once he moves out to uni shortly. I don't know if I can bear it. The day passes so slowly without him asking what food we have in. All I have is the tedious task of clearing everything out. Having the whole weekend alone with nothing better to do has been successful in that respect. The spare room is completely cleared, and there is no longer any trace of all the stuff we have kept and not needed over the years.

When I eventually hear the key in the front door, I am relieved. It is nice to have human company once again. Not that Monty isn't the best of company too.

I promised myself that I wouldn't quiz Dylan about the weekend away. However, when he arrives home, I can't help myself.

'How was it?' I ask before he can sit down.

'Yeah, cool.'

I ask about the match at first. Pretend I am interested in who won and then get down to the nitty-gritty.

'So did you meet Dad's friend then?'

'Yeah, I told you we were going for dinner.'

'Yes, but what was she like? Was she nice to you?' Please let her at least have been pleasant to my gorgeous boy.

'Yeah, she was all right. Boring really.'

A glimmer of satisfaction spreads through me. She was boring!

'Ooh, boring. Like what?'

'I don't know. They just kept talking about books and stuff.'

'Books? Since when has your dad been interested in books? Rugby books are the only thing that he ever reads.'

Please tell me that he hasn't started becoming interested in new things and is evolving into the best version of himself. Whenever I tried to tell him about a great book I was reading, his eyes would glaze over.

'Don't know, they seemed to be banging on about some Jane Austen book… Or maybe *Jane Eyre*. I don't know. Jane something and some other weird book.'

What on earth would Will be talking about books like that for? Just like Dylan, he doesn't know his Jane Austen from his *Jane Eyre*.

'How many times did I try and teach you that *Jane Eyre* is the name of a book, not an author? It's by Charlotte Brontë. What are you like?'

'Whatever. I'm starving. Anything for tea?'

Satisfied that it doesn't sound like the most romantic of dates with Dylan sat there whilst they talk books and Will's eyes surely glazing over at some point, I feel a little more at ease.

'Whatever you fancy,' I say.

'Even a fish finger sandwich and chips?' says Dylan. His eyes are wide in anticipation. It is very rare that I don't insist he eats vegetables, but tonight feels like a treat night.

'Even a fish finger sandwich and chips. I think I'll join you,' I say, smiling.

I head into the kitchen and start peeling the potatoes for freshly homemade chips. I am happy again. My boys and fish finger sandwiches are what make my world go round.

Chapter Twenty-Five

Another Monday morning brings with it further tribulations. Before I can even wake up properly, the estate agent is on the phone.

'Would it be okay if we popped around this afternoon to do some measurements? I know contracts haven't been exchanged yet, but Mr and Mrs Thompson want to measure out the kitchen properly. It seems there's a six-month waiting list for the units they want so they wish to order them at the earliest.'

In my head, I want to refuse. But I remember how keen Will is to sell up and how he also needs a permanent roof over his head. So I politely agree and make the necessary arrangements for them to come over. This time I make a promise to myself that I won't set off any stink bombs. Although when I see Elaine standing on the doorstep with some kind of trap in her hand, my resolve is definitely tested. I look at her in horror.

'Would you mind if I put a mole trap down now? I don't want them doing any further damage to my lawns.'

'Well, I don't really agree with killing animals,' I say. I don't mention the fact that there are no moles and I am simply a strange human being who dug mole hills all by herself whilst the neighbours weren't watching. Besides, she hasn't even paid for the house yet. They're not legally her lawns. They are mine.

'It's keeping me up at night. I'm so worried. I know it doesn't seem to matter to you because you're selling up, but please understand that the garden is very important to me. I don't want any more damage than necessary.'

If I hadn't rolled my eyes so much over the past few weeks, I would have given her a gigantic mother of all eye rolls. Instead, I smile and agree that she can put a trap down. After all, she won't catch any. So, once again, as Dylan says, 'Whatever,' I mutter to myself.

Gerald tries to be a little more polite and shows me the tape measure he has brought along to measure the kitchen.

'I do hope you don't mind. It's just when Elaine has an idea in her head, we have to roll with it. She's fallen in love with her dream kitchen and, you know what they say, "Happy wife, happy life." Anything to keep her quiet,' he says, laughing.

'Right,' I agree. She sounds like a bit of a bully if you ask me.

Dylan pokes his head around the living room. It is the first time he has met the owners-to-be.

'All right,' he says to Gerald.

'Aye, you okay, mate? Enjoying the school holidays?' asks Gerald.

'I'm no longer in school.'

Dylan looks thrilled as he says this. He is a real grown-up now.

'Oh, right. You in uni?'

'Yeah, starting in Cardiff in a few weeks.'

'Oh, brilliant. Our son studied in Cardiff. He's an engineer with a big air-conditioning company in the Far East now. I think Callum wanted to escape his mother's moaning so went as far away as he could, to be honest,' he says, laughing.

Perhaps I got Gerald wrong. He seems to be quite a good bloke who is simply trying to keep his wife happy, which I can't imagine would be easy.

'What was that, Gerald?' says Elaine.

'Talk of the devil, and you know what they say,' he mutters.

Elaine might be a bit of a battle axe, but I think poor henpecked Gerald will look after our beautiful home. Anyhow, I guess I don't know what issues Elaine has. Maybe there is a reason she is such a diva. You never know with people.

'Thanks. We've taken up enough of your time. We'll be off then. I'm sure the next time we'll be here will be when we have the keys,' says Gerald.

'Now there's a thought. Well, I wish you the best of luck. I'm sure you'll be very happy here,' I say.

Just because I can't manage to hold onto the house, it doesn't mean I should resent Gerald. He might be happy here, but I am not so sure about Elaine. I get the feeling that she will never be happy anywhere. She will just move about and still be unhappy with everything around her. God help any moles that get in her way on her house-hopping journey.

I am relieved when they have left and I can close the door on them. Hopefully, I shouldn't need to see them again. I turn to Dylan. I think we need more comfort food after that.

'I know we've been a bit naughty recently, but how do you fancy an ice cream with your mam?'

'Are you serious? Fish finger sandwiches, ice cream. What did you do with my mam? I'll get my jacket,' says Dylan.

We take Monty with us and the three of us head for ice cream in Tenby. It is the same place I went for the date, and I cringe as I think about it. But the thought of the ice cream makes up for it. I don't know what it is about the ice cream here, but it really is something special. Even plain old vanilla tastes like it was handmade in some special Italian gelateria. We struggle to choose the flavours as I keep an eye on Monty, who is tied to a post outside. He is already licking his lips as much as we are when we head back onto the pavement with our cones. I remove the lid and pop Monty's doggy ice cream down for him. Dylan's treat is piled up with scoops of vanilla and chocolate, and I have a retro raspberry ripple.

'Delicious,' we both say at the same time.

Tenby is starting to get busier now. The tourist season will be over before long. The tourists are trying to cram in the last of their holidays before going back to school and work and so we struggle to find somewhere to sit down. Eventually we find a spot near the bench where Will and I used to sit. I have managed to avoid that for some time now. I look across and see a couple snuggled in together sitting on 'our' bench. I hope they don't end up the same way as we did.

'Hey look, there's Dad,' says Dylan. Monty jumps up and goes on high alert. Then he wags his bushy little tail as he spots him. I am almost scared to look in case he is with Tinder Woman. I am not ready to see them walking hand-in-hand in the same town we all live in.

'Dad,' shouts Dylan.

I look up to see Will heading in our direction. Thankfully, he is alone. Monty gets more excitable and much more vocal, much to the dismay of a passer-by.

'Hello, you having an ice cream? Lovely,' he says.

'Come and join us. If you give me a couple of quid, I'll go and get you one,' says Dylan.

Will fishes in his pocket and hands over some loose change. I would rather Will went and got the ice cream. I don't really want to sit here alone with him. I don't have much to say.

As Dylan heads off, we sit in awkward silence for a bit until Monty leaves us no choice but to laugh, embarrassed, as he does a stinky love puff. I think that's a much nicer term than what the boys like to call them.

'Nothing changes,' says Will, laughing.

I want to say that *everything* has changed but bite my lip.

'Dylan was saying at the weekend that he can't wait to get to uni now,' says Will.

'That's good. It will be a great adventure for him. He always has been a free spirit, needing his own space,' I say.

'We've been so lucky with them. But, then again, their mam brought them up well. You can take credit for the way they've both turned out.'

'Oh, we both can,' I say quietly.

'Well, you especially. I was busy with the shop. You're the one who took them to rugby, after-school clubs and made sure they were fed and watered. Fair play to you.'

'Thanks,' I say.

'You know, I'm so sorry about the way things turned out. I want you to know that,' says Will.

'Me too,' I say.

Will and I look at each other. For a moment, I see a tiny glimmer of the love we had for each other in his eyes. Then Dylan arrives back with the ice cream.

'They ran out of chocolate. It's heaving in there. Salted caramel okay for you?' he says. He begins to hand over the ice cream, but not before teasing his dad first and pretending that he is going to splat his nose in it.

'Lovely,' he says. The three of us sit on the bench with Monty at our feet. It feels just like the good old days. That is until Will looks at his phone.

'Oh no, is that the time? I lost track seeing you here. I was on my way to meet a friend. I'm going to be late.'

My heart sinks. A friend? If it was one of the boys or our mutual friends, he would have surely said their name. I know all of his friends. Except for Tinder Woman. He must be off to meet her again. He was only with her over the weekend!

'Oh, you don't want to be late for your special friend,' I say. I can't stop it from coming out sarcastically.

Will ignores me and throws the ice cream cone in the bin, uneaten. 'Got to go, can't keep her waiting.'

I try to keep a neutral face as I take in the word 'her'. I knew it.

Will ruffles Dylan's hair and runs off in the direction of one of the pubs we always used to go to together. I hope he doesn't have the audacity to take her to our favourite haunts too.

'Come on then. We'd better get you home,' I say.

I take Monty's lead and we head back to the car. However, as I start walking in that direction, I turn around. I shouldn't take the long way around when Dylan needs to get back home as one of his friends is due to be calling around, but I can't stop myself. I need to know if Will is in the Fox and Arrow. Dylan will just have to be late.

As much as I don't want to see Will with someone else, a weird part of my brain needs to know. I have to see if he is in our favourite pub with Tinder Woman. I don't know if I'll remember her from that glimpse on Tinder, or that night in a dark car, but I do know that she has very blonde hair and I don't think I would mistake that, even if I don't recognise her features.

'Where we going, Mam?' asks Dylan.

'Oh, thought we'd go around the scenic way. See if the tide is in,' I say.

'Past the Fox and Arrow?' says Dylan. This boy is too smart sometimes.

'Yes, all right. Past the Fox and Arrow. And don't roll your eyes like that,' I say.

'Dad's only gone for a drink,' he says.

'Did you know he was going for a drink in town?' I say.

'Well, yeah. But I wasn't going to tell you that or we wouldn't be able to go for ice cream. You'd have said no in case we bumped into him and you got sad,' says Dylan.

'I'm not sad. I'm perfectly fine,' I say.

'Why are you stalking Dad then?' says Dylan.

'I am definitely not stalking your father, Dylan,' I say.

'Yeah, all right. Whatever,' he says.

As we get closer to the Fox and Arrow, I get more nervous. What if I see them kissing? I couldn't cope with that right now.

I try not to show Dylan how nervous I am and keep walking with Monty.

However, Monty soon decides it is time to go to the toilet. Of all places, he chooses to on the pavement right in front of the window of the Fox and Arrow.

'Great timing, Monty,' I say, absolutely mortified.

I look up at the window and am grateful that nobody is sitting there to see me right now. I don't want anyone to be put off the fabulous pub grub they do there.

As I clean up after Monty, I notice Dylan waving to someone. I look up, and to my horror, I notice that Will and a female companion are now putting drinks down on the table by the window.

Will smirks at me, and the female companion – who is most definitely not bleached blonde – seems quite expressionless. Did they have to see me like this with my bum in the air clearing up after Monty?

'Oh, Monty, the joys of being a dog owner,' I say.

Monty wags his tail as if he has done something to be proud of and I couldn't possibly be cross with him.

Dylan finds it funny, and I tell him to stop laughing. When he has stopped mocking me, I can't resist asking him if the woman is the same one that he met.

'Yeah, that's her. The boring one who went on about books,' he says.

'There's nothing boring about books,' I remind him.

What I am surprised about is that it is most definitely not Tinder Woman. Even if she has undertaken a make-under, with her dark short bob and bright green eyes, this is most definitely not the person I saw on Tinder, or indeed in the car that night.

'Two dates in a few days. He must be keen then,' I say.

'Dunno,' says Dylan, playing on his phone.

I can't believe Dylan can be so nonchalant about it all. This could be his future stepmother.

'I need to know who she is, and I'm going to make it my mission to find out,' I say to Dylan. Let's face it, it isn't as though I have anything better going on with my life. A little social media stalking is always fun, although not sure how fun it will be when I find the answers.

'Whatevs,' says Dylan, not really listening.

But I am paying attention. More attention than anyone will ever know. From now on, I am going to make it my mission to hunt for every clue until I find out who the man that I am still married to is taking on dates to our favourite pub. Who is that woman and why does she look slightly familiar?

Chapter Twenty-Six

When I meet with Emily for our weekly cawl, she is glowing again. I don't know that I have ever seen her so happy, not even when she was first married to John.

She tells me how she has met Jade and what a lovely girl she is. How they went shopping together, and it was like being around the daughter she had always wanted. Although, she says it is important Jade realises that Emily doesn't want to step into her late mother's shoes. Emily has always loved her shopping so I can just imagine she was a fun companion for Jade to have around.

'Jade said I should wear a more neutral-shade lipstick. What do you think? I picked this up in John Lewis with her,' says Emily, pouting her lips.

'It looks lovely. Always nice to have advice from someone who follows beauty trends. As long as she doesn't get you to put lip filler in next. You don't want a trout pout,' I say, laughing.

'No, she wouldn't dream of doing that,' says Emily. She almost sounds defensive of her, and I realise that she is already genuinely fond of her.

'So, how's everything with you? Divorce coming along nicely?' asks Emily.

'Well, it's all in the hands of the solicitors. They expect it to go through in a few months. Might even be the start of the new year. Got to finalise the sale, then all the other bits of paperwork. I can't believe how pedantic everything is. So many different bits to sort out. You know how it is,' I say.

To think that what started out as marrying the love of my life has ended up in a bureaucratic nightmare of paperwork to end it all. So much for us being in love for the rest of our lives like we thought we would be.

'Yeah, don't I just remember? You're lucky; things are moving fast. Mine took two years, but that's because John kept hiding the bank accounts,' says Emily.

The waitress delivers our steaming hot bowls of cawl, and I am glad that they are a little too hot to tuck into right away as I wanted to get Emily's thoughts on Will's 'friend'.

'I need your help, Emily,' I say.

'With what?'

'I need to know who Will is seeing.'

'Why on earth would you want to know that? It's no longer your business. You filed for divorce. It's up to him who he sees.'

'I know. But what if it gets serious and she becomes a stepmother to Dylan and Ewan? What if she's some kind of monster?'

'Will has done some things in his past, but I doubt he is dating a monster,' says Emily.

'Well, she could be one. I need to make sure she is okay to be around the boys.'

Libby takes my hands in hers and looks at me.

'Look, I think you're overreacting. Besides, it's not like they're five-year-olds. They're old enough to stay away from someone if they don't like her. This is completely out of your control and you're going to have to accept it.'

Emily's words might hurt, but I still want to know who she is.

'But she looks slightly familiar. Now I am wondering if he could have been seeing her before. Why do I recognise something about her?'

'I don't think Will ever cheated on you. He was always a devoted family man until the business thing. He's just not the type. I don't know why she seems familiar. Perhaps she works somewhere that you go to. Asda! You're always in there looking for bargains. Perhaps she works in Asda.'

'No. For some reason I can picture her with a briefcase. Like, a bag, and Dylan said she keeps talking about books.'

'The library then. She must work in the library.'

'Nope. I never used to have time to go to the library. I've not been there for years. Definitely not the library,' I say.

'A book shop,' says Emily, exasperated. 'Does it really matter?'

'Yes, it does. It's driving me potty not knowing where I know her from,' I say.

'Come on. It's time you focused on your own life, not hers,' says Emily.

She takes a sip of her cawl and puts her spoon down, looking at me seriously.

'Do you think it would be better to perhaps put your energy into looking for a new home rather than trying to find out who this woman is?'

'No, I don't,' I say.

'Well you're going to be stuck when that house goes through and you have to leave. Where will you go?'

'I was hoping I could stay with you for a bit, perhaps,' I say.

'I don't know how much longer I'm going to stay around here, to be honest. It turns out that Nick has the most beautiful thatched cottage in Cowbridge and I seem to be wanting to stay there more and more now. I know it's a bit of a whirlwind, but we can't seem to stay away from each other. I'm so happy.'

I am shocked at how quickly she is willing to commit to someone. Emily has never been particularly impulsive and has been on guard for so long that I don't recognise the new version of her. I am quite taken aback. Not to mention that the thought of her moving away fills me with horror. Who will I go and have cawl with? My circle seems to be closing in more and more, and with Dylan going to uni, I won't have anyone left. I should be happy for Emily, and I am to an extent, but I also feel a tinge of jealousy. Even though she was alone all this time and I had a happy family to go home to, I am actually jealous, which makes me feel like the worst sister ever.

I feel even more awful when I get home and casually mention Will's 'friend' to Dylan. He is the only person who may have a name for her, or some hint of where she works so I can find out more. I broach the subject as he sits in the kitchen looking over some books he bought ready for uni. I feel like some kind of evil mother, but I can't stop myself.

'Have you heard any more about Dad's friend?' I ask.

'No. Why would I?' he says.

'Oh, I don't know. I just wondered if you'd made any plans to all meet up again or anything.'

'Umm, no.'

'Ah, right. What was her name, anyway? I must stop calling her "his friend". I'm sure she has a name.'

I feel ashamed to ask as I realise it is wrong of me to quiz Dylan. This lady is nothing to do with me, yet I am compelled to find out more.

'I don't know. I think Dad called her Sarah,' he says.

'Sarah! Hmm. Did you get a surname?'

'Why would I get her surname?'

'Sorry. I don't know. Anyway, what do you fancy for tea?'

'Mam, I'm trying to read here. Whatever. I'm going to my room.' Dylan grabs his books and leaves the kitchen. It is clear I shouldn't be doing this.

'Sorry, love. I'll make a nice treat for you.'

I desperately try to take my mind off my obsession with Sarah, but once I pop a lamb curry in the oven, my thoughts immediately go back to her.

In a fit of anger, I removed Will from all my social media a while back. Now I regret it as I may have found something out. He isn't on Instagram, but I remember he is on LinkedIn. When I was trying to increase our customer base, I even made an account for the shop. I remember the password because, of course, it is 'Monty', so I can easily access the account. I am a genius! Would he have a love interest on his account? I have to quickly find out.

I can't wait a moment longer to get into the account. I click on his profile and begin to go through his contacts. I put in 'Sarah' and she comes up right away.

Sarah Crookell, Antiquarian.

It all makes sense with the book talk they have been having, and I recognise her photo as the woman he was with at the pub. This is definitely her.

It does surprise me that someone who has never cared for books is hanging around with an antiquarian! He never sold books in the shop, so what is his interest in them now?

I want to click on her page to find out more, but I daren't, as then she will know that I have been checking her out, or at least the shop has. Why does LinkedIn do that and show people that you have viewed their profile and are effectively a stalker? So I google her and it seems she is quite a success. The headlines show that she is obviously very ambitious.

> Sarah Crookell gets record-breaking deal for rare book.

> Antiquarian sells rare hardback for record cash sum.

She can't be short of money if that is the type of thing she does. She must get some kind of huge commission. What if Will is with her for her money? It is certainly not their common interest. I begin to feel sorry for her and wonder if I should warn her.

I look at her photo a little longer as I wonder how old she is. She is certainly a lot younger than Will. I would imagine she is in her thirties. Will would have been around twenty when she was born. In fact, we were practically about to meet then!

As I look at her closer, I remember where I know her from. It hits me in an instant. It is funny how you can think and think where you know someone from, and then, when you least expect it, you remember. The shop! She has been in the shop. I can see her again carrying a briefcase. She came in one day asking to meet with the owner. It was quite some time ago. Maybe two years or so. Have they kept in touch all these years? I didn't really give her any thought when she came in. She just seemed like a normal rep-type person who came in sometimes, trying to sell us stuff or seeing if we had anything to sell them.

Will had never dealt in books. He preferred dealing in bigger items, such as furniture and ornaments, so now I remember that he took her card and explained that he didn't sell books.

At the time, I didn't think it odd that he kept her business card. Now I wonder why he would take someone's business card when he didn't deal with that product.

What if he took a shine to her there and then? What if it was love at first sight, two years ago? I have shivers down my spine as I think about it. The old me would have admonished this thought right away. But I never thought he would sneak into the safe and remove Dad's watch either. What if he was planning on running away with her and was going to use the money from the watch? Stranger things have happened. There was a guy who pretended he had died canoeing, wasn't there? Then suddenly he appeared again. Perhaps Will was planning on running away and was going to pretend he had died and was off to spend my watch money with Sarah? Surely Will would never dream of doing such a thing, and he was just hoarding business cards, as he did with everything else. I would certainly like to think so, but I just don't know.

My phone rings and startles me. It brings me back down to reality and the fact that Will would never have thought of all of that. That would probably be a bit too conniving even for him. My imagination has been ruined by watching too many true crime Netflix programmes and I am spiralling out of control.

'Hello, sorry to ring so late in the evening,' says the estate agent.

'It's okay. What's up?' Half of me hopes that Elaine and Gerald have had a change of heart. What if they no longer want the house?

'I've just had word from the solicitor that we are about to exchange since there is no chain. Is that okay? What date would you be ready to move out?'

How on earth has everything moved so fast? Sometimes I think the universe wants me to move on. First the court date was given to us quickly, and now the house. What happened to sales falling through and hitches and glitches along the way?

The moment has arrived far too soon. I have to sign away the house and hand Gerald and Elaine the keys. I start to panic slightly.

'Well, can they wait for me to find somewhere else to live?'

'Absolutely. Shall we say around November/December for them to be able to move in? I think that would suit them as their new kitchen will be delivered soon after that. They should be all set by Christmas.'

Christmas! I hadn't even thought of that. There will be no invite to all our friends for drinks around the Christmas tree this year. Instead, a new family will be doing their own take on Christmas in my home. What if Elaine is the type to have a fake plastic tree? Oh heavens. I always had my annual six-foot Norway Spruce. I'll be lucky to have a two-foot one this year.

'That'll be fine. Please thank them for giving me some time to sort myself out. I appreciate that.'

'I'll pass that on. I know that Elaine is a bit of a…
Well… she likes things her own way, but they are both
quite fair, really.'

'Sure, thanks,' I say.

I put the phone down as Dylan comes back into the
kitchen.

'All right, Mam?' he says.

'Yes, I'm okay.' I try to smile, but my eyes are about to
spurt out tears that I really don't want to show Dylan.

'You sure?' he says.

'No, not really.' He knows his mother too well. I wish I
could hide my sadness, but I feel so deflated. First, I found
out that my husband is dating a successful antiquarian and
then I am told that the timer is ticking for us in this home
we have loved for so long. It was all inevitable and driven
by my filing for divorce. I have to accept this now, but I
just wish I could have known how horrendous it would
be.

I have probably made the biggest mistake of my life,
but it is far too late for regrets now. I simply have to live
with the consequences.

Chapter Twenty-Seven

For the time I have left in the family home, I make the most of every moment. When I am not making jewellery, I am picking up more boxes to pack away the remainder of the things I will take to the charity shop, sell or take with me to whatever home I eventually find.

I still have a bit of time left, but it takes forever to pack up a lifetime of memories that I had put away to reminisce about one day in the future. Yesterday, I found some of Dylan's old schoolbooks from primary school. They were full of gold stars, and I remember being so proud when he would come home with them. Now he is off to university. Tomorrow he leaves for his new adventure. How did time go so fast?

I have made good progress in my clear-out whilst Dylan has been saying goodbye to his mates and enjoying the last of the summer days in Tenby. There are faded areas on the carpet where cabinets have already been moved and sold. The good thing about having a clear-out is that at least there is some money in the bank.

Tonight I am holding my last dinner party to celebrate Dylan's forthcoming departure for uni. I try not to think about how it is the final party I will hold here. I consider Nick's wife and the illness she succumbed to. I am reminded that there are much worse things than not being able to hold a dinner party in the family home.

Ewan and Nia are home for the night, and I decide on a truffle chicken and potato gratin for the main course as it is Nia's favourite. It is lovely having them stay with me once again, even though I am mindful that I probably won't ever have a big enough home for them to do this again.

'Do you need any help?' asks Nia as I sprinkle over the parmesan and spread some sage leaves on the top layer.

'No, I'm all done. I tell you what though. You can open the wine if you like,' I say. I reach over and touch her arm fondly. It is so good to have a daughter figure in the house. I always wanted a daughter. I hope that we would definitely stay in touch if anything went wrong between her and Ewan. I certainly hope it doesn't, though.

Nia hands me a glass of wine.

'Cheers,' we say to each other. We clink our glasses, and then Nia leans over and gives me a hug.

'I know it can't be easy for you having to leave this house. I know how much you love your dinner parties. You're so strong. I admire the way you've handled everything.'

'Thank you. That's kind of you to say.'

'You know, Libby, I love this family more than anything, and this house. But I think it is you that makes this house so warm and cosy. Any house, or flat, will be the same with you in it,' she says.

'Oh, Nia. You're going to make me cry now.'

'What are you two gossiping about now?' says Ewan.

'Nothing,' I say, trying to smile.

Ewan puts his arm around Nia. It is clear to see he cares for her as much as I do.

'Welcome to the family, Nia,' I say.

'What? I haven't asked her yet,' says Ewan.

'Asked me what?' says Nia.

'Oh, Mam. Why did you have to say anything?'

'I haven't said anything. You've lost me now.'

Ewan rolls his eyes, and I have no idea what he is on about.

'Never mind. Where's the beer?' he says.

'Where it usually is. In the fridge,' I say. He is strange sometimes.

Nia and Ewan take their drinks to the dining room when there is a knock on the door. I wipe my hands on my floral pinny and go to see who has arrived.

Will is standing there with a lovely bouquet of colourful mixed roses.

'My favourite, thank you,' I say.

Given the fact that this is our last dinner party and all the family were coming, Ewan had asked if he could invite his dad. I would never be a woman to stand between my sons and their dad, so naturally I agreed.

'Thought they'd look nice on the dining table. I know how you always like your centrepiece,' Will says with a smile.

'That's very considerate of you.'

Will comes inside and, for a second, it feels as though nothing has happened. We are all the same people in the same house, but the elephant in the room is the divorce paper that is being drafted between our respective lawyers.

I am about to offer Will a drink when the doorbell rings again. Monty is practically hyperventilating at having Will back in the house so doesn't run to the door in his usual manner.

Emily stands with Nick on the doorstep. She wears a beautiful handmade silver shawl over a slinky black dress. Nick wears an expensive-looking tie, and they look as though they were made for each other. If you passed them on the street, you wouldn't ever know that either has had the sadness they have both experienced. They look like a well-to-do couple who have everything at their feet and have never known suffering at any point in their lives. It reminds me that none of us knows anyone's situation and I promise myself that I will be kinder to Elaine.

'Come on in. You look amazing… Both of you.'

Nick hands over a bottle of vintage wine.

'My goodness. This must have set you back,' I say.

'He has a wine cellar, and it's very lovely,' says Emily.

I have never met anyone with a wine cellar before.

I introduce Nick to Will, unsure how they might get along. Will can sometimes be a little prickly with people who have more than him. He has always been the same as he strives for success but doesn't always make it. He seems to see himself as a failure. But I guess it isn't for me to worry about any longer since he isn't hanging around. He will be leaving after dinner, and who knows if he will be straight on the phone to his beloved Sarah, telling her how much he missed her?

As we sit across the table from each other, I try to forget about Sarah. Tonight is about us as a family.

Everyone enjoys the crab lollipops I made as a starter, and it fills me with joy as I take the empty dishes into the kitchen.

I am getting the main course out of the oven when Ewan sneaks up behind me.

'Mam. Can I ask you something?'

He sounds serious.

'What, my love? Is everything okay?'

'I want to ask Nia to marry me. I've bought a ring, and I wanted to ask her after dinner. Do you think it's inappropriate because tonight's about Dylan going to uni? Maybe it should all be about him?'

I am so excited that I want to shout it to the world. But I try to stay calm and not give the game away.

'So that's why you were acting weird earlier.'

'Yes, I couldn't believe you said that about welcoming her to the family and then I was planning on proposing. It was as if you knew.'

'Ha. I must be psychic. No, I just meant it because you two are so cute together.'

I hug my boy, who has grown up so quickly. Stepping back, I admire the handsome young man in front of me.

'Oh, Ewan. I am so thrilled for you both. You can see you two think the world of each other. It's important you seize this chance of love right in front of you. Nobody knows what the future holds, and you have to make the most of every moment together. You and Nia remind me of me and Dad... Well, you know, in the better days.'

I think back to those better days. For all that we are going through, I no longer regret the past. In fact, there are still some days that I would do anything to have them back.

'I know things didn't work out with me and Dad, but I want you to know that he was the best thing to happen to me all those years ago. I mean, look at the gorgeous boys we had.'

I start to feel a little emotional, so I play with a tea towel on the work surface.

'Anyway, I just wish you'd have warned me and said something earlier. I'd have got something bubbly in to celebrate,' I say.

'She hasn't agreed yet,' says Ewan, laughing.

'Oh, I'm sure she will.'

I am an emotional wreck, so I run into the cloakroom to dab my eyes. I am going to give the game away in no time if I keep on like this.

When I have composed myself, I plate up the food and feel immense pride when I see everyone's reaction to my offering.

'Oh, this smells divine,' says Emily.

'Goodness, is that a compliment from my own sister?' I say, laughing. Nick has definitely been a good influence on her.

I watch everyone tucking in, just like the old days. When they finish, there are empty plates all around. My heart wants to burst with happiness at the lovely people around me. Nia is right. It might be my last dinner party in this place, but my recipes and some of the family will be coming with me. I may not be able to fit as big a dining table in the next place, but I can still have the same satisfaction from looking after my boys and their future families.

I am surprised when Dylan tells me to sit down as I get up to get more wine for everyone. He isn't usually that attentive at the dinner table as he is normally too busy eating every last bite and asking if there are any leftovers. Dylan rushes into the kitchen and brings in a bottle of champagne that I didn't know we had.

'It's time for the good stuff that Ewan got in,' he says.

'But I think Ewan wants to say something first.'

I soon realise that I am not the only person in on Ewan's secret this evening. I wonder if Will knows too.

Ewan stands up, and I see his cheeks start to flush. He clears his throat and starts. 'I want to do something very important tonight, and I want to say this in the house I grew up in. This is where so many milestones have happened, and I suppose this will be my last milestone here. Dylan's off to his student accommodation tomorrow. I'll be heading off with Nia. I wanted tonight to be special for everyone… Including Nia.'

Nia smiles at Ewan with no idea he is about to propose. I hope she doesn't say no. I smile at her encouragingly as Ewan goes down on one knee.

'Nia Evans, you complete me. I didn't know what that meant until I met you. You are the most gorgeous, sweet girl I have ever met. You are perfect in every way. I mean, you even get on with my family, so you must be a special kind of person, because we're all a bunch of muppets, really—'

'Oi,' interrupts Dylan.

We all look at each other, and there is gentle laughter in the room.

'What I'm trying to say is, Nia, will you marry me?'

'Oh, my god. Are you serious?' she says.

'Um, yes. I'm serious,' says Ewan. He is starting to look rather nervous, and so am I. The room goes deadly silent as we await Nia's response.

'Of course I'll marry you. Yes, yes, yes!'

Thank goodness for that! She had me worried for a split second there. We all clap and cheer around the table. I look at Will, who definitely didn't have an inkling by the look on his shocked face.

'Well, you dark horse. I had no idea that was on the cards. But wow. Congratulations,' he says. He hugs Nia and Ewan, as we all do in turn.

'Did you know about this?' he asks me whilst everyone is excitedly chatting.

'Only just found out.'

'Remember when I proposed?' he says.

'How can I forget? Putting a ring in someone's chocolate fondant dessert is never a good idea,' I say, laughing.

'I thought I'd killed you. Thankfully, that guy on the table next to us knew the Heimlich manoeuvre.'

'Well, you know me and chocolate. I just gobble it down. I never thought to check for a beautiful diamond solitaire hidden in it.'

We both laugh and look at each other fondly.

'Good times,' says Will.

'There were indeed,' I say, smiling.

'Were…' says Will quietly.

It suddenly gets awkward between us so I make my excuses and move away from Will to plate up the desert.

'Nana's pavlova,' I say with a smile as I start handing out the bowls.

It had to be done for our last dinner party here.

'Aww, I'm going to miss this at uni, Mam. Can you deliver me bowls down there?' says Dylan.

'We'll see,' I say, smiling.

Even though a new dawn beckons tomorrow I can't think about it yet, or the day after that. I want to enjoy this special moment tonight as we sit around together for one last time.

Then suddenly there is the biggest bang. I look at Monty, but thankfully, he isn't startled by the noise. The fireworks at Tenby Harbour that mark the end of summer have begun. We rush out into the back garden where we can get a bird's-eye view. The display happens annually, but I forgot that they were on this evening. Being able to see them from here has always been one of the highlights of this garden. We never had to stand amongst the crowds, jostling for a space, as we have always been able to watch it from the comfort of our patio.

The sky fills with gold and red as we hold our champagne glasses tightly. As we look up into the firework-filled sky, it feels like the final send-off for our family and our much-cherished home.

Chapter Twenty-Eight

Nia and Ewan are still fast asleep at lunchtime when we have to leave for Cardiff. It was lovely watching them enjoy the evening and finishing off the champagne last night. Even if they will have sore heads today.

I try my best to put my feelings of uncertainty about the future aside as we leave the house to deliver Dylan and what stuff he has left to his student accommodation. Will and I may no longer be together, but I am glad we have managed to put aside any resentment or awkwardness, for today at least.

Our youngest born is leaving the nest and moving to the capital. It was hard enough when Ewan left for university, but this is so much harder. I begin to think empty nesters need some kind of support club. Perhaps it should be mandatory that universities support lonely mums as well as their students. I remember when I was a class rep for Dylan in primary school. That didn't even seem so long ago. Could I possibly ask the uni if they would allow me to start up a mums' group for the parents in Dylan's subject? I smile to myself as I think how Dylan would most certainly disown me if I dared.

We pack the car up with the rest of Dylan's stuff. I look back once again at my youngest boy's bedroom. It is more or less empty now. Tomorrow his bed will be moved into storage as he will no longer be coming back here to stay.

Now he will have to stay at whatever rental flat I get for the time being, or at Will's. I haven't asked Will what his long-term plans are and I don't really want to know.

'So you looking forward to starting then?' says Will as he packs the last of the things into the boot.

'Can't wait. I'm going to be in that student uni bar quicker than you can say "What're you studying?".'

'Well, not too much drinking, please. I've heard of all sorts of things happening to students from drinking too much. Did you know you can choke on your own vomit?' I say.

'Yes, Mam. I know.'

'Don't worry, Libby. He'll be fine. He's a good lad.' It is nice to hear Will say my name again. I have missed the way he says it.

As we drive towards Cardiff, we reminisce about old times. We talk about all sorts of escapades Dylan got up to, including when he got his head stuck in a fence right outside the doctor's clinic.

'At least you were in the right place,' says Will, laughing.

'Oh, I tell you. I really thought they'd have to call the fire brigade. Luckily the doctor had such a knack for getting kids' heads out of railings. I was mortified having to walk into reception alone and explain that my son was there to see the doctor but currently had his head stuck.'

'Well, it didn't do me any harm,' says Dylan.

'I wouldn't be so sure,' teases Will.

'Oh my god, do you remember when you took me to rugby training and the car broke down? The ref stopped and gave us a lift home and I had to sit on your lap in his two-seater. Every time we passed a police car, you'd both shout "duck down". Nobody believed me in school. They said he was far too straight for that,' says Dylan, laughing.

'That's incredibly naughty of all of you,' I say.

'We had our seat belt on. It just had to stretch over two of us,' Will says, laughing.

'Oh goodness. I am glad I didn't know what you two got up to sometimes. Now I am really going to worry about uni.'

'Oh, Mam. It's time to look after yourself now. Stop worrying about everyone else,' says Dylan.

'Yeah, you've always been a worrier,' says Will.

'That's what I always used to say about you. Well, I can tell you, I wasn't worried when I did my skydive. Quite the opposite! Exhilarating, in fact,' I say.

'I'm glad I didn't see it. I'd have been worried sick,' says Will.

'Would you?' Our eyes meet, and then a car cuts in front of us.

'Bloody idiot,' shouts Will.

'You need to watch where you're going,' I warn him. I forgot how testy he can get on the roads. 'Right, what music shall we listen to then?' Music always calms down road rage.

'None of that old stuff you listen to, please,' says Dylan.

'Do you mean to say that you don't want to listen to the golden oldies' channel?' says Will.

'Nonoo,' says a disgusted Dylan.

'Mam's favourite Eighties classic tracks then,' I say.

'Maaam,' says Dylan.

Will and I laugh in the front of the car. It is so easy to wind a teenager up.

'Why don't we just switch the music off then? Let's play I spy instead,' I say.

'I spy?' says Dylan incredulously.

'Yup. If we can't agree on the music, let's play I spy.'

'Maaaam. It's getting worse. Just put the Eighties hits on then,' says Dylan.

'Yay. I knew I'd get my way with that threat,' I say, laughing.

I put on the Eighties station and notice Dylan tapping his hand on the back of the seat.

'You're enjoying this, admit it,' I say.

'Urgh, no I am not,' he says.

I smile all the way to our destination as I make the most of this time on the way to uni. How I will miss teasing Dylan.

When we arrive, Will helps take everything to Dylan's room. Some friendly students smile at us, and I am reminded of junior school and Dylan's first day. Only then I would try and matchmake friends for Dylan. I won't make that mistake again. I remember approaching a five-year-old in the playground and asking him if he wanted to play with Dylan.

'Oh, he looks like a nice boy. Why don't you go and play with him?' I had said. Only the boy was a mini-terror, and the two of them ended up enemies until the last day of school.

What I have learned since that day in primary school is that I have to let Dylan make his own way in life. I can no longer try to control things and wrap him up in cotton wool. He is his own person and he needs to spread his wings without his mam interfering.

Saying goodbye to him is awful. My boy, who has only generally stayed away from home when he was on a school trip, is not coming home with me tonight. This is his home now. I promised myself I wouldn't cry in front of him, so I keep strong until I leave. I don't care if I sob all night, but I don't want Dylan to know.

'Oh, Dylan. You look after yourself. You know where I am. If you need anything at all, I'll be there for you,' I say.

'I'll be fine, Mam. Don't stress now, okay?'

'No, I'm not stressing. Just want to make sure you'll be all right,' I say.

'Come on, Libby. Let's leave him to get on the lash then,' says Will.

'William!' I say. I don't know when I last called him that. It must have been many years ago.

'See, Dylan. She still tells me off, and I'm getting on. You've no hope, son,' says Will, laughing.

'Right, well, you take care of yourself,' I say.

'I will. Now stop worrying,' says Dylan.

'Just do me a favour and go on WhatsApp from time to time so I can check when you were last online. That way I'll know you're still alive. If it's more than two hours I'll call the police,' I say.

'Mam, my lectures will be more than two hours.'

'All right, three hours,' I say.

'Mam!'

'Okay. Okay. Six hours. If you haven't been online for six hours – not including bedtime – then I'll call the police to check on you.'

Will and Dylan shake their heads and laugh.

'Now, come on. Let's leave him to start his new life,' says Will.

Dylan waves goodbye, and once we are out of sight, I hear the door slam shut.

'Fancy a quick bite to eat before we head back?' says Will.

'Well, I could definitely do with a drink. Just the one though,' I say.

There are so many bars and restaurants near the accommodation that we don't have to walk far to find somewhere. We come across a lovely small Italian restaurant. It reminds me of the ones in Venice.

Will pulls out a woven bistro chair for me and I sit in front of the small table with its red candle that is already lit. I am glad of the flicker of light to help me see the menu as it is quite dark in here. My eyes are also struggling with the small print, and I remind myself that with more time, one of the things I need to do is schedule that optician's appointment.

'Do you know, I haven't had gnocchi since we were in…' Will was going to say Venice. He looks up at me and then quickly looks back at the menu.

I don't say anything and order myself the mozzarella and tomato salad. I don't seem to have much of an appetite. However, the wine I order helps calm down some of the fears I have about my new life.

Will is quiet over our meal and, just like me, seems as though he has a lot on his mind. I begin to wonder if he is thinking of Sarah. Is he looking forward to getting back to her? Are they meeting somewhere later? I suppose it was me who filed for divorce and maybe it is time to accept that Will has moved on a lot more than I have. So I decide I have no choice but to accept her. If he likes her that much, who am I to get in the way?

'So how's young Sarah?' I ask as we finish off our meals.

'I didn't know you'd be so interested,' says Will.

'I'm not. I'm just enquiring how she is.'

'I'm meeting her after I drop you off, actually. Some important business to sort out.'

Will has a glint in his eye as he says this, and I realise that I have lost him. He loves her! What if the important business is that he is about to propose and they marry as soon as the divorce is through? He can be quite impulsive. I know I said I would accept her, but I am not sure how I feel about that already.

I decide that I don't want to go back in the car with Will. I don't want to sit there beside him all that way, knowing that he is off to see his girlfriend the minute he drops me off. So I make an excuse to leave him.

'You know what? I think I'll do a bit of shopping before I leave Cardiff. You head off. I'll get the train back to Tenby.'

'It's already four thirty. You won't have much time to shop. Do you want me to hang around for a bit?' says Will.

'No, you go. I'm pretty sure it's late-night shopping today. I'll stay and enjoy the shops. It's not often I get down here.'

'Well, if you're sure,' says Will.

'Absolutely. You head off and meet Sarah,' I say.

I smile, just like I did to Dylan, as I try to hide the sadness I am really feeling.

The truth is that there is no late-night shopping tonight. So I make a run for the next train. Besides, Monty will be needing his evening walk by the time I get back.

All the way home to Tenby I manage to keep my composure. It is only when I open the front door and give Monty his usual fuss and his dinner that I start to quiver. I shout for Ewan and Nia, but, as I thought, they have already left to head back home. It is just me and Monty.

He chews at a new toy I have given him and ignores me when I call him for a *cwch* on my lap. I understand. He, too, needs his space sometimes.

I put the television on for some company, but all I seem to find are dramas with families sitting around dinner tables. It seems hard to believe we, too, were like that not so long ago.

I walk into the empty dining room so that I feel close to the memory of last night when everyone was all around me. It is all quiet now, and the table is bare and ready for picking up in the morning as it has already been sold. It won't fit anywhere that I could afford to move to.

I stroke my beloved table. Oh, how it has served our family. I hope the new owner will have wonderful dinner parties around it too. How quickly a family can diminish in the blink of an eye. I am glad of a message from Dylan to take my mind off things.

> See Mam, checking in. Still alive. No need to call cops xx

I laugh. He might not be living at home any longer, but it doesn't mean to say we can't have the same close relationship with all the banter.

I hold the phone to my chest. It makes me feel close to Dylan. I might not be able to give him a real hug, but my phone is the next best thing.

Chapter Twenty-Nine

As I wake up to a home empty of any other human inhabitants, I realise that it's going to take some time for me to adjust. Moving out will take some adapting too – although that has unexpectedly been delayed by a few months. Maybe the universe was kind enough to give me a little longer here.

The lawyer for Elaine and Gerald has been in touch to inform us that there is a little spanner in the works. After all that gardening, Elaine suffers from a dodgy hip and has been on a waiting list for a few years patiently waiting for a hip replacement. She has finally been called but is rather annoyed with the timing as her operation date is when they are supposed to be moving in. So they have asked if they can hold off the completion until her expected recovery in the new year. Although the house is now half empty and I was gearing myself towards the inevitable move, it will be nice to have the home for a while longer, so I happily agreed.

In the meantime, I keep myself busy by getting ideas for rental properties until I decide where I want to live permanently.

I love it around here, but if Emily is going to move in with Nick eventually, and the boys are away, I am not sure what there is for me here any longer.

However, when the time draws closer to my move, and Elaine eventually recovers from her successful operation, I find myself hunting for the right home during a dark and dismal January.

The first property I enter with the rental agent is cold and damp. I could never manage a harsh winter here, so I decide right from the start that this one isn't for me. Then we visit a small bungalow. It is quite modern and mostly quite nondescript. It makes me realise how lovely my home is. It has so much character, and I like that about a home. I will miss the beautiful red-brick inglenook fireplace that I enjoyed toasting my feet in front of all these years.

I am about to give up hope of finding something I actually like until we visit the final property of the day.

It is only two bedrooms, but at least that means that the boys can come and stay as there will be a spare room for them. As soon as I walk in, I feel as though this could be the one. There are cobwebs on the walls and stains on the carpet, but I take no notice. There is nothing that can't be cleaned up here.

I check out the stone walls and beamed ceilings and know that this is just the type of place I could call home. I don't quite know what it is, but immediately it feels safe and homely. There are so many things this little cottage has that make it perfect. I have already fallen in love with the period sash windows, the garden that will be perfect for Monty once it has been cleaned up, and the wood-burning stove. It just feels right.

'It's available right away,' says the agent. He can obviously see that I am keen.

'I'll take it,' I say.

The agent says that he can get the contract across by the end of the day, which means, following some security checks, I can move in whenever I want. It feels good to know that I finally have somewhere to move my taped-up boxes to.

I rush to the cashpoint and pay the deposit before anyone else can grab it. There is such a shortage of good rental properties nowadays.

Finally, I feel as though I have some control over my new life and remind myself that home is what you make it.

Walking to the cashpoint means that I have to pass the shop. I have tried to avoid it until now. But, today, I don't make a detour as I normally do. I face my fears and am taken aback when I see closing-down sale signs. I have purposely not spoken to Will, or anyone else, about how the shop is doing. I presumed it was doing as miserably as ever. It has been such a liability and the cause of all our problems. So it has felt like a curse that I didn't care to ask about. Finally, it looks as though Will has seen the light, but sadly it is too late for us. I am glad for the sake of his sanity though. Hopefully, he can finally have peace of mind and no longer struggle with something that was untenable.

Through the window, I spot Will with some boxes. He appears to be throwing some things in there that I recognise have been in the shop, gathering dust, forever. I am tempted to pop my head around and tell him how pleased I am that he has finally seen sense. No business is worth that amount of stress. Sometimes you have to admit defeat. Perhaps it was Sarah who advised him that the time had come to say goodbye to the family business. If so, it is really hurtful that a new person in his life could have such an influence when he wouldn't listen to what I had been trying to tell him. The only mistake he made is that he should have done it years ago. I walk on and hope that he hasn't seen me, but then I hear his unmistakable voice call my name as I am about to turn the corner.

'Libby!'

He calls again. I ignore it and continue walking. I don't have time to stop; once I get the cash out to pay the deposit, I am on a mission to get to the travel agency before they close. I have decided it is time to treat myself to a break. After all, the money for the house will be in the account in the next week, and after everything we have been through, I feel that it is time to treat myself.

'Libby!' shouts Will, even louder this time.

'Oh, hello. I didn't see you there,' I say when he finally catches up with me.

'How are you doing? Did you find somewhere to live yet?'

'Yup, I'm just about to sign the contract so I'll be out of the house in time for the deadline. Don't you worry. You'll get your share of the money soon enough.'

'Great,' says Will.

My hackles rise once again. It's all about money to him. He doesn't care that we no longer have the home.

'Well, you'll have plenty of money once that shop of yours is closed down and you no longer have to pay the rent and have all those outgoings hanging around your neck.'

'Yes, about that. I have something to tell you.' Oh no, don't tell me he is relocating to a cheaper shop. I thought it was closing down completely. Perhaps he will never learn.

Will is about to speak when I spot my favourite butcher walking in our direction along the pavement. Usually, I would love to stop and chat, but this is the first time I have seen him since Will and I broke up. I try to pretend I haven't seen him at first, but then he makes an exaggeratedly surprised look at seeing me.

'Ooh, well, hello, Mrs Jones. Haven't seen you in town for ages! Oh, sorry, do you prefer *Ms* Jones now? Have I put my foot in it?' He has obviously heard of the imminent divorce and looks back and forth between Will and me.

God, I hate how women are pigeonholed by their titles.

'It's still Mrs,' I snap.

'Oh, right. Yes, of course. Anyway, better leave you be then,' he says.

I feel terrible for snapping, but I am not in the mood for such a conversation. It also makes me feel like a failure. Poor Ms Jones.

I turn back to Will.

'What were you saying, Will?'

'I… Oh, never mind.'

'Look, I'm in a rush. See you around, yeah?' I say.

'Okay.'

Will smiles at me and looks like he wants to tell me something further. However, I am in no mood to hear what he wants to say. What if it is that he is moving in with Sarah? Whatever it is, I do not want to know.

–

Despite my hold-up, I manage to make the travel agent's just before it closes. A friendly young woman greets me.

'I'd like to book a holiday, please,' I say. I feel rather silly when I say it. Talk about stating the obvious!

'Well, you're in the right place. Any idea where you want to go?' she asks.

'Now let me think…' I smile to myself. I don't really need to think. I just want to be sure I am doing the right thing before I say it out loud.

'Venice.'

'Okay, and for how many people?'

'Just the one. I'm looking for something that doesn't have too much of a single supplement.'

'Do you know, we have just received an offer for a package to Venice with no single supplement. Do you think you could travel in February? Otherwise, it's going to be a bit more expensive for a single traveller.'

It is a little bit sooner than I planned, but as long as Will or Emily can look after Monty, I might be able to make it. I would have to work super hard moving out of the house and into the new cottage though. Plus, I need to get some jewellery made up for the shop so that I can at least earn something whilst I am away.

I quickly ring Will to confirm he can look after Monty. He is half his dog after all.

'It's just for five days in two weeks' time. It's urgent. I'm in the travel agent's now,' I say.

'You're going on holiday?' he says. He sounds shocked.

'Yes. I can go on holiday by myself, you know.'

'Yeah… Yeah. Sure. Where are you heading?'

'Venice, but look, I just need to know if that date's convenient for you. I'm in the travel agency now. Yes or no?'

'Yes, no problem.'

'Great. Let's book it,' I say to the travel agent.

The agent presses 'Confirm', and in a moment I am booked to go back to Venice.

'So, any particular reason you chose Venice?' she asks as she attempts to make small talk whilst she prints out the receipt.

'I've got some important business to take care of. Closure, I suppose,' I say.

'Oh, right. Well, here's all the stuff you need. Have a fab time.'

'Thank you. I will.'

I clutch the travel documents she has given me and feel a glimmer of hope. In two weeks' time I will be in Venice, and I know where my first stop will be.

Chapter Thirty

It is astonishing how quickly I can move when I have to. I have never been a particularly speedy person, and I would consider myself slow and steady. But when the thought of packing up my home, plonking it all down in my new place and travelling soon is weighing on my shoulders, I can move at the speed of lightning. Besides, keeping frantically busy takes my mind off things.

It doesn't take me long until all the boxes I need to take to the charity shop are packed up and dropped off. Boxes that are carrying my clothes and the bits and bobs I am taking with me have been packed into my car and driven over to the new place fifteen minutes away. Before long, my new cottage will look like a proper home. I blast out my favourite Eighties hits, pop the rubber gloves on and give the house the biggest clean it has probably ever had. Soon there are no longer cobwebs in every corner. I have even managed to start the unpacking, and the stone fireplace now has cheery, colourful candles around the base. It isn't quite as impressive as the inglenook fireplace we had, but it already looks homely and will look nice enough when it is all lit up. Everything is starting to fit together, even though I haven't quite moved in. The furniture removal company are booked for tomorrow, and then I fly out to Venice after I spend my first night in my new home.

I have been a little nervous that after the drama of the past few months there could be a spanner in the works. I was worried that one of the removal men might have done their back in and they'd have to reschedule, or that the house payment wouldn't arrive. However, it has all been plain sailing. All the planets have aligned, and Will is picking Monty up before the removal men arrive. I felt it best to have him out of the house as I don't want him too unsettled when he sees strange men come in and take what is left of our belongings. Monty is the easiest-going dog ever, but I can't imagine what would happen if he bit one of the removal men on the bottom because he was taking away his basket. I would be mortified!

I am getting Monty's dog treats and food ready to hand over to Will when I notice he is calling me.

'Hi, Will. Everything okay?'

'Listen. I'm so sorry, but I won't be able to look after Monty. Something's come up.'

'Are you serious? I leave in less than thirty-six hours, and I don't want him here when the removal men arrive.'

'I know. That's why I wanted to let you know at the earliest. I have to be somewhere tomorrow.'

'What could possibly be more important than looking after Monty? Oh, Will. How on earth could you do this to me?'

'Look, I can't apologise enough, but it can't be helped. I've spoken to Emily and she's willing to help out, okay.'

Whilst I am enraged with him, I don't have time to argue as to what could be more pressing than making sure our dog is looked after.

I call Emily to confirm she has agreed. Monty couldn't cope with kennels. He has always stayed with family members.

'Yes, it's not a problem. I don't know why you didn't ask me from the start.'

'Oh, Emily. Thank you. It means so much. I really need to get out there. You're an absolute superstar.'

I don't tell her exactly why I have to be on that flight to Venice. Nobody knows the real reason for my trip.

The next morning, Emily arrives early to pick up Monty. She is driving away just as the removal truck comes up the road.

I welcome them in and make them a brew. It feels strange as they remove all the big items that have taken up so much space in this house for years. Bit by bit, I see it all start to accumulate on the truck. I realise that I may have been a little over-ambitious with the amount of stuff I thought I could take. I can already see that my precious Welsh dresser is never going to fit in the living room, as it does here. I may have to put it up for sale.

After a few hours of hard work and a van full of our furniture, there is nothing left to remove from our old home.

'Right then. That's the lot,' says a man called Phillip who appears to be the head removal man.

His voice echoes around the empty room. This is really it. There is nothing left but an echo and the dust that the removal of all this stuff has created. Fortunately, I kept the broom and some cleaning equipment here for this bit. I would hate for Elaine to complain that I had left the house in any kind of mess. I am sure she would be onto the lawyers asking for compensation for a cleaner, especially when she is taking it easy after her new hip.

I sweep up whilst the removal men head over to the new house. When it is all finished, there is nothing left but faded marks on the walls where paintings and portraits of the family have been. I wonder what colours Elaine will want to paint my magnolia walls. I have always liked neutral, calm colours. She may prefer deep purples and reds. I am sure I won't recognise the house after she has put her personal touch on it.

I have always been a bit of an overthinker, but I swore to myself that the skydive would change all of that. What with the freedom of flying through the sky like a bird with a backpack and then hearing about Nick's wife, I swore I wouldn't worry about the things I couldn't control any longer. So with that thought in mind, I lock up the front door and stroke the handle one last time.

'You've been a happy home. Thank you,' I say through my tears.

I keep walking until I reach the car. There is no point looking back; it will only serve to hurt me.

I drive on and focus on the future. I live in a new home now. Elaine and Gerald have paid for the house; now it is entirely their choice what they do to it.

I move a bramble away from the door of my new cottage. I am amazed the removal men don't scratch themselves on the way in with all the overgrowth. A bit of TLC and I will have the overgrown garden as good as new. I may even try and plant some new potatoes and make a vegetable patch. That would save money on the exorbitant supermarket shops for a start.

Inside, the house smells musty. Once the sofa is in the right place and I have made the bed, the first thing I will do is light my beautiful scented candles.

'Where do you want the bookcase?' asks Phillip.

'I had hoped I could get it into that little alcove over there,' I say. The alcove was another of the things that attracted me to the house, along with the window seat where I imagined I would be able to sit and read a good book.

'We're not going to get it in there. It's too tall,' he says.

'Oh.'

'Anywhere else you had in mind?' asks Phillip.

'Nope. There's no room. Can you take it out to the back porch, please? I'll have to just squeeze past it for now until I figure something out.'

'We already left the dresser there, as you asked.'

'Oh. I don't know what to do with it. There really is no room here, is there?'

'Nope. We can take it back and charge you for storage if you wish?'

'I think you'll have to.'

I watch as my beloved bookcase heads through the door once again. What will I do with all my books? Perhaps I should ask Sarah to sell them for me. Although I don't think I would have the classics that she would want. They're more bonkbusters than the brainbusters she auctions.

When the removal men have finally put everything into place, I search in a drawer that has already been crammed full of my belongings for a lighter for the candles, but I can't find one. There is only one box left that isn't unpacked, and I open it up to see the lighter lying on the top. I light my candles carefully until the fireplace looks beautiful. I am sure it is a long time since it had this much attention.

With everything sorted, I treat myself to a glass of wine. It will be just the one as I have a flight to catch tomorrow. As I sit down, I think of the box that still hasn't been unpacked. I should probably go through it so that when I return from holiday, there is nothing left to face.

Although I promised myself that I wouldn't look back, when I look into the box, I can't help myself. An old camera of mine is amongst the many items I forgot I had packed in the rush. My goodness, I haven't used a camera for years! I always take photos on my phone nowadays. I can't resist opening up the camera case and looking at it. The camera almost feels like a prehistoric creation! Removing the chip inside, I pop it into my laptop. Immediately, family photos that I had forgotten about come up on the screen.

I touch the screen and stroke Dad's face gently as a photo of him on holiday in Portugal with all of us comes up. It was the last holiday we would ever have as a complete family. How special. I promise myself that I will print it off and put it into a frame. It can take pride of place over the fireplace.

Looking through the photographs makes me realise what wonderful memories they are of a life passed by. There are so many photos of the boys growing up at school and days out. Other photos show Will with his arm around me fondly, proving just how much has changed since these photos were taken.

I stop for a moment and look up at the living room. Not even Monty is here tonight. It is just me and a pile of old memories. Wonderful memories, but sadly a time in our lives that has now passed. I go upstairs to pack the camera safely away in my luggage. I will take it with me, ready to make new memories, which will start tomorrow in Venice.

I tuck the camera away carefully, alongside the final divorce paperwork that is waiting to be signed. We started our married life in Venice; it is only fitting that it will end there too.

Chapter Thirty-One

Returning to Marco Polo Airport is strange without Will by my side. I keep wanting to say, 'Ooh, remember seeing that last time?' whenever I spot something familiar, but there is nobody standing there. So I just smile at people and make my way to the bus for the water taxi terminal. There is no fancy boat this time either.

I have never been one of those people who go to places alone. I suppose I have been lucky that, until now, I have always had family around me. Even when I popped to the supermarket, I would always bump into someone who knew me from the shop, or school. Now I am truly alone in a foreign country. The one thing this forthcoming divorce has taught me is that I am learning to enjoy my own company.

When I get to the special offer hotel, it is not as glamorous as the past ones we have stayed at. There are no views of Rialto Bridge or Piazza San Marco, just an alleyway which gives off the whiff of pizza from a takeaway every now and then. But I am not purely here for the beautiful Venetian views, or the food; I am here for something even more special. In fact, I drop my bags off, have a quick freshen up and try and get my bearings so I can begin my mission to the jeweller's without delay.

I am not so familiar with this side of town, but fortunately, there are signs for Piazza San Marco that I can follow. I figure if I can find my way there, then I can work my way to the shops.

I walk fast through the chilly winter breeze as I realise the shops will all be closing soon. Some of the shutters are already coming down as I rush ahead.

The crowds are sat enjoying their Italian biscuits with their hot drinks at Caffè Florian, but there is no time to stop at Venice's oldest cafe for a coffee to warm me up. I recall the story that a guide told us on our honeymoon about how it was one of the first cafes to allow women, back in 1720, and that it is the second oldest cafe in the world. Even Casanova and Charles Dickens are said to have been there! Once I get what I came here for, I have promised myself an espresso there.

I pass some traders who seem to be arguing with each other. They shout in Italian, and I wonder what they are talking so heatedly about. I don't have time to waste worrying about other people though; I must find the alleyway I am looking for.

Then I see something that looks familiar. I make my way down the alleyway but can't seem to find the jeweller's. A terrible thought occurs to me that they could have even closed down. Then I will never find the man I am searching for.

I remember there were two alleyways that looked similar. So once I have completed my search of the shops here to no avail, I try the other one. If I don't find it along this other alleyway, then the store must have closed down. It was definitely one of these.

I am halfway down when I see it. I recognise it straight away. All this time the store frontage stayed in my mind, but I couldn't place the name on the sign. It is in Italian, so I am not surprised I couldn't remember it. I am relieved to find the shop still exists, after everything else that has changed in the world since we were last here. The only bad news is that it has already closed for the day.

I make a note of the opening hours and will make sure I am here as soon as it opens in the morning. In the meantime, there is nothing else to do but head to Caffè Florian for that treat.

Below the arches, I enter the cafe. It's stunning and so sophisticated, with a pianist playing beautiful classical music. Despite the generous seating area outside, I opt to warm up in one of the ornate rooms with its gold elaborate décor on the walls and red velvet seats. I still get the view of the square, but also the luxury of the beauty and warmth of the interior.

The waiter, with his white jacket and black bow tie, serves me immediately. I get the impression that hundreds, if not thousands, of tourists flock here. The waiter looks so stylish, and I laugh to myself as I think how different the uniform is here to the chippy back home – although, to be fair, there is a huge price difference too. The uniform alone looks like it cost a bomb.

'Espresso, please,' I say.

When I was with Will, I never had much time to people-watch. However, now that I am twiddling my thumbs, I find myself watching everyone and wondering where they flew in from and what their lives are like.

Take the man who rushes past the window. Where is he going? Is he late for an important dinner date?

Then there is a couple who look madly in love. I would say they are on a romantic break, honeymoon even. I wonder if this is what Will and I looked like all those years ago. We were so engrossed in each other I don't think we cared less if anyone was looking at us. It is sad to be here without him, but no matter what, Venice will always be my special place. How could anyone not fall in love with this magical city?

'One espresso,' says the charming waiter, placing it down in front of me.

'*Merci*,' I say. Why did I just speak French to him? I was trying to be cultured and elegant and now the wrong language has come out! How uncouth of me. What on earth is the word in Italian for thank you? I try to remember the name of that magazine. What is it called? The one Nia is always reading. *Grazia*! That's it. Word association always helps.

'*Grazia!*' I shout.

'I think it's *grazie*, not *grazia*,' says an American tourist sitting beside me.

'Yes, yes. Of course,' I say, laughing. Fortunately, the waiter is long gone and didn't even notice my mistake.

'First time to Venice?' she asks.

'No, it's my third actually.'

'Gee, practically an aficionada then,' she says.

'Yup.'

'Do you mind if I join you? I'm backpacking around Europe alone.'

'Oh, no. It would be great to have the company,' I say.

Marcie provides great companionship at the table despite our age gap. She must be in her late twenties. If only she were a few years younger, I would be setting her up with Dylan.

Marcie is from Florida, and we chat about the time we took the boys to Orlando when they were small.

'Hey, I am going to a masked ball tomorrow night. I have a spare ticket, if you'd like,' she says.

She digs in her bag and pulls out two tickets for a ball at a fancy palazzo.

'Wow, how on earth did you get your hands on these?'

'My parents. They gave them to me as a surprise, but I didn't want to tell them that me and my boyfriend split right before the trip. So I have a spare one. You seem like a nice lady, and I've not met anyone who will stop and chat with me yet. You may as well have it.'

I think about how I impulsively packed my beautiful blue and gold mask at the last minute. I couldn't come to Venice without it, just in case a miracle happened and I could attend another ball somehow. This is the moment I was waiting for. It seems too good to be true.

'I would love that. I really wanted to go to one but didn't have anyone to go with. That would be amazing.' I dig out my purse to pay for the extra ticket.

'Oh, I don't need money. It's fine. It's a present from me,' says Marcie.

I am taken aback by her generosity. I remember how expensive these tickets were the last time. However, Marcie insists she doesn't want anything for them. We eventually agree that I will give a nice donation to her favourite dog charity in the States. I definitely couldn't argue with that.

We agree to meet at a central point tomorrow night, and Marcie heads off to visit Basilica di San Marco, leaving me alone with my empty espresso cup. I grin to myself like a Cheshire cat. Tomorrow is going to be wonderful. I can feel it already.

'Madam, can I get you anything else?' asks the waiter.

'Nope, just the bill, thanks.'

I see a message from Nia on my phone. She is so considerate and wants to check I arrived in Venice okay and whether I have been to the jeweller's to search for the watch yet. I message back to let her know I am safe and hitting the jeweller's again tomorrow. She is the only person I have told about my plan. Then I send her some photos. I take pictures of the cafe and then one of my ticket for the ball.

> Oh wow. I've always fancied going to one of those.

> You'll have to come to Venice with Ewan. Maybe on your honeymoon, like me and his dad!

I pack the ticket safely away and head back to the hotel. It has been a long day of travelling and I am in need of an early night. Besides, I want to be up and about early to see how I can get Dad's watch back.

Chapter Thirty-Two

I struggle to eat my continental breakfast at the hotel as I have butterflies in my tummy. I have so many questions for the man in the jeweller's. I wonder if he remembers the watch? Will he remember me, and what can he tell me about Will?

I practically fall over my laces as I rush to the shop. I slow myself down before I end up falling in my haste. That won't do me any good. Tourists walk in front of me, slowly taking in the views. I start to get impatient as someone stops in the alleyway to take a selfie. Oh please, don't take a selfie now! I jostle my way around her and can see the shop in view. My nervousness starts to peak as it gets closer and closer. I attempt to be confident as I push the heavy glass door. A woman is working behind the jewellery counter, and I take a deep breath.

'Hello, how can I help you?' she says.

I look at the displays and see that there is no watch resembling Dad's. Then again, what would I expect? It has been a year since Will brought it in here. It is a beautiful piece; it was bound to be snapped up.

'I'm looking for a watch,' I say.

'Okay, we have a nice selection. Is it for yourself?'

'No, not any watch. I'm looking for a specific watch. There's a guy who works here. Does he still work here? He may remember the watch I'm looking for.'

'Leonardo? Ah, yes. He is the owner of the shop. But he is off today. Can you call in tomorrow when he's back?'

'Well, I was hoping I could find the watch today. Can you call him?'

'Ah, it's a family christening today. I can't disturb him.'

'No, fair enough.'

I describe the watch to the lady and ask if she remembers anything. She says she knows the watch but doesn't know where it is.

'The cursed one,' she says, laughing.

'Sorry?'

'I think this watch brings bad luck, no? Is this the watch?'

'No. It is a very good watch,' I say.

'I don't think. Anyway, why don't you come back tomorrow.'

I am sure we are lost in translation here. She is obviously confused and has got things the opposite way around.

She tells me what time she expects him to be in tomorrow and I arrange to be back at ten a.m. sharp.

'Please, will you tell him I'm coming? Perhaps he can get the watch back for me.'

She nods her head and starts polishing some pieces of jewellery in front of her without any concern for my dilemma. The watch may not mean much to her, but it means so much to me.

This wasn't quite how I planned the morning, but I suppose there is no reason that Leonardo would be at the shop every hour they are open. I should have thought of that before instead of getting so over-excited and thinking he would be there waiting for me.

I message Nia to tell her the disappointing news.

Ah, no way. Never mind. Enjoy the ball tonight and take lots of pics for me, she says. I spend more time messaging Nia than I do the boys sometimes. At least Dylan's WhatsApp is showing he is still alive. Although I would put money on it that he has been staying out late, as he isn't checking his phone until lunchtime most days. The little lazy bones.

Since I have a day of leisure, I decide to visit some art galleries. Paintings were never really Will's thing, although even he was impressed the first time we went to the Doge's Palace. But he still kept saying he wanted to grab an ice cream as we walked around. So, the benefit of being alone means that I can go to places like the Dalmatian School in Castello. I read an article about it in the in-flight magazine on the way over and decided I had to visit. It sounded like just the thing the *real* me – rather than the mum-and-wife me – would love.

I wasn't sure I would manage to find it, but the barrage of alleyways and bridges across the canal eventually lead me to the small church building. It doesn't face the Grand Canal, like many of the tourist places, but this is what I think makes it a bit of a hidden gem.

When my eyes finally adjust to the darkness from the bright daylight outside, I am stunned by the Renaissance artwork inside the building. On the ground floor, the paintings by Vittore Carpaccio take my breath away. I imagine Will's response if he were here now. He would probably complain about the darkness and say his eyes were hurting him and ask a member of staff where the nearest gelateria was. But I don't need anything when confronted with such beauty, and I understand that art needs to be protected from the light.

A painting of George slaying a dragon leaves a lasting impression on me. I must ask Marcie if she is interested in art. If so, she would love it here. She seems like someone who likes to visit different things and not just the super-touristy stuff.

I don't know where to look in here. The walls, the ceilings. Wherever I glance is a work of art. It might not be the biggest place to visit, but I still spend ages in there. Every time I step away from a painting it lingers in my thoughts, and I feel compelled to return to it to then notice more features. One of them has a white dog, I notice. The painting might be from the sixteenth century, but I laugh to myself as I think how, aside from the colouring, he reminds me of Monty! I am so glad I read about this place.

Eventually, I head out onto the street. My eyes have to adjust to the sunlight again. I stop at a trattoria for some tiramisu, again sending Nia a photo. I message Dylan, too, and tell him how much Mam hopes he is behaving. I can't resist teasing him.

After a walk along the Grand Canal, I head back to my room. I worry that I don't have a fancy outfit for the ball tonight as there was no way I could manage to organise the costume hire in time. I also don't want to splurge too much as I need money to somehow buy the watch back. However, I did pack a nice long blue silk dress that I have, which matches my mask.

As I look in the mirror, I am quite pleased with the outfit and make my way to meet Marcie.

Luckily, she is exactly where she said she would be at the time we agreed, which makes me relieved. It was only afterwards that I realised we hadn't exchanged any contact details and all I knew of her was that she was a young American called Marcie. I would never have tracked her down. Marcie looks absolutely stunning and has dressed up in the full regalia for the evening. She stands out, and I notice both men and women who pass, giving her admiring glances. I feel like the Ugly Sister!

Oh, to have that beautiful, flawless young skin she has. I want to tell her not to take it for granted because there will come a time when even the best of skin creams won't help revitalise that half-century-old sun-damaged skin. But she wouldn't understand at this stage in her life. Now is the time for her to enjoy the youthful beauty she has.

When we arrive at the palazzo, people are queuing to get in. Many are dressed up, but thankfully, some are wearing nice dresses and suits rather than costumes and ballgowns, which makes me feel less underdressed.

Already, people are quite merry inside, and it feels like one of those times when you are late to a party and the last to walk in.

A handsome young man soon leads Marcie onto the dance floor, and as I stand near the bar on my own, a chap in a gold brocade jacket, short trousers and a red dickey bow bumps into me.

'*Scusa*,' he says. Then he pops his mask on and rushes off to the dancefloor.

I don't blame him for rushing off. As an Italian soloist sings the most beautiful, haunting-sounding tune, I can't help but sway my hips. Unlike at the art gallery when I was happy to be alone, I begin to think of Will and how I wish he was here to dance with me. We always enjoyed a dance together.

I am on another planet when a man in a mask who looks like a sexy highwayman startles me and asks me to dance. I don't think he speaks English as he gestures with his hand. He must have taken pity on me, pathetically watching everyone else have a good time.

'Why not,' I say. Still, he doesn't say anything.

By the time we reach through the crowds to the dance floor, the song is almost over. I feel a little embarrassed that the man may want to sit down as the song ends, and I am unsure what to do. However, the highwayman gestures to stay on the dance floor.

We dance to the rest of the song and then I suggest I sit down. Once again, he gestures to keep dancing. This time the song is slow, and he moves towards me to take me in his arms. I can't say it doesn't feel strange dancing so closely with a highwayman. But, apart from that, there is something comforting about his embrace. I tell myself not to be so silly. How can a highwayman in a cloak be comforting?

The man moves his arm around my waist and my stomach does a little somersault. Goodness, what is that all about? I haven't had such a feeling for years. He then touches my shoulder and goosebumps hit every part of my body. Oh, good grief. I step back to look at him. I ask him what his name is, but he doesn't answer. Instead, he quickly spins me around in a fancy dance move. He definitely doesn't speak English. I may not know what he looks like, but I feel this amazing chemistry between us. I can't believe that I finally meet someone I connect with and we are unable to communicate. How could this happen? His arm slides down to my lower back and I can hardly take any more. I feel like ripping his mask and cloak off! I force myself to remember that I am a mother of teens who would be disgusted with the thought of their mother ripping a stranger's cloak off in a fit of passion. Not to mention that those divorce papers aren't even signed yet. My emotions are all over the place. I need to get over Will completely before I think about anything else. So I step away from him. I can't do this. It wouldn't be fair to the tempting highwayman anyway. I have far too much baggage.

When I move away from him, he nods his head, as if to say thank you. I go back to the bar, where Marcie and the young man are now in an embrace. I buy a drink and take a sip, my eyes scanning the room. The man has disappeared into the sea of masks. He is nowhere to be seen. I look at my shoes and giggle as I think of dropping one here for this mysterious Prince Charming to find. But I tell myself that he is a highwayman, not Prince Charming.

Still, for the rest of the night, I can't get it out of my mind that he was certainly charming. Very charming indeed.

Chapter Thirty-Three

The next morning, I have the biggest smile on my face as I make my way to the jeweller's. Whilst I hope that today there is a teeny chance I will get closer to being reunited with the watch, I know that the extra fluttery feeling and the cheesy grin are thanks to the highwayman. I haven't been able to stop thinking about him since I left the party.

I hadn't realised until now how much I had missed someone giving me attention. The way he touched my back will stay with me for a long time. My Prince Charming awakened the romantic side I forgot I even had. Until now, I was just fine with the fact that the only living thing I have curled up with in recent months is little Monty!

If only I could have found out Prince Charming's name and that there were no language barriers between us. I suppose, at a party in Venice, he could be from anywhere. How lovely it would have been to know more about him though. I suppose he will have to remain my mystery Prince Charming. Still, I grin like a Cheshire cat as I open the door to the jeweller's where I spot Leonardo, the shop owner, right away.

'Hello, was it you who came in yesterday asking for the watch? My colleague told me someone was asking about it,' he says when he sees me.

'You remember me?' I say.

'Of course. How can I forget you?'

'Am I that memorable?' I ask.

'It's not every day I put my foot in it with someone,' he says, smiling.

'It's okay. It isn't your fault. You did the right thing speaking to me that night. I'm glad I found out.'

'So why do you want to ask about the watch after such a long time?' he says.

'I want to track it down. I really want to get it back.'

'Ah, but you came too late. It sold again.'

'Again?'

'Yes, this cursed watch. It has sold two times now.'

'How did you sell it twice, and why is it a "cursed watch"?'

'The man who bought it said he had nothing but bad luck afterwards. Everything went wrong for him once he left the shop with it. He threw it down at me after one week and demanded a refund.'

'So it came back to you?'

'Yes. Since then, nobody wanted it. Until two days ago. Then I sold it again.'

'What? You sold my dad's watch two days ago?'

'I don't know whose watch it is. But I know that I hope it doesn't come back here again.'

'Okay, but please, you have to tell me who bought it. I will buy it back,' I plead.

'I'm not having that watch in this shop again. Whenever it is in here, I get bad sales. I think this man is right. It is cursed watch.'

'It's not cursed. It just didn't want to be sold. It needs to belong to the right family. Ours!'

'Okay. Maybe it is a bit cursed though. This man who bought it fell and broke his finger, then he had his car windscreen smashed by a stone, after this, his fridge broke… Everything broke. Finger, fridge… You see what I'm saying?'

'A broken fridge is hardly a curse.'

'As you like, but I am telling you he was afraid and upset.'

'It must have been my dad's spirit wanting it back where it belonged then,' I say.

'Maybe. I think you are right.'

'Okay, so please help get it back to me. Where it belongs.'

'I'm sorry, but I can't break this confidentiality. Remember last time I said too much? Your husband was very mad with me.'

'You spoke to him after I saw you?'

'Yes, he rang me shouting that I shouldn't have said anything. That it was confidential.'

'I am so sorry.'

'Now I also shouldn't have said that. Look, please, if you want answers you have to ask your husband. Not me.' He stands with his hands on his hips and looks more determined than ever that I am not going to get another word out of him.

'Look, he put us all in a difficult position. I understand. It isn't your fault. I really don't mean to put you in the middle of all of this. If I give you my phone number, perhaps you can call me if the watch comes back? Maybe put me in touch with the new owner? Do you think you could at least ask them if they'd be willing to speak with me?'

'I must keep my mouth shut. You understand.'

'Yes, I understand, but just take my number and ask the new owner to contact me.'

'I'll see what I can do. I am not giving any promises.'

'Yes, absolutely. Please just ask them. Look, whilst I'm here I'll buy some more gemstones. I make jewellery now. I got the idea when I first came here. You sell the most gorgeous stones.'

'Well, I like to please my customers with unusual things. That's why I bought the watch from your husband.'

'I know. It's a very beautiful watch.'

I pick out some pink, jade and coral stones and he wraps them up carefully together.

'My customers will love these,' I say. I would never have believed that one day I would have repeat customers for my designs.

Isn't it funny how it is impossible to get your life sorted in every direction? Every day, life is like having unruly eyebrows. You flatten one long hair and another will spring up, and this time it could be even worse and be grey! My sons are sorted with uni, I have launched a little jewellery business, and I have fulfilled my dream of doing a skydive. Then I look around at a time I should be spending with my husband, and he is not there. He is probably too busy having fun with Sarah. I bet he isn't even thinking of me as I visit the place we always loved so much.

When I leave the shop, I am a little less positive. The highwayman was just a fantasy. I will never see him again, just like Dad's beautiful watch. I have no chance of getting it back now. I find myself secretly hoping that Dad *has* put a curse on it, and the person runs back in with it demanding a refund again. The curse would need to hurry up, though, as I fly back the day after tomorrow.

'Please, Dad, do your best,' I say, looking up at the Venice sunlight.

When I get back to the hotel and look for something to wear for dinner, I see the divorce papers untouched in my bag. I think how Will has moved on and how so much has changed. The time has come to sign them. I may as well get it over with.

I reach for the papers and sit at the desk in the room. The complimentary cheap plastic hotel pen is all I need. It doesn't work at first, so I have to use the small notepad that is beside it and scribble until I get the ink flowing.

The pen scratches along the paper, finally leaving its black mark with my signature.

'There you go, Will. You're free to do what you want now,' I say to thin air.

I need a stiff drink after that so I decide to revisit the bar that I liked the last time I was here and bumped into Leonardo. I could definitely do with a few Limoncellos after signing those papers.

As I make my way downstairs, my mobile is ringing with a number from Venice. The only person I think it could be is the jeweller. Who else would call me from here?

'Hi. It's Leonardo. From the shop, yeah?'

'Yes, I know who you are. Thank you for calling so quickly.'

'Good. Well, I wanted you to know that I spoke to the person who has the watch.'

'Yes, and what did they say?'

'They said they want to talk to you about it. It's your lucky day. They want to meet with you.'

'They want to meet me?'

'Yes. There is something they need to tell you.'

'Oh, I hope they're not going to bang on about this stupid curse you all believe in.'

Did Dad's spirit do something already? I'm sure he wouldn't do anything mean though. I know there is no way he would want someone's finger broken.

'I'm not getting involved again. I am just doing what everyone is asking of me. I gave the message to them and they said they will meet you tomorrow. That's it.'

'Thank you. I really appreciate it. That's just amazing. Where do they want us to meet?'

'I will send you a message on your phone with the address,' he says.

'Amazing. Thank you. Do you think they'll sell it back to me?'

'I don't know. Please, this is all I know.'

'No, of course. Sorry. I'm just a bit over-excited.'

As I walk into the bar, I have renewed hope. I have a feeling that I can get the watch back. All I need is to be able to meet the new owner and explain how it is the most awful mistake. Surely nobody would be that mean not to hand it over for a price once they know the truth behind it. Besides, if they get awkward, then I will tell them about the spurious curse.

I order my Limoncello and sit down at the window overlooking Rialto Bridge. I look around at some men sitting near the bar. What if one of these was my mysterious highwayman? Wouldn't it be incredible to be reunited with the watch and my Prince Charming?

Chapter Thirty-Four

I copy the address that the jeweller has given me and put it into Google Maps. I can see that it is not too far away from Piazza San Marco, which is good news. I do have a few hesitations about meeting a stranger in such circumstances, but I have messaged Nia with the address and told her to check up on me if I go silent. Fortunately, it looks like a very public place.

The area has lots of bars and cafes, and I look for the name of the place we are to meet. It is a cute little restaurant. I wonder if perhaps it is the owner of the restaurant who bought the watch and that is why he wants to meet here. I realise that the jeweller only gave me the address to meet the buyer of the watch and not the name of the person I am actually meeting. With no idea of whom I am looking for, I sit down at a table by the window so that I can keep an eye out for anyone who is looking around as curiously as I am.

For ten minutes nobody approaches me. This is silly. Two strangers are expected to meet in a restaurant and neither knows anything about the other one? Whose idea was this? I start to pack up my handbag. The jeweller has sent me on a wild goose chase.

As I stand up to leave, I see someone familiar hurrying through the restaurant door. I can't quite believe what I am seeing. It can't be, surely.

'*Siwmae*,' says the voice.

'Will! What on earth are you doing here?'

'Same as you,' he says.

'Meeting someone?' I ask.

'Yes. Can I sit down?'

My hands start shaking. I tell myself not to be so silly. It is Will. There is nothing to be nervous about. I can't seem to help it though. I suppose it is the shock of seeing him here.

I look around and nobody else seems to be approaching me, so I agree that he can sit there.

'I was just about to leave, but I am surprised to see you here,' I say.

'Do you want a bite to eat whilst we're here?'

'Well, it depends. I was supposed to have an important meeting, but the person hasn't turned up.'

'Hasn't he?' he asks.

I look at his face. He has a strange expression that tells me he is involved in all of this.

'Right. What's going on? Do you want to tell me now, Will?'

He moves his hand into his pocket, pulls out a box and puts it on the table.

Immediately, I know what is inside. I snap open the box, and there is no mistake. Dad's watch has been polished and looks better than ever. I clutch it to my heart. It's back where it belongs.

'I'm sorry. I did the most foolish thing of my life and I owe you the biggest apology. It was a moment of sheer madness. I—'

'Excuse me. Do you want to order something?' interrupts a waiter.

'Oh, er... I suppose we should. Libby, we could order your favourite Italian wine?' says Will.

'I...erm, yes, why not?' I say.

Will orders the wine and informs the waiter that we will have a look at the menu in a bit. I hope he leaves us alone for a minute as Will and I have got a lot of talking that needs to be done.

'What were you saying again, Will...?'

'Right, well, basically, to be honest, I was in so much debt trying to keep the business afloat that I got further into trouble. I couldn't tell you. I mean, I couldn't face up to it myself, let alone tell anyone else about the predicament I was in. I kept thinking all it would take would be to sell this bit or that bit of stock and it was an ever-increasing circle that just got worse and worse. I put more on credit in the hope of attracting sales with new stock and then it all spiralled out of control until I ended up absolutely desperate.'

'You should have spoken with me, Will. I know how much the business means to you. And I know we were struggling. But Dad's watch. How could you take that? Of all the things to do.'

'I know. I was disgusted with myself. It was the lowest thing I've ever done. But you have to realise, by the time we were planning Venice, I was in far too deep. I wanted to celebrate our wedding anniversary, and I'd promised I'd always look after you. I messed everything up.'

As the waiter arrives with our wine, I see that Will is crying. He never cries. This then makes me cry and we both sit with tears running down our faces.

'Oh, Will.'

'Now that I'm being honest with you, I realise that I chose my family's legacy over yours and that was terribly selfish of me. It's just that all I could think was how my father would have been so disappointed in me for losing the business. I was always a failure in his eyes. I can imagine what he would be saying if he saw the state I got the business into.'

'You're not a failure, Will. Don't say that. Nothing could ever please your parents, let's be honest. It didn't matter how successful you'd have become; they'd have always found something to disapprove of. You've been living in the shadow of their expectations for far too long.'

'Do you think so?'

'I know so,' I say. I sit back for a moment and then lean forward towards Will. 'Look, you have to remember that the business wasn't doing very well by the time your dad died. Then all the older regular customers died, and times changed. It wasn't you. It was just that it was a different era. Fashions change. Sometimes you need to diversify,' I say.

'Yes, well, that's what I thought I was doing by buying more trash nobody wanted.'

I do feel for him. Will looks so worn down.

'I shouldn't have taken the watch though. It was just that I stupidly thought it would make everything better. All it did was make everything a million times worse.'

My head feels like it is going to explode. Today has definitely not gone as I expected.

'Now that I'm telling you everything, I have to be completely honest. The stress was making me ill. I mean, I had chest pains and everything...'

'Oh, Will...' I lived with Will and slept beside him every night and had no idea how bad things were. I knew he was stressed, I knew he worried, but I didn't see that he had made himself so ill... It's another reminder that nobody knows what anyone is secretly battling. Even when it is the person you are closest to in the world. I can't believe I didn't know how bad it had got for him. I wish I could have made things better.

'I was just desperate to find something that would solve it all. I kept thinking that there must be something I could sell somewhere. I searched the house for anything. Absolutely anything I could find. The watch was my last chance.'

'The business wasn't worth any of this. It wasn't worth damaging your health. I'd much rather have my family well.'

Will and I are both sobbing. At times, there is no doubt that I have hated him for what he has done, but when I hear about how much he went through physically and mentally, it hurts so much. If I had only known, I could have somehow helped or talked sense into him. Nothing in the world is worth the pressure and stress he has put on himself.

The waiter appears, hovering around us and then puts the wine down. Thankfully, he politely ignores the fact that we are both in floods of tears. 'Did you want to order some food?' he says.

The menu is the last thing on our minds. We haven't even glanced at it. I don't think I can eat anything right now. Will wipes his eyes, clears his throat and straightens up.

'Do you want some tagliatelle? There must be something like that on the menu,' he says.

'I'm not bothered what we eat. I think I've lost my appetite.'

The waiter finally leaves us alone, and I rest my hand on Will's arm.

'Why didn't you tell me any of this? I would have helped.'

'I was so ashamed. As I say, I was a complete failure. Couldn't even keep the family business alive. What sort of husband and father am I?'

'A bloody wonderful one, you were.'

'Were?'

'Yes, well, things have changed now. We were a wonderful family together. It's such a shame it all had to end like this.'

'I know, and I'm so sorry. I never meant for things to escalate so badly. I panicked when you found out about the watch here in Venice. I thought if only I could keep quiet until we got back you may not notice.'

'Might not notice Dad's watch was *missing*?'

'Yeah, exactly. Like I said, I really wasn't thinking straight at that point. I just kept living a lie day by day. Each night I'd lie awake and worry about how I'd cover my tracks the next day. It was like the biggest snowball, and then, finally, a huge avalanche smashed me in the face. I got what I deserved.'

'I get it. I'm sorry you've been through all of this, and it breaks my heart that I couldn't help you. You've always been a proud man, but you really shouldn't have suffered in silence. Are you getting help with managing your stress levels? Can I do anything?'

'Thanks, I can see that now. I'm fine. My friend, Sarah, gave me the number of someone. I actually have a therapist now.'

His 'friend' Sarah has got him help? I suppose I should be grateful to her, but those words cut like a knife.

Even so, I get up to give him a hug. It feels lovely to be back in his arms again, and I don't want to let go.

But, I remind myself, the divorce papers are ready, and he has another woman who is helping him work through his issues. Everything has changed. We are not who we were any longer. I quickly let go of him; he is with Sarah now and not me.

I wonder why he never told me any of this before. Then again, I can blame myself. I didn't give him a chance to explain and blocked any attempt he made of trying.

I sit back down awkwardly, and Will takes a sip of his drink. Things were never awkward between us when we were married. Now I find myself not knowing what to even say. It is Will who breaks the silence first.

'Just for the record, when you asked for a divorce, I was horrified. But then, as time went on, I realised I was a failure, and you were better off not married to me.'

'Please don't say things like that.'

'It's true, Libby. You deserve better. This divorce is for the best.'

It is hard to imagine how any of this situation could be deemed 'for the best', but I don't have the strength to argue. Tears leap into my eyes again. So many tears that I begin to wonder where they all come from.

'Don't cry, Libby. It'll all be okay. I promise. Everything will be okay.'

Will leans over and strokes my hand. All I can do is trust him, even if that is something I am finding hard to do.

Chapter Thirty-Five

As we are on different flights back, I tell Will that we will catch up when we both arrive home in Wales. I am relieved we are not flying back together, as I couldn't bear it if Sarah was picking him up at the airport. It would be too much seeing her with a big smile as she welcomes her boyfriend home, especially after the revelations he and I have shared of how stressed he was when he sold the watch. We were so close again for that short moment.

On the train home, I take the watch out of my hand luggage and look at it. I keep needing to know that it is still safe with me. I sneakily pull it out, careful that nobody notices it. I can't even imagine what I would do if someone stole it after all it has been through. I did offer Will the money that he paid to get the watch back, but he wouldn't take it. I suppose it is fair enough since he took it from me and it wasn't his to sell. He said that I owed him nothing. I am so incredibly happy to have the watch back where it belongs and know that Dylan can rightfully have it passed on to him on his twenty-first birthday.

I begin to get the feeling that everything might work out okay after all. I have the watch back, and Will is thankfully getting support for his stress. He has even admitted that the palpitations he would get in bed, which he never told me about before, have now stopped. I hate to admit it, but Sarah seems extremely supportive of him, and this has certainly helped.

I pop the watch safely away in my bag when Emily calls me.

'Hello, just checking what time you'll be back. Monty wants his mam.'

'Won't be long. Just pulling into Carmarthen. How's he doing?'

'Oh, great. All good here. Now, are you going to finally tell me what you've been up to on this trip of yours?'

I consider telling her that the watch is safe again but decide against it. I will show it to her when I see her. It will be such a lovely surprise.

When I eventually arrive at Emily's, she insists I stay for a cuppa whilst Monty doesn't stop jumping all over me.

'Oh, I've missed you, my boy.'

Seeing him again reminds me that he is off to a new house with me tonight. I hope he settles okay in the new cottage.

'Sooo, anything exciting happen in Venice? Or did you just mope about art galleries alone?' asks Emily.

'Emily! I didn't mope about. I saw some fascinating art, actually.'

I tell her about all the wonderful things I saw at Dalmatian School, and then I can't wait any longer to show her the precious item I have brought back with me.

'Look what I've got.' I take out the box and open it.

'Dad's watch!'

'The guy in the shop said that whoever bought it from him thought there was a curse on it and brought it back. Ha! It mustn't have liked the fact it was no longer where it belonged.'

'My goodness. Who'd have thought, hey?' Emily removes the watch from the box and holds it in her hands. 'Welcome back, precious,' she says, stroking the gold strap. 'So, do we finally forgive Will then?'

'Yes, I think so. It was Will who got the watch back for me. He told me all about why he took it when he was in Venice. Can you believe he was there the same time as me?'

Emily puts her mug down and touches my hand. She looks as though she is about to tell me something serious.

'He called me as soon as he found out you were going to Venice. That's when he asked me if I could look after Monty.'

'Huh?' I am so confused.

'Will said that you called him to look after Monty and when he heard you were going to Venice, he couldn't let you go there alone. He wanted to be there too. But he didn't want to let you down with Monty. So he checked with me first.'

'Why didn't you tell me?'

'Will said he wanted to surprise you. He said he had spoken to the jeweller and paid for the watch over the phone before he left. He seemed determined to get the watch back for all of us. To be honest, even I finally forgave him after we spoke.'

'I can't believe you knew all of this. I've been under so much pressure, determined to get the watch back, and you didn't even tell me? And you were the one who told me to divorce him before I could cool down in the first place! Unbelievable,' I snap.

'Don't be like that. Look, he told me not to tell you and I was sworn to secrecy. I didn't know that's why you went to Venice. You never even told me you were going to get the watch back. I'd have told you not to bother anyhow as I thought it was lost forever by now.'

'Ooh, do I hear a pair of squabbling sisters?' says Nick, walking in.

'No, I was just leaving,' I say.

'Not on my account, I hope,' says Nick.

'No, not at all. I think Emily and I are finished here. Come on, Monty.'

'Look, wait,' says Emily.

'Just leave me alone, okay? Thanks for taking care of Monty.'

I arrive back at the new home with Monty sniffing around as he tries to work out where he is. I unpack my luggage whilst he is preoccupied with his new adventure. The first thing to be unpacked is the watch, and I lock it safely away. I even change the combination on the safe three times, in case anyone could guess it. Then I get out the divorce papers I signed. They're ready to be hand-delivered to the lawyer's office tomorrow. I pop them by the front door ready so that I can slip out with them in the morning.

Monty is still scooting about, unsure where to go by the time I finish the unpacking, so I move his basket into a corner, and he eventually settles happily near the fire.

'That's nice and cosy, isn't it,' I say. Monty finally settling into his new home is a big relief.

He's lucky, as I am unable to rest in my bed at all. I toss and turn as I think about how Emily knew about the watch and Will coming to Venice and didn't tell me. My own sister! The other thing that plays on my mind is that Will didn't want me to go to Venice alone and yet on the other hand he felt that he didn't deserve to be married to me. That has really shocked me. Is his self-esteem really that low? I have so many questions.

Why would it even bother him that I was in Venice by myself? Where was he in Venice until now? Was he stalking me around the city? I certainly didn't see him following me around corners like some weird stalker in a brown mac. I try to think. The first time I saw him was at the arranged meeting. There were no other times he could have seen me. Then I remember the ball. Everyone was dressed up. Could he have been there spying on me in a mask?

I grab my phone quickly. I punch in Will's phone number. I need to speak to him immediately. I am still his wife until tomorrow, and I need answers.

'Hi. Did you get home okay?' says Will.

'Yes, yes… No problem. Listen. I need to ask you something. I know that you told Emily you were in Venice. She said that you didn't want me there without you. Why would she say that when the divorce papers are signed and ready for tomorrow morning?'

'I suppose I wasn't entirely open with you. There were some things I didn't say. Perhaps we need another talk,' says Will.

'I think you're right there. I don't understand anything that's happening with you. I can't believe you'd follow me to Venice,' I say.

'Can we meet first thing in the morning? Please don't take the papers to the lawyers until we've spoken. Can you promise me that?'

'Okay.'

'Thank you. Let's meet on our bench. Get some sleep and I'll see you tomorrow,' says Will.

'I shall, but I need to ask you something first.'

'It's late. Can't you ask me tomorrow?'

'No. It won't wait or I'm not going to be able to sleep.'

'What is it that's so important it can't wait?'

I swallow nervously before I begin.

'Right, well… This might sound a bit strange, but you weren't dressed as a highwayman at a ball in Venice, were you?'

The phone line goes quiet for a while. Then Will takes a deep breath.

'I have no idea what you're talking about. Let's chat tomorrow, hey?'

Chapter Thirty-Six

I can see that familiar head with the pointy ears as soon I turn the corner. Will is already sitting at 'our bench' when I reach it. He is looking out to sea, across to Caldey Island, just like the old times.

'Peaceful, isn't it?' I say.

'Always. I came here so many times on my own when I was in a bad state. I wanted you sitting beside me, but I was too weak to tell you the truth.'

'You were never weak, Will.'

'I certainly felt weak.'

'Well, that's not true. You managed to keep the business afloat as long as you could. That took determination and strength.'

A flock of seagulls suddenly gathers around us and squawks noisily at some litter they spot nearby.

'I can't hear myself think. You want to go for a walk along the beach?' says Will.

'That would be lovely. I should have brought Monty along. He's allowed back on the beach at this time of year,' I say.

We head down to the Blue Flag beach. The sea reaches out for miles.

'This feels just like the old days,' says Will as we walk alongside each other.

'It does. Except everything is different,' I say.

Will stops walking and turns to me. He takes my hand and looks directly at me.

'I know we've hit a bad patch. A very, very bad patch, but it doesn't mean to say we have to submit those papers,' he says. He looks down at his feet and lifts his head slowly. 'It's a huge document. There's no turning back once they're in with the lawyers. I just feel we should think carefully before we do anything we may regret in the future.'

'We're bound to have last-minute nerves. But we've sold our house, we practically lost everything, and now you're with someone else,' I say.

What is he thinking? We have gone too far to stop now.

'Hang on. Let me stop you there. I'm with someone else? What on earth do you mean?'

'Well, first you had that woman on Tinder…'

'Let me tell you, I went on *one* date with that woman from Tinder, and that was only because I thought you were seeing some farmer. We had nothing in common whatsoever and all I thought about all night was how I wanted to be home with you. I didn't want to be out dating, making small talk. I wanted to be sat on the sofa with you, watching rubbish on TV with Monty trying to blame his stinky farts on me.'

'Oh, Will. Don't be rude. You know I hate that F word. Monty doesn't do stinky… You know he does love puffs. But, wait, you only went on *one* date with her?'

'Believe me, that was enough.'

'I agree. It isn't easy trying to go on dates with strangers that you have nothing in common with,' I say.

I am tempted to tell him about Simon and his gnome collection, or Terry and his tortoise ashes, but I decide against it. I wouldn't want to make a mockery of the poor man.

'Well, you might have only gone out with Tinder Woman once, but now you have your girlfriend Sarah, who seems to have helped you a lot. I don't think she'd appreciate you talking here with me, asking to delay the divorce papers.'

'Sarah? What Sarah are you on about?'

'What is wrong with you? She helped you with a therapist. You introduced her to Dylan at dinner. And you met up with her when I saw you in town. Your *girlfriend*, or have you suddenly forgotten about her?'

'What? Sarah with the books? My friend, Sarah?'

I am not sure quite how much I should know. I don't want to show Will how I have been snooping on her, so I act coy.

'I don't know. Does she have books?'

'Don't you remember her, Libby? She came into the shop a while back and left her business card. Surely you remember?'

'No. I don't know. Not really.'

I mean, it is not like I haven't spent hours scouring her social media. I may even know more about Sarah than she knows about herself.

Will gestures to a big rock and we sit down together.

'You didn't really think I was dating her, did you? My goodness, she must be twenty years younger than me for a start.'

'Well, I know what men are like. Always looking for a younger model,' I say, narrowing my eyes at him.

'Don't be so silly. You should know me better than that. What would we have in common? She wouldn't have even heard of the music I like.'

'No, well it is all a bit prehistoric,' I say, laughing.

'Not to mention all the legendary rugby players I've always loved. She probably wasn't even born when half of them passed. Oh no, I would never date someone younger.'

Could I have got the wrong end of the stick? Will isn't actually dating that lovely young antiquarian? How come they were so friendly though?

'Well, you seem pretty cosy with her. You have obviously had some very personal conversations for her to help you like that. Why do you meet up with her so often then? You have plenty of friends. Why Sarah?'

'That's the thing I wanted to talk to you about. You remember I bought that box of stock just before we went to Venice for our anniversary?'

'The one when we were walking and the seagull pooped on my head?' I ask.

'Yes, that's the one. It was one of the last buys I did for the shop. We didn't have room to put it out, so I left it in the back.'

'What has Sarah got to do with that box though?'

'Well, when I started clearing things from the shop... When I finally realised that closing down was inevitable, I opened the box. There wasn't much in it...You know, the usual stuff from a house clearance. Nothing of any particular value. But there was a book in there. You know what I'm like, don't know Jane Austen from *Jane Eyre*, but something about this book stood out. It looked tatty and old, but when I flicked through it, I noticed inside that it was a first edition from 1922. Well, I thought then I may have struck lucky, and it might have some value. So I searched for Sarah's card and called her up. Sometimes it's good to hoard things,' says Will with a smile.

'And so you took her for dinner?'

'Yeah, well, she was in Cardiff that weekend and asked if she could see the book. I was at the rugby all day and was there with Dylan. I couldn't really work out how we could meet unless it was at dinner. For one night I figured I could be like one of those hot-shot guys who entertain their clients over dinner and then deduct it for expenses. So I invited her along to dinner with me and Dylan and brought the book along to show her.'

Dylan did say that they talked about books all night.

'What did she say about it?'

'She was so excited when she saw it, I thought she'd fall off her chair. I'm not great with books, but even I could tell that it was practically an antique. But I wasn't quite expecting that response. I knew when I saw her face that I was onto something. It turned out to be some book that had previously been banned and had some big history. Sarah was banging on about its importance, but I wasn't really listening. It was only one of a thousand copies.'

'What book was it?'

'*Ulysses* by James Joyce. Never heard of him myself.'

'Wow. That must have been worth something.'

'It was. Sarah said she would do some digging that weekend and find out what the value would be. She travels all over the place with auctions and things, so she came down to Tenby that Monday you saw us together. She wanted to tell me in person how much it would fetch. She had already found a buyer for it. She was so excited. That's when I burst into tears and told her all about the problems I'd been having. So she suggested I see this therapist she knows.'

Sometimes I wonder if I will ever keep up with Will's confessions. So much has been happening without my knowledge.

'Can you believe the collector was willing to pay forty-five thousand pounds? If only I'd have opened the box sooner and found it before, none of this would have happened. I'd never have done the terrible thing I did. Nothing would have saved the shop, I realise that now. But that book would have been the answer to the mounting debt. That is why I burst into tears when she told me.'

To think the answer to our troubles was in that box all along. Maybe the seagull that pooped on my head really was trying to tell me he had brought us some luck that day.

'I'm just glad that you got through all of the worry and stress. I'm sorry you felt you couldn't share any of this with me before. I was to blame too. I suppose, in a way, I was too busy keeping up appearances to notice. I wanted to be the perfect wife, mother, neighbour. I suppose we all wear our masks. Which reminds me...'

Will puts his arm around my back, and when he touches me, I don't need to ask the question that I was about to. My body shivers in exactly the same way it did at the ball in Venice.

'You're the highwayman, aren't you?'

'Highwayman? What are you on about?' says Will.

'You know jolly well what I'm on about.'

'No comment.'

'Why didn't you say something that night?'

'Because I didn't think you would ever forgive me for what I did. I wanted one more evening of being close to you. I didn't dare open my mouth or my Welsh accent would have let it slip. So I had to be the strong, silent type for the night. It killed me walking away from you. I wanted to take you in my arms and back to the hotel. It was quite hot playing the role of two strangers, though, don't you think? Maybe we should do it again.'

'Oh, Will. Shh. Someone will hear you,' I say, giggling.

Although looking around the beach, I can see it is deserted apart from an older man walking his golden retriever.

'Well, don't tell me that you didn't enjoy it as much as I did?' says Will.

'Yes. I couldn't stop thinking about our little… well, dalliance, I suppose,' I whisper.

'I know dogs have good ears, but I promise nobody can hear you,' says Will, laughing.

I step back a moment.

'Hang on. Just one thing though… How did you know I was going to be at the ball?'

'Ah. That was thanks to the lovely Nia. The boys, along with Nia, knew my plans for Venice. Nia very helpfully forwarded me a copy of the ticket you sent her. Thank goodness you updated Nia with your every move.'

'Nia knew about all of this too?'

I can't quite make my mind up about whether I am angry at Nia or impressed with her deviousness.

'Just wait until I see her,' I say, smiling.

'Come here. I've missed you so much. Every single day without you has been sheer torture,' says Will.

'I know. For me too. I just had to try and get on with it. I hated living life without you.'

'You know what I think? Instead of a divorce, how about we renew our vows?'

'Renew our vows?'

'Yes, come on. In Venice. We could go together properly this time. And I wouldn't need to wear a mask to seduce you – at least I hope not,' says Will, laughing.

'I don't know. I think it's going to take time to get us back to where we were. Why don't we take things step by step? Let's take things slowly.'

Will kisses me, but then I move back a little.

'Step by step,' I remind him.

'But we're supposed to get all the papers in by today. Time isn't on our side. What do you want to do?'

'What do *you* want to do?' I ask.

'I just told you what *I* want to do.'

I look out to the sea and then turn to him.

'I think tearing them up is the best option,' I say.

Will punches the air.

'Let's never do anything stupid like this again, okay?'

'I agree.'

'So who's going to tell the lawyers?' says Will.

'I suppose we both should. We are in this together, after all.'

–

When Will arrives with the rest of his stuff the following morning, the divorce papers are still lying on the table. They sit there in shreds, ripped into tiny confidential pieces, ready to be thrown into the fire. Will hangs his jacket on the stair banister, and suddenly there are reminders of him all over the house. His things may all be the same, but this time they are in a different home. I suppose this will be a reminder of what we have been through. The scar that tears through our marriage will always be a reminder of the journey we went on together.

Monty plays excitedly with one of Will's slippers that he has already put down by the sofa. I look at them with a fondness that I never did before. I am ashamed to admit that I used to kick them out of my way when he had left them somewhere inconvenient, which he frequently would. It would annoy me that he had left them somewhere someone could trip over them. Now I am just glad to see them. I am sure it won't take me long for those little niggles to annoy me again, but for now, I am just grateful for them.

'Did I ever tell you how much I love these tatty worn things?' I say, picking up the slipper that Monty hasn't got his little paws on. 'Perhaps it's time you had some new ones though. Look at the state on the sole. I know what you're having for Christmas this year.'

'Ah, no. Monty loves them, mun. It wouldn't be the same with a new pair of slippers. Just as it wouldn't be the same without you. Come here.'

I am not sure we have ever held each other tighter. A relief runs through me from the top of my head to the tips of my toes as I relax in his familiar arms. It has taken until now to realise that home is all about *who* you are with rather than *where* you live.

'Oh my gosh, Will. Let's never fight again.'

'No chance. I promise to communicate with you for the rest of my years. I don't ever want to be without you again. Not even for a day.'

'Well, that is something we can definitely agree on.'

We kiss like new lovers. All the passion that faded over the years is suddenly rekindled. Will leads me upstairs, and Monty wags his tail excitedly.

'No, you're staying down here, Monty. Play with Dad's slipper,' I say.

I follow Will to our new bedroom, and the sexual drought we have had for so long is broken. We no longer have that over-familiar relationship of being best friends and not lovers. The spark between us is rekindled and I don't want it to go out ever again. It is then that I realise that none of us is perfect. We all have our moments, and sometimes relationships with people can be difficult. Marriages aren't all plain sailing, and there are definitely times when you have to look into your heart for forgiveness.

Chapter Thirty-Seven

Six Months Later

I hold Will's hand tight as we stand on the terrace of the hotel overlooking the Piazza San Marco. He only lets go to remove the vows that are written on a piece of paper he has carefully stored in his pocket. As we renew our vows, he looks at me with the love he did on our wedding day. Then he puts on his reading glasses.

'Sorry, I didn't need glasses the last time we said vows to each other,' he says, laughing.

I look over at Dylan, Ewan, Nia, Emily and Nick, who are all grinning from ear to ear. It is their first time in Venice, and they are loving it here, just as much as we do. I just wish we hadn't had to leave Monty at home with Nia's mother.

Will starts to read from his paper.

'Libby, we have been through so much, and I want to tell you that I love you more than anything in the world. Sometimes we get caught up in everyday life and lose sight of what is important. Having you beside me is all that matters. I will never disappoint you again.'

Will turns to look at Dylan and Ewan, then he continues with the vows.

'The beautiful boys we have brought up are a credit to us. They are the bond that means we will never break.

Libby Jones, I never knew it was possible to love someone so much. With each year that goes by, I love you more and more. When we got married, I promised to love and protect you. I don't know that I protected you as much as I should have, but I promise that I will never stop making you happy from this day forward.'

Will leans over to kiss me, and everyone claps. Then a waiter rushes up from nowhere with glasses of champagne for us all.

As Will gives my hand a squeeze, we smile at each other. I can't even imagine that we could have been divorced today and living separate lives if we hadn't finally communicated with each other.

Even if we have lost our home and are still renting until the right one comes along again, I have no regrets. Sometimes, something bad has to happen to make you both realise what you mean to each other. After so many years, we had gotten to the stage where we took each other for granted and were no longer communicating. I will never let it happen again.

Emily and Nick are the first to congratulate us. We made up when I finally realised that she had my best interests at heart.

'You look so beautiful, Libby,' says Emily.

'And so do you.' Emily looks as glamorous as always in her silky gold dress and skyscraper heels. I would definitely fall over if I wore heels that high. I don't know how she does it. Will leaves us to chat for a while and heads over to the boys.

'Such a beautiful day makes me think we should get married, Emily,' says Nick.

I look at him with surprise. Oh my goodness, I hadn't ever imagined Emily re-marrying.

'Ah, now. What did I tell you? This is Libby's day. It's not about us.'

'No, don't mind me. You carry on and propose to her if you want. I'd be delighted.'

'Libby, no. I wouldn't hear of it. Today is your day and I have no intention of taking the limelight from you. Make the most of it, as it doesn't happen often,' says Emily, smiling.

'Well, I'm very happy for you both if that's what you decide.'

I give them both a hug and smile over to Nia. Looking at her brings back the memory of the messages I sent her about the ball I went to the last time I was here. It reminds me that I must get Will to dress up as a highwayman again sometime. He makes a beautiful highwayman. Perhaps that is something for tonight. After all, there must be some kind of honeymoon after renewing your vows, surely?

Will chats with Ewan as Nia comes over and hugs me. I try not to spill any of my champagne over her, or the long ivory silk dress I am wearing. This dress is so different to my previous meringue one. I adjust the pink Morganite beaded necklace I made especially for today and notice that Nia and Emily are wearing the necklaces I made for them all that time ago. What a dream come true to see people wearing my jewellery on such a special occasion. Life couldn't possibly be better.

Dylan, Ewan and Will come to join Nia and me, and it is only then that I notice everyone has a drink except for Nia.

'Where's your drink, love?'

'Oh, I'm okay. I've asked the waiter to get me an orange juice.'

'Don't you want something stronger to celebrate? That's not like you.'

'I'm fine, honestly.'

'Is something wrong?'

Nia looks at Ewan, and he nods his head.

'What is it? Are you ill? Are you going in for something?'

'Well, not really, no,' says Nia.

'What then?'

'I'm pregnant,' she says with a smile.

I grasp at Will's arm.

'What? How long? Oh my gosh! You've got to tell me everything.' I search for a chair to sit down. What a shock. A nice shock, but such a surprise.

'Four months. Sorry, I didn't mean to tell you today,' says Nia. I get up from my chair.

'Oh, come here. Let me give you a hug. This is the best news we could ever wish for. Now it really is the perfect day.'

I look at Will, who seems as chuffed as I am.

'Wow. We're going to be grandparents,' I say to Will.

'We're going to be grandparents,' he repeats excitedly. His eyes are sparkling and his cheeks are getting redder, just like when he is excited at a rugby match. I can tell that he is definitely as delighted as I am.

'Gosh, there's so much to think about. You'll need a nursery and, of course, a babysitter. You know I'd love to volunteer. I only wish the house was big enough for a nursery and our grandchild could stay over. The old house would have been perfect for grandchildren.'

'Oh, Mam. I forgot to tell you. Did you know the new owners are selling?' says Dylan.

'Already?' I say.

'Yeah,' says Dylan.

'Wow. Well, the estate agent did say they were regular customers of his. They're serial movers.'

They will probably be asking far more than we sold it for with all the renovations they had planned.

'Well, it's a lovely thought, but we couldn't afford it anyway. So it doesn't really make much difference if it is back on the market or not,' I say.

'Of course we can afford it. I sold the book. We still have most of the money from the house sale. We can put it all back into the house again,' says Will.

'Wow, do you really think this is our chance of getting the final part of our old lives back?' I say.

'Well, not really. It'll be different this time. It can never be the same,' says Will, drawing his eyebrows together.

'Don't you think?'

'No, it'll never be the same because the last time we lived there my priorities were all wrong. I was so focused on the business and money that I wasn't there for my family.'

Will looks at Dylan's wrist. We decided to give him Dad's watch before we left for Venice. A few years earlier than planned, but I am sure Dad would understand given everything the watch has been through.

'Take care of that watch. It's magic, that is, Dylan,' says Will.

'It's beautiful, but I don't know that it's magic,' says Dylan, laughing.

'Oh, but it is. It has magical powers that teach you the biggest lessons in life. Maybe that was the reason your grandad left it to us.'

A Letter From Helga

I hope you enjoyed this story featuring beautiful Venice. It is a magical place that is perfect for the setting of any story. Of course, I have to include the stunning landscapes of Wales, too, so, for this book, we are also in Tenby.

As always with my novels, I wanted to feature real-life issues. *My Heart is in Venice* looks at the dynamics of a long-term marriage. Being married isn't always easy and sometimes the person you love the most can annoy you the most! Sometimes there are surprises, and the person you think you know so well does something that might shock you to the core.

I do hope you enjoyed this story of Libby and Will's relationship and the turmoil that ensues.

I am always very responsive on social media, so please feel free to contact me if you enjoyed the story. You can contact me via:

www.twitter.com/HelgaJensenF
www.facebook.com/helgajensenfordeauthor
www.instagram.com/helgajensenauthor

Acknowledgements

As usual, the biggest thank you to Keshini Naidoo at Hera Books, who was responsible a few years ago for allowing me to bring my stories to life. I will be forever grateful for the opportunities she has given me. As an additional bonus, she truly is one of the most amazing people to work with. Huge thank you also to my amazing, super-duper editor, Jennie Ayres, to whom this book is partly dedicated. Everyone needs an editor like Jennie. Another thank you goes to Jennifer Davies for a wonderful copy edit, Lynne Walker for the super proofread and a big thank you has to be said to Diane of D Meacham Design for yet another stunning cover.

As ever, thank you to JK and Mr B for your support. Also, thank you to all my wonderful friends, special people, and writing buddies. To my writing buddy Jenny, your support means so much. As I always say, I have the best people in my life, and I am so grateful for that.

Finally, the biggest thank you goes to every reader who takes the time to pick this book up. You wonderful readers mean so much to me, and I can't thank you enough for choosing to read my stories.

Happy reading x